THE WESTON WOMEN

THE WESTON WOMEN

The Second in the Pendragon Series

Grace Thompson

This first world edition published in Great Britain by
SEVERN HOUSE PUBLISHERS LTD of
9–15 High Street, Sutton, Surrey SM1 1DF.
First published in the USA 1996 by
SEVERN HOUSE PUBLISHERS INC of
595 Madison Avenue, New York, NY 10022.

British Library Cataloguing in Publication Data
Thompson, Grace
    The Weston Women. – (Pendragon Island : 2)
    1.English fiction – 20th century
    I. Title
    823.9′14[F]

    ISBN 0-7278-5176-4

Typeset by Hewer Text Composition Services, Edinburgh.
Printed and bound in Great Britain by
Creative Print and Design Ltd, Ebbw Vale, Wales.

Chapter One

Walking from the Court a free man was such a relief that Arfon Weston wanted to cry. That would really make him look an old fool after his masterly performance these past months. He coughed, spoke irritably to his wife to "hurry up, Gladys," and "stop fussing" and marched to where their taxi waited. After months of waiting, of delays and postponements, of sleepless nights and stressful days, he was free.

Not without a hefty fine and costs that would cripple him, but the air in the South Wales town had never smelled so good.

"The first thing I want to do when I get home is to walk along the sands and get some deep breaths into my lungs," he said when the taxi was on its way through the streets of Cardiff.

"Walk on the sands? When did you ever?" Gladys said disparagingly. She was feeling hurt. He hadn't hugged her and thanked her for her support. The tender scene she had envisaged hadn't happened and even though they were well into their sixties, they still showed affection without embarrassment. She wondered with concern, if Arfon was going to return to being the unattentive husband he had been when they were first married, concentrating all his energies on building a business and making money. They needed that sort of dedication, she knew that, with most of their money gone and debts to pay, but she didn't think she would cope with it all again. Not now.

Then there had been the babies to enjoy, their twin girls, Sally and Sian, now married, Sian with a son Jack, and Sally with twin daughters of her own, her dear Weston Girls, Joan and Megan.

She tuned in to Arfon's voice beside her in the leather seat; he was chuntering on about the unfortunate choices their twin daughters had made, when they married the lazy Ryan and the thieving Islwyn.

"What did we do to deserve those two, Gladys?" he boomed as the car stopped outside their house. Then, "Well, this is it, the new beginning. Tomorrow I start all over again building the family fortune. The Westons aren't finished yet, my dear and this town of Pendragon Island will soon find that out."

"How exciting, dear," Gladys smiled, while wondering where they were going to find the money for anything other than survival. The family were all there to greet them, their twin daughters, Sian and Sally with their husbands, although Islwyn couldn't look them in the face. Even their grandson Jack had turned up, and their lovely twin granddaughters, Joan and Megan, who, although not bearing their grandparents' name were always referred to as 'the Weston Girls'. She hugged them all, even Islwyn, who had brought them to this sorry state, then hurried to make sure Mair had tea ready and hadn't forgotten anything.

She checked the tray the maid had prepared and frowned over the lack of polish on a teaspoon. Really the girl was nowhere near as good as Victoria Jones had been. Such a pity she'd had to leave. She adjusted the display of small cakes in her finicky way then nodded approval. "Very well, Mair, you can take it in now and please try not to overfill the cups or dribble tea into the saucer."

"Thank you Ma'am." Mair wondered what she was thanking her for. The rules on what she must say on every occasion were so ridiculous.

"Well, Grandfather, what now?" Jack asked when the maid had left them.

"First of all I want to know what you two are going to do." Arfon looked at his sons-in-law. "Ryan?" he asked. "Isn't it time you got back to work or are you going to retire permanently at the age of forty-five?"

"I can't be expected to go back and accept Viv Lewis as manager, Father-in-law, you can't expect that of me."

"Why not? He's a better manager than you were!"

"But it was he who got us in this mess. If he hadn't gone to the police with evidence of you burning down your own shop for the insurance money—" he faltered as Arfon's eyes bulged as if about to explode.

"Well, it doesn't seem right, Daddy, Viv Lewis being given a share of a business he all but ruined," Sally added in support of her husband.

3

"The business was in the hands of a lazy man who did as little as he could get away with," Arfon glared at Ryan. "And," he turned his fierce gaze on Islwyn, his other son-in-law, "a man who thought he was justified in stealing from his own family."

Islwyn stood up as if his seat were on fire and almost ran from the room. His wife Sian followed, calling back abuse at her father.

"I don't think you can count on my father to help rebuild Weston's Wallpaper and Paint, Grandfather," their son Jack said casually, staring at the door swinging shut after his parents. "I'm afraid he isn't up to it. Best if you leave it to Viv if you ask me, he knows what he's doing and is utterly trustworthy."

"Trustworthy and – loyal?" his Auntie Sally demanded. "They go together don't they? Honesty and loyalty? If he finds something a bit irregular, what makes you think he won't go to the police again?"

"If Viv is running things there won't be anything – irregular – will there?" Jack replied.

"Vivian Lewis stays in charge and if you decide to start earning your keep again, Ryan, you do as he says, right?" Arfon glared again at Ryan and at his daughter, Sally. "He had his chance, Sally, love, and he failed me, you, all of us. I'm keeping a tight hold of the reins from now on and Viv Lewis runs the business. What he says goes. Right?"

Ryan shuffled his feet but didn't reply.

"Will our allowance have to be reduced?" Arfon's granddaughter Joan asked. She and her twin sister,

Megan, tilted their heads on one side and looked at their grandfather appealingly.

"Heavens above, Joan. You don't think I'd survive your grandmother's wrath if I suggested that, do you?" Arfon laughed. "Cutting back on expenditure, yes, but touching your allowance? It's more than I dare do."

"More tea anyone?" Gladys enquired after a conspiratorial smile at her granddaughters. "I'll ring for Mair, shall I?"

Arfon felt the elation of seeing the end of the court case sliding from him as he thought about his sons-in-law. Ever since their twin daughters had married, he and Gladys had given them an allowance. It would have to stop, at least until the firm was on its feet again and he wondered whether Ryan and Islwyn were men enough to compensate for the loss of both allowance and wages and keep their families without his support. Sadly he thought not.

"Until now, your grandmother has refused to discuss it," he told Jack confidentially. "She's convinced that everything will be all right, that the finances will magically revert to how they were before the revelations that have beggared us."

"Grandmother will cope, once you explain exactly what the situation is," Jack said. "Don't try to cover up the severity of it, she'd hate that."

"I'll have to talk to her – and soon, Jack. I keep hoping it won't be as bad as I first thought. But I've done my sums over and over again and I can't kid myself anymore and you're right, it isn't fair to kid her."

He watched his wife as she criticised the maid for stacking the china with less than perfect orderliness, and sighed. Gladys would find it harder than the others to deal with poverty. At sixty-six she had the right to live comfortably as she had always done. Perhaps he'd wait a while and see exactly how they were fixed before discussing the economies he needed to enforce. He knew nothing would magically change, that he was being cowardly, but seeing Gladys in her drawing room, enjoying being a generous hostess to her family made him weak. Damn it all, he'd let her down.

Islwyn took his wife home then went to Glebe Lane to see Ryan.

"What are we going to do?" he demanded when he and Ryan were alone.

"Nothing," Ryan smiled. "The damned Westons have made us into lackeys, insisting on running our lives for us, so let them get on with it. Let's see how Old Man Arfon deals with this situation with only Viv Lewis to help him."

"You're right. He's led us by the nose since we married his precious daughters, so he can dig us out of this mess. After all it's his fault."

"And yours, you damned fool! Fancy helping yourself from the till."

"Righting the balance, that's all," Islwyn retaliated. "Gladys spends hundreds on your daughters, her 'Weston Girls', and my Jack hardly sees a penny piece."

"Well, anyway . . ." Ryan sat and allowed his thoughts to drift.

"Bloody Viv Lewis and his righteousness," Islwyn muttered. "He's got the fault and now he's a partner in the firm. Well, we'll see how long he lasts. Little upstart."

Viv Lewis, the subject of Ryan and Islwyn's displeasure was in the office of Weston's Wallpaper and Paint at that moment. There was a lull in the shop and he had run up to his desk to make a few phone calls while he had a chance. He did as much office work as possible before and after the shop closed, as he believed in making the customers aware that although he was the manager, he found time to take a real interest in their purchases. And at the moment he was carrying out an experiment, timing his various tasks to see how much more of his time he could spend on the shop floor.

He saw Victoria Jones, the Westons' ex-maid come in and he went down to see what she wanted. She didn't look like a customer. The way she looked around her wondering which of the assistants to approach made him think she wanted to see him. He rapped on the office window, waved, then ran down to meet her.

"Hello Victoria, looking for me?" he asked.

Her cheeks reddened and she whispered, "Yes, well, if you aren't busy. Would you rather I came back?" She stepped away from him towards the door.

7

"Come up to the office, we can talk there," he said, taking her arm. Such a thin arm that the sleeve of her worn coat lacked substance. He glanced at her and saw how pinched and pale her face had become. What ever sort of employer Gladys Weston had been, she had fed the girl. Victoria didn't look as if she had eaten a good meal since she left. He called to one of the assistants to make them a cup of tea. "No sugar, mind," he said. "Mam can't spare any more of her rations."

"I was wondering if you had a job going? Cleaning perhaps?" Victoria began as they waited for the tea to arrive. "Evenings or early mornings would do."

"I thought you had a job?"

"I have, but I could do a few hours besides the shop. A shoe shop isn't hard work and I've plenty of energy."

"Saving up for something nice, are you?" Viv asked.

"Well . . ."

"All right, I don't want to know your business. Let me think about it, shall I? I'll let you know after the weekend, when I've talked to Mr Weston."

"I'll pop in on Monday then, save you coming to the house."

Glad to be gone, she ran down the stairs and out of the shop without waiting for the tea. Viv wrote a note to remind him to speak to Arfon and wondered idly if Victoria was saving to get married. She was only sixteen but she'd probably be glad to get away from that awful family of hers.

He heard that the trial was over and Arfon had been fined and awarded costs, from Jack, who had called in after leaving his grandfather's house and the family gathering.

"I'm glad he wasn't sent to prison, Jack," Viv said, avoiding his friend's eye.

"Are you?"

"Yes I am. I've grown to respect the old man and although I can't honestly say I regret reporting what Basil Griffiths found out, I am glad he didn't have to face prison. At his age it would have been hard."

"You don't think it's hard losing all his money and having to start again at his age?"

"Not if it makes your thieving father and your Uncle Ryan do something useful instead of scrounging off him, no I don't!" Unable to keep his temper any longer, Viv reminded his friend that, "Justice is for all and that includes the precious Westons!"

"You've done well enough out of it, Viv Lewis! A partnership isn't it? A partner of the man you snitched on?"

"Come off it, Jack! 'Snitched on' indeed! It wasn't a game. He burned his property down!" Anger rising due partly to his uncomfortable guilt, he went on, "Don't look down your nose at me, boy! Old Man Arfon trusted your father, Jack. And all the time he was stealing from him. And Ryan was hardly honest, was he? Taking wages and doing sod all! What right have you to come in here and sneer at the likes of me? I'll help him and do all I can to put this shop on it's feet again. What are you going to do? Any of you?"

A moment passed and they were aware of the three assistants silent and listening. Lowering his voice, Viv asked, "For a start off, what will your father do to earn his keep? Arfon won't have him back here, for sure."

Jack's shoulders drooped as he submitted to the truth of Viv's tirade. "He won't even go out in the daylight. I can't see him finding a job anywhere."

"And your Uncle Ryan?"

"He says he won't work for you."

"Good on 'im. I don't want him wandering round here telling me what I'm doing wrong and idling his hours away. The fact is, Jack, the business won't stand it." He pointed down into the shop where the assistants were serving a small trickle of customers and said, "One of those will have to go. Maybe two. I'm trying to decide which. I thought I'd take on a cleaner and let the highest paid assistants go. Pity for them but they'll soon find something else. There's no other way if I'm to make a profit for your grandfather, Old Man Arfon."

"Mr Weston to you!" Jack swung on his heel and hurried out.

Viv doubted whether he and Jack would ever return to the close friendship they had once enjoyed. Although they spoke now, there was always an undercurrent of anger in Jack to which Viv's temper was quick to respond. Impulsively he ran after Jack and saw him standing at the corner of the road. Cooling his temper, he is, Viv thought, recognising in his friend a feeling he knew very well.

"Fishing? Sunday morning?" he asked.

"All right, seven o'clock start."

"OK."

They parted with a little less anger, a continuation of the slow thaw.

When work finished for the day, Viv sometimes called in for a drink on the way home, but today he was earlier than usual, having managed most of the book-keeping before the shop closed. Home first, he decided, and have a bite of tea to fortify myself for the visit to Arfon and Gladys Weston.

He looked in on his sister in the sweet shop, Temptations, on the corner near their home. "Any off-ration sweets, miss?" he teased.

Rhiannon smiled and threw him a toffee from one of the jars on the shelf behind her. Then he ran to their home just three doors away, number seven, Sophie Street.

At six-thirty, Mair opened the door to Viv and, as usual, requested he wait in the hall until she found Mr Weston. As usual Viv ignored her instruction and walked past her to sit down in the library-cum-study leading off the hall, where Arfon found him a few moments later.

"Congratulations, I'm pleased you don't have to face prison," Viv said at once.

"My instinct is to thank you for your good wishes, but I don't think it's apt, really, d'you?" Arfon growled.

"I'm pleased it's over," Viv said. "Now the real

reason I wanted to talk to you is about the staff. One must go for definite and I really want to get rid of two, at least for the time being, and take on a part-time cleaner."

"Sack two? But that leaves you with only one assistant? How will you manage?"

"I'll do what I've been doing for weeks, get in early and leave late, then I'll be available to help in the shop. If your granddaughter, Joan, would demean herself to working, she might like to come in on Saturdays for a while to help out."

Arfon ignored the rudeness and said, "Joan? Well she did work there for a while but, a Saturday . . ." He pursed his lips and shook his head. "Girls seem to be frantically busy on Saturdays."

"This is an emergency, Mr Weston. You've looked after the family really well for years, now they must start giving something back."

"I'll have a word with Ryan and—"

"No bloody fear! I don't want them two hanging around looking superior and doing sod all, thank you very much!"

"Viv, you're damned rude."

"Yes, and you think the same and don't deny it." Viv grinned unrepentantly. "It wouldn't work. They'd undo all I've done and you must admit things are looking up."

"A cleaner you say?"

"You know Victoria Jones, who used to work for Mrs Weston? She called to ask for a few hours cleaning before or after her day at the shoe shop. I think she needs to earn a few pounds more."

"All right, boy, do what you must and I'll support you. Now will you have a drink to celebrate the fact that you didn't ruin me completely?"

"Smashing."

Half an hour later, Viv poked his head into The Railwayman's Arms and saw that Basil Griffiths was there with his brother Frank and their cousin Ernie.

"Eleri all right?" he called.

"Being looked after by Mam, she's fine. Rhiannon's with her now. Doing each other's hair or something I mustn't witness. I'll tell her you were asking."

Eleri had once been married to Viv's brother who had been killed in a car accident and she was now the wife of Basil Griffiths. Although no longer related, Viv and his sister Rhiannon remained close friends of Eleri. Rhiannon and Eleri particularly, spent a lot of time together.

Basil and Eleri lived in a flat in Trellis Street but with Eleri's baby due in November, she and Basil had closed up their flat and gone to live temporarily, with Basil's parents.

The Griffiths family lived on the edge of the town in a house that was shabby but always filled with people. Janet and Hywel's son Frank and their nephew Ernie lived at home, and their daughter Caroline also shared the limited accommodation, with her son Joseph.

Hywel Griffiths had extended the place by building a corridor to join up the house with a brick building

13

that had once been a garage, and this had become a bedroom for Frank and Ernie. Even with that addition, there wasn't much room, but somehow eight disparate people lived in close proximity without disagreements or even irritation.

Basil was the only one who had a job. He had worked as a nightwatchman ever since he had asked Eleri to marry him. The rest lived very comfortably on the occasional 'deal' and on what they could scrounge, barter or 'borrow' – their euphemism for steal.

Viv glanced at his watch, almost nine o'clock. He walked slowly to the corner of Goldings Street and St Margaret's Crescent – which, since a bomb had obliterated the curve, was no longer a crescent but two short terraces. Eight years since the end of the war the scars remained. He stood in the shadow of an overgrown hedge until he heard footsteps.

"Joan," he said in greeting and Arfon and Gladys Weston's granddaughter took his arm in a cuddly embrace and lightly kissed him.

"Family conference over then?" he asked.

"Will it ever be? Poor Grandfather, he's so ashamed of my father and Uncle Islwyn, isn't he? Uncle Islwyn did the stealing, but my father wasn't much better, doing so little to justify his wages. That was stealing too; taking Grandfather's money and doing nothing."

"Except torment me!" Viv added.

They walked along the damp roads, to where a bus stop made a cosy seat out of the draughts and where few people passed. Behind them was a park

14

and rustlings were heard as small animals foraged for earthworms and insects amid the fallen leaves of autumn.

"I asked your grandfather if you'll come and help in the shop on Saturdays," Viv said and he smiled in the dark, guessing at the outraged expression on her pretty face as she exclaimed,

"On Saturdays?"

"That's what he said!" Viv chuckled. "But if you are really ashamed of your father and uncle, you must be willing to help the family recover."

"All right, so long as I don't have to deal with boring customers choosing pink for bedrooms and beige – so practical – for the hall."

"I'll leave you to enter in the goods we receive. I'm trying to work out a better stock control system so we don't have too much money lying idle. I'll put all that aside for you to do each Saturday. Right?"

"Oh, all right," she said, touching her lips against his. "But you'll have to keep me sweet or I'll forget to come."

"I'll come and fetch you, drag you to my lair, still wearing your nightie."

"Oh, Viv. Sometimes you're impossibly common!"

In the park behind them, Joan's Uncle Islwyn disturbed the branches and looked to see who was using the bus stop seat. As he guessed, it was his niece Joan and that Viv Lewis. He'd bide his time, and tell Joan's father when it would have the most effect, like when Ryan was at his most righteous and unforgiving.

15

"What was that?" Joan whispered in alarm. "I thought I heard someone in the bushes."

"Probably a rat," Viv said and was rewarded by Joan clinging even tighter.

Islwyn accepted the remark as an insult and glared angrily through the damp branches before slipping silently away.

Viv walked Joan back to her parents' house in Glebe Lane and headed for home. It was after ten o'clock and Mam wouldn't go to bed before someone came in. In the doorway opposite number seven, a form was visible in the poor light from the street lamps.

"Night Maggie," Viv called, and an arm waved in response. Maggie Wilpin hated night-time which, for her, was filled with an irrational fear that she wouldn't see the next morning. She would sit outside prolonging the day as much as she could, and shortening the time of danger. Behind her a wireless played softly, and above, her great-grandson Gwyn, who delivered papers for the local shop, lay restless, waiting for her to settle to sleep. When she was in bed, he would climb out of the window and creep along the dark roads trying car doors to see what he could steal. His father had shown him how, and Dad would be out of prison soon. Gwyn smiled in the darkness thinking of the pleasure of showing his father his hoard of successful snatches.

The Lewises' house was still when Viv stepped inside, the clock ticking abnormally loudly on the wall. His father was dozing on a chair in front of the fire but woke when he spoke to him.

"Your mam isn't well again," Lewis Lewis told his son. He nodded towards the grate where a teapot stood covered with its hand-knitted cosy. "Cup of tea fresh made. I'm waiting for Rhiannon to come in then I'm off to bed."

"I'll wait if you like, Dad," Viv offered but was relieved when Lewis shook his head.

"Promised your mother," Lewis explained with a pained look in the direction of the bedroom. These days they all avoided upsetting Dora, as she lost her temper faster than usual.

Since discovering that Lewis and Nia Martin, who owned Temptations, the sweet shop on the corner, had been having an affair, Dora had been very difficult and on occasions had needed a sedative to calm her, so they all took extra care not to upset her. The situation had been exacerbated by Rhiannon working for Nia Martin, successfully running the sweet shop for her.

Rhiannon arrived before Lewis and Viv had drunk their tea and she looked upset.

"Everything all right, love?" her father asked.

"Oh, I'm a bit fed up that's all. Eleri is all right, the doctor thinks she might not go as long as they first thought though. She's getting impatient to have this baby."

Lewis poured her a cup of tea and said no more. Rhiannon must be thinking her own chances of marrying and having a child were slowly fading, even though she was only twenty. She loved Barry Martin, Nia's son, but Barry was married and although he was promising to seek a divorce, it

17

was probably upsetting for Rhiannon to see Eleri and Basil happy, and awaiting the arrival of their first child, while she and Barry were having to wait years for him to be free.

Footsteps were heard from upstairs and the trio waited with some trepidation to see what mood Dora was in. She smiled and their shoulders relaxed.

"Hello Rhiannon, love, is Eleri all right?" Reassured on that she turned to her son. "Where've you been, Viv, out with someone nice? When are we going to meet her?"

"Who? There's no 'Her' in my life, no time for courting. Good heavens, with all the hours I work? Who'd put up with that?"

"Oh some girls might," Rhiannon said with a sly wink.

"I went to the pub and had a drink with the Griffiths boys, before that I went to talk to Old Man Arfon, to discuss giving a few peasants the push," he joked, "that's about all." He explained properly then, about having to lose two assistants.

"It does make sense to cut down on your wages bill, son," Lewis agreed.

"It seems I'm the only one able to drag the Westons out of the mire, Dad," he said with some pride. "Old Man Arfon trusts me and listens to what I suggest. I must admit it feels good."

"What about Islwyn and Ryan, when are they going back to work?"

"They aren't. At least, not with me they aren't. I told Old Man Arfon flat, I don't want two snooty,

18

idle passengers while I'm trying to rescue the business they demolished."

"And he takes that sort of talk from you?" Dora asked.

"It's only banter, he knows I don't mean any disrespect, he enjoys a bit of cheek coming from the working classes," Viv grinned. He touched his mother's arm and looked at her seriously. "Mam, you ought to find a job you know. There's a real shortage of reliable people. Someone good at book-keeping like you are would be a real asset to a struggling firm."

"Your father can keep me, Viv. Less for him to spend on that Nia Martin then, isn't there?"

"Nice try, Viv," Lewis said softly as Rhiannon and her mother went upstairs.

When Viv had left the Westons' house, Arfon sat in his study for a long time, contemplating his future plans. That Viv Lewis would feature in them was in no doubt. He had done well to offer that young man a partnership. He was working many more hours than he was paid for, planning and scheming to make a success of the business far more energetically than if he had been on a normal employee status. And the promise of a share of the profits was nothing more than a joke at present, no more than a carrot to urge the boy on to better efforts. Besides the expediency of making him a partner and getting more work out of him, Arfon liked the fiery young man.

He often wondered why he had so much less liking for his own family. He didn't have to explain things to Viv, or listen to hours of griping about how difficult the job was. Viv met difficulties like a hole in the road, he either bumped across and suffered the slight inconvenience, or went around them. His useless sons-in-law Islwyn and Ryan complained and abandoned the journey. Pity sons-in-law couldn't be sacked like useless employees!

Gladys popped her head around the door before she went up to bed, to see if he needed anything. Mair had gone home, the maid didn't sleep in but arrived at eight in the morning and left after preparing supper.

"Is everything all right, dear?" she asked.

Arfon decided that this was a good time to explain to his wife the seriousness of their situation. "That court case is behind us, Gladys and that's a relief I can tell you, but no, everything is far from all right." He reached out and took her hand. "It's serious, my dear. We've absolutely no spare cash. In fact we might have to sell up."

"Isn't Viv Lewis doing what you hoped?"

"Oh it isn't Viv, he's doing marvellously. Got a flare for business that boy has. If only ours were half as keen and clever we wouldn't be in this mess. No, the shop will survive, unless we have some real bad luck. It's just this house and all we do for the family. We'll have to stop the allowances to the girls straight away, and as for this place," he looked around him at the warm cosy room in the house where he had brought Gladys as his bride. "It will have to go, dear. We have to sell up and look for something smaller."

"Nonsense, Arfon. I'm not extravagant, we live comfortably, that's all. You must admit I've never pestered you for a grander house up at the park or near the sea. I've been content to live here, where we began."

"But we keep this large place so there's room to feed the family several times each week, and accommodate the family at Christmas and so on. And we do support them generously, don't we?"

"A little perhaps."

"Gladys, love, we have to point out to Ryan and Islwyn, firmly, that we can do so no longer. It might make them look to their own skills to support their families at last."

"I suppose it is about time," Gladys admitted. "But I don't know whether they are up to it, do you? They've always had the business to lean on. A safe and steady income to support them."

"They don't realise it yet, but that support has gone and they've just fallen over!"

Chapter Two

Old Man Weston hated facing his daughters and telling them he was without funds. Ever since his twin daughters were born he had given them an allowance and it hadn't ceased upon their marriage and now after forty-one years it must.

Gladys had given one of her demands for the family to gather, and in the large sitting room, where so many family affairs had been discussed, he told them there was no money.

"We can no longer manage your monthly allowance," he told Sian and Sally sadly. "And," he added with a glare of disapproval for his sons-in-law, "of course the firm can no longer pay wages to Islwyn and Ryan. It's a long time since they earned it anyway!" he growled.

"Arfon, dear," Gladys whispered, "you promised not to upset the girls."

"I've paid most of my debts and I am clear of any further punishments, thankfully," Arfon went on in his portentous manner, his voice booming out as if he were talking in a large hall instead of his sitting room. "There is precious little left in the kitty, and I have to make sure we have reserves in case of problems." He turned to his wife and said jokingly, "If you break a window, Gladys my dear, we'll have to use some of the net we used during the war to hold it together, we can't afford a new one!"

"Tell Mair, not me," Gladys hissed, glancing towards the door. "I only have to say 'good-morning' to Mair for her to drop whatever she's holding!"

"She'll have to go," Jack said, but his grandmother shook her head.

"I can't manage this house without help."

"That brings me to another thing. This house," Arfon began, but Gladys shook her head more urgently and he finished, "– but perhaps another time."

It was clear that their daughters were concerned. Having an income from their parents had been so casually accepted that they had never thought about it. Now, the idea of losing both the allowance and their husbands' wages was frightening. How would they manage? they demanded, Sally petulantly and Sian with some aggression.

"You have husbands, the responsibility is theirs," Arfon reminded them gently. "It has never been ours, mine and your mother's, not since you married. We've been glad to help, but the responsibility is Ryan's and Islwyn's, surely?"

"What if we want to marry, Grandfather, will there be money for that?" Megan surprised them by asking.

"You don't even have a serious boyfriend so why ask that?" her mother demanded.

"About time they did," Gladys said. "And don't worry, dear, we wouldn't allow you to suffer a Register Office wedding. No, whatever the circumstances, your grandfather and I will see that you and Joan have weddings the town will remember."

"How?" Arfon said in exasperation. "Damn it all, there's me telling them there's no money and you put your oar in and suggest we've got a secret hoard!"

"It doesn't matter, there isn't anyone in their lives," their mother said confidently. "I'd know if there were, they're just tormenting you and making sure they won't miss a share of whatever's going. Wicked you are, Mother, the way you indulge them."

"Only until they make a successful marriage, Sally dear."

Islwyn gave an unexplained laugh then called Mair to fetch his overcoat. He was always the first to leave. He grabbed his coat as if accusing Mair of trying to steal it, and hurried out into a night that was dark and thick with a fog that almost swallowed up the glow from the street lamps. Melancholy in the darkness, the fog horn gave its wooo-ump, wooo-ump. But even that seemed quieter; deadened by the damp air. Islwyn's footsteps faded as quickly as his figure dissolved in the gloom.

Making her excuses, Sian went out in search of her husband, but with little hope of seeing him until the small hours.

Jack watched his mother go after his father and sighed. "D'you really imagine my father will find work and keep her, Grandfather?" he asked. "You spoilt them for too long."

Arfon shrugged and said, "Facts have to be faced and I am in no position to support them any longer. Damn it all, Jack, they should be helping us at our age, not the other way about!"

"I agree," Jack said, "but expecting them to take your bounty and at the same time become independent was some hope, Grandfather. Coming for a drink? I'm going to The Railwayman's for an hour."

"I think I'll go to the club. I don't fancy much company tonight. I'll find a corner and hide behind a newspaper. You've all made me feel more guilty than that judge did!"

Some hours later, the fog precipitated into rain that chilled the night air and made the street lamps almost useless, so walking became almost as hazardous as the wartime blackout. Arfon stood outside his club fastening his coat against the steady drizzle. Not far to walk, but far enough for him to wish he had brought the car. The shiny wet pavements were deserted. Only a couple arm in arm, strolling along as if the night were warm and bathed in moonlight. Fools, he chuckled, remembering how he and Gladys had done the same thing more than forty years ago.

As he watched, the couple parted after a brief embrace and the girl ran, on ridiculously high heels, to a bus stop. A single decker loomed out of the night spitting water away from its tyres like wings,

25

and Arfon decide to catch a bus for the two stops between the club and his home.

Glancing briefly to check on traffic, he crossed the road in front of the bus which slowed as it approached the stop. A man alighted, calling to his friends and Arfon stepped onto the platform. It was as he was settling into his seat that he realised the girl had disappeared. He looked out of the steamy window and saw her limping in the direction he was travelling. Damn it all, the young woman might not have had the fare on her. He could easily have given her tuppence or thruppence if she needed it.

Around the next corner the girl leaned against a wall and took off her shoes, she hestitated only briefly before pulling off her precious nylons too. She'd have sore feet anyway, no point in ruining her stockings as well! What a hoot, almost bumping into Grandfather Weston like that. He'd have had something to say about her kissing a boy on the street, even if it had been dark!

What more he would say if he knew it had been Viv Lewis who was one of grandfather's employees! Grandfather Weston had strong ideas about class, and Viv Lewis was most certainly not suitable company for one of Grandmother Gladys's Weston Girls.

Their name wasn't Weston, but affectation made her grandparents insist they used it. Megan and Joan Fowler-Weston they were called and their father, Ryan Fowler, had accepted that his name was not good enough without demur. Weston money soothed their way through life and Ryan was not one to complain about that.

Her twin, Megan, was at their grandparents' house and if necessary, Joan knew she would cover for her absence but she did want to be back in time for supper, which Grandmother usually served at nine-thirty. Joan and Megan had just come that day to stay with Gladys and Arfon for a week, while their parents were visiting their other grandmother, Grandmother Fowler, in Penarth. Probably in the hope of some money, she and Megan had surmised.

Reaching the gate she waited in case her grandfather had stopped in the porch for a final cigarette before going inside. She had been caught by that little habit of his before! When she was sure all was clear she slipped in through the kitchen door, where the maid, Mair Gregory, working late for the week of their stay, turned away and pretended she hadn't seen her. With a whispered, "Thanks, Mair," Joan ran up the wide staircase to the room she shared with Megan.

Although Joan had escaped the notice of her grandfather, someone else had recognised her as she ran away from the bus stop. Her Uncle Islwyn.

"And there's old Gladys talking about them marrying sucessful," he muttered with a wry smile. "A shop boy from Sophie Street. That'll impress her for sure!"

Although he was only forty-four Islwyn walked in the shuffling gait of an elderly man. He had followed Joan around the corner, darting back as he saw her raise her skirt and begin to slip off her stockings.

"Really," he muttered, "the Weston Girls have no sense of what's right, no restraint. Ruined proper they've been, by their doting grandparents."

When he dared to look again around the corner of the fence Joan was gone. Islwyn strolled on, wondering vaguely which of the twins it had been. Joan probably. She had always been the worst of the two.

Islwyn rarely left his house except at night, apart from when summoned by Gladys. Since the police investigation and the revelation that he had been stealing from the family's wallpaper and paint stores, he had become an empty husk, compared with the haughty and unbearably smug man he had once been. Resentment had caused him to take from the firm to compensate for the lack of money his son Jack received compared with those flighty nieces of his.

Jack hadn't minded his twin cousins being fêted with clothes and entertainment and treats practically every day of their lives, but Islwyn had. Resentment had grown over the years until he'd had to do something to redress the balance for his son. Jack used to laugh and say that it was what made Grandmother Gladys Weston happy, and it gave him pleasure to watch.

Now the small nest egg he had built up for Jack had been confiscated and he had narrowly escaped a court appearance. The fact that he had escaped facing a judge and jury hadn't prevented the publicity. The papers had reported the affair to the exclusion of everything else – or so it had seemed. There had been so much talk he rarely felt able to show his face. As for working, how did his father-in-law expect him to find work, with everyone knowing he'd been accused of taking money? Money that in any case rightly belonged to him, or at least to his son.

Sian pretended to be concerned for him when there were people about but in fact didn't speak to him when they were alone, except when absolutely necessary. He was living a half-life, hiding away until night time enabled him to leave the house and the recriminating eyes of his wife, and take some exercise.

For no reason at all, he followed in Joan's footsteps to the Westons' big house on the road overlooking the docks, and stood for a while imagining the look on Gladys's and Arfon's faces if he told them that their precious granddaughter was meeting Viv Lewis, that perfidious little man who worked in their shop.

Smiling at the imagined scene, he wandered up the hill to the main road and on around the town, a lonely, shabby figure lit occasionally by street lamps and the light from house windows. He hadn't eaten since breakfast and he wondered idly whether Sian had left him anything for his supper. He hoped not. He wasn't hungry, eating was too much of an effort.

The rain had stopped. He walked on over the beach, half frightened by the empty, dark place where the ghosts of holiday entertainment seemed to watch him from the shadows; where echos of laughter hovered on the wind, mocking his misery.

After supper, during which Gladys Weston demanded to hear all about the twins' day, Megan and Joan escaped to their room.

"Did you meet him?" Megan whispered.

"I did and we went for a walk in the rain," Joan replied.

"Hardly exciting!"

"Viv Lewis is hardly exciting at the best of times, all he talks about is Grandfather and the business. He's a good dancer though. Pity we can't go with him more often, instead of the boring people Grandmother approves of. I enjoy his company more than most. He doesn't kowtow to us like so many of our friends.

"Most of our so-called friends ignore us! No one kowtows to us since the accusations against Uncle Islwyn and dear old Grandfather, do they?" Megan said sadly. "D'you know, I still can't believe Grandfather would set fire to his shop to save his business. That's criminal and how can you put Grandfather Arfon in that category?"

"That letter Viv Lewis and Basil Griffiths found, with the confession of the man who actually struck the match seemed so undeniable."

"Don't talk about it now, tell me about Viv."

"We talked about Uncle Islwyn, which is why I mentioned him now, I suppose. Viv feels so bad about it all."

"Rubbish! He's responsible, isn't he?"

"Hardly, Megan."

"He told on him."

"That's hardly being responsible, is it?"

"Poor Grandfather. And poor Grandmother. It's worse for her than any of us. We'll probably marry and be free of this worry about money, but she loves being important and this has made her a figure of fun." Megan smiled then, her carefully made-up face not quite hiding the young girl behind the sophisticated mask. "Let's plan a surprise for her, shall we? Something special to take her mind off it all for a while."

"Such as?" Joan arched a brow indicating it was a futile hope.

"Viv gave me the idea. He thought a trip into Cardiff, lunch out and a wander around the shops, you know how she loves that."

"Oh, very exciting that would be! You heard Grandfather telling us there was no spare money. She won't be able to go shopping for years, if ever."

"We could treat her, and take her to the theatre."

"Us pay, you mean?"

"Why not, Joan? She's given us plenty in the past."

"It's a novel idea, but would she agree?"

"We'll tell her it's all booked and insist she takes it or risk hurting our feelings."

Joan shrugged. "All right. We'll ask her." She turned then and glared at her sister. "Megan, exactly when did Viv give you this idea? When did you see him? I thought we'd agreed that you were tired of him and I was going out with him – until I grew tired of him?"

"I called into the shop to collect some papers for Grandfather. We talked about Grandmother then. Don't worry. Viv Lewis is all yours!"

"So is that face cream! So hand it back. Now!" Joan retorted.

*   *   *

31

Gladys Weston sat up long after Arfon and the twins had gone to bed. She sat near the low fire and thought sadly about how her dreams were fading. She was sorry for Jack of course. He must have had to cope with a lot of abuse, with his father accused of fraud and his grandfather of arson. His career as a school teacher might not be much, but he seemed to enjoy it. But it was far far worse for the twins, her Weston Girls.

Jack was her failure she had decided long ago. He wouldn't conform to her idea of making the Weston name more important, a name which made people sit up and take notice. She remembered sadly how hard she had tried to persuade him to become a solicitor or a doctor or a financier – she had always thought that sounded rather grand – but he had laughingly refused to consider anything she suggested.

"If you want me to have power, Grandmother," he had chuckled, "I'll become a bus conductor, there's a smart uniform and everyone will take notice as I ring my little bell and stop and start the bus. Now there's power for you!"

No, it was useless and a waste of time to try and make something of Jack, she thought with a sigh.

"You all right, Grandmother?" a voice whispered and Megan peeped around the door. "I hadn't heard you coming up and I wondered if you needed anything. A nice cup of tea? Or Horlicks?"

"Thank you Megan, a cup of Horlicks would be nice. Then you must go to bed. Even someone as lovely as you needs her beauty sleep you know."

An hour later, the drink cold and untasted, Gladys still sat near the revived fire thinking. But now her face had lost its sadness. Her eyes glowed with excitement; she had decided what to do. The year of 1953 was almost out, but it could be the year in which the engagements of Joan and Megan and Jack would be announced. Or at least the year in which they started courting in real earnest.

She would show everyone that the Westons were not hiding away in shame. Planning the weddings would bring them to the notice of their one-time friends and make them wish they hadn't abandoned them when disaster had struck. She pulled out a note book and began to write down the names of all the eligible men she knew.

It was already October, so she could count the time in weeks only, but by the time the fire had issued its last dying flame and settled into grey lifeless ash, her first big plan had been born. She crept up to the room she shared with Arfon and slept like a baby.

Viv Lewis opened Weston's Wallpaper and Paint Store, and went at once to the small office which jutted out from the top of the stairs and overlooked the shop floor. It was an hour before the place was open for customers and half an hour before the rest of the staff arrived.

He liked this time on his own, time to sort the post, if Henry Thomas wasn't late again, and deal with some of the bookwork that needed his full attention. By coming in early, he was able to spend more time on the shop floor, dealing with customers himself when he could, and always listening to make sure the staff looked after them properly. Although, after next week the staff would consist of only one.

Viv loved his job. He had started there as an odd job boy supposedly observing and learning the business but he had soon shown himself capable and enthusiastic, offering ideas to Arfon when he appeared and infuriating Arfon's sons-in-law. They had not been able to accept his abilities, even now when he had made a remarkable improvement in the business they had all but killed.

It had been Viv who had brought them to the brink of disaster, hadn't it, they reminded anyone who would listen, by bringing to light the truth about the fire which had burned down the premises many years before? And through that – Islwyn said so often he almost believed it – the police had delved deeper and mistakenly thought Islwyn had been stealing from his father-in-law's firm for years.

Rightly or wrongly, Viv had been sacked, but Arfon had soon realised that if he were to save the business for when the court cases were over, he needed someone like Viv to restore it and build it up.

Viv knew that by offering the job and eventually making him a partner, Arfon had made enemies for him, of both Ryan, and Islwyn. Being found guilty of cheating on his father-in-law didn't stop Islwyn hating him and blaming him for his thieving becoming public knowledge. In Islwyn, Viv knew he had a dangerous enemy.

Which was why it was fun to meet the Weston Girls in secret and to enjoy calling Jack his friend. For a while he thought he had lost Jack but they were gradually reverting to their previous comradeship, although both avoided the subject of fire, theft and the vagaries of British justice.

Now, in the quiet shop, he watched as Henry Thomas bent down and stuffed the morning's post through the letter box and shouted, "Sorry I'm late, boy, the alarm clock called me so quiet I never heard it. Too soft it was, so was the bed!"

Viv waved and went down to see what needed immediate attention. Today was half-day closing and he hoped to finish on time and meet Jack after school closed, for a spot of fishing.

The letter, with its large, bold handwriting stood out from the rest and he opened it, a smile flickering around his lips. Joan!

'*Eight o'clock on Sunday. Usual Place.*'

That was all it said, and he tore it up into small pieces and threw it in the bin. He would join the boys for an hour first, meeting them at the Griffithses, from where he could run across the fields to the corner where they usually met. That way he had an alibi of sorts, although he'd have to be careful not to drink too much of Hywel Griffiths's home-brew!

To his surprise he had a second invitation that day. Friday was his birthday, his twenty-first, and Jack had remembered.

"I thought you might like to come out for a meal," he said when he called at the shop after school closed at lunch time.

"Thanks!" Viv was pleased. Apart from a gift from his parents and Rhiannon, he hadn't expected his twenty-first to be very different from the other birthdays.

"I've booked a table at Montague Court over the beach."

"Dining with the crachach are we? I hope I don't forget and use a knife to eat my peas!"

"Just don't drink out of your saucer!"

"My grandfather used to, Jack," Viv said. "Bless his socks, he started work early and if he overslept, my Gran would make a cup of tea then pour it into four saucers to cool it and he'd go along the line slurping it up."

"Clever, but I don't think they'd like it at Montague Court, d'you?"

"Dare me?"

"No, Viv! I don't!"

Gladys Weston wore her fur-trimmed coat and carried her most expensive leather handbag. Her shoes and gloves were best leather too, and she walked tall and looked with disapproval on everyone she passed. So many of her smiles had been ignored in recent weeks she no longer offered any.

Going into the bank, she sighed to see several other people waiting. Even Caroline Martin, the sister of the awful Griffithses, was opening a bank account.

36

Really she thought, a frown folding creases in her brow, there was no knowing who you'd bump into in a bank these days. So many common people knowing your business. She pushed her way through the small group of people waiting and sat in the chair near the counter.

"I have an appointment to see the manager," she announced loudly. She had no such thing, having disregarded his constant plea to telephone first, but she had no intention of standing in line behind the likes of the Griffithses.

"Oh, good morning, Mrs Weston. I'll go and see if he's free." The man behind the counter abandoned those waiting and scuttled into the back room. He came back a moment later and with a face reddening in embarrassment, said, "I'm sorry, Mrs Weston, but there seems to have been a mistake. No appointment has been made."

"Then you'd better make one quickly hadn't you!" Gladys sat glaring around her while the other customers stood in line and patiently waited.

When she was shown into the manager's office, she announced without preamble that she wished to withdraw her money and close the account.

"But, why, Mrs Weston? There isn't anything wrong is there? If we have been remiss in any way—"

"I have no wish to discuss my affairs with you, young man, if you would please arrange for me to receive the money in two days time I will call then and collect it."

"But – it's rather a large amount. I wouldn't be happy allowing you to walk out carrying it."

"No one would know what I was carrying – unless you plan to tell all and sundry." Gladys drew herself up and added, "No one would dare to attack me, if that's what you were thinking."

The manager couldn't disagree. The woman was probably made of granite!

Gladys had been saving what she could, to add to her personal account for many years, imagining some really spectacular birthday present for the twins on their twenty-first. That hadn't materialised, as their other grandmother in Penarth had arranged something for them there. Now she hoped the party would be an engagement celebration. She planned to introduce her Weston Girls to all the most eligible young men in Pendragon Island. Now Arfon was safe from a prison sentence she could begin her campaign to find husbands for her girls. And a wife for Jack of course. At least he wouldn't be so costly!

Having collected her money two days later, she went to the house of her daughter Sian. She hoped Islwyn wouldn't be there. She'd heard he spent most of his time in his room, only going out at night. And that, she thought, is a very good thing. Stupid man, robbing from his own family! He deserved all he suffered. How her lovely daughter Sian could have got herself married to a stupid man like Islwyn she had never understood. Islwyn had completely taken her in. She would make sure Joan and Megan were better suited.

Sian was in the kitchen, a smudge of flour on her cheek revealing her activity. A good cook, Sian spent a lot of time in the kitchen. Even with food still rationed, Sian enjoyed making attractive and nutritious meals. Gladys sniffed disapproval, what a waste, using such wonderful skills for someone like Islwyn!

"I am planning a party, dear," she told Sian. "I don't know exactly when it will take place but probably some time towards the end of the year."

"Mummy, d'you think it's wise to arrange something now? Wouldn't it be better to wait until memories fade and people have stopped gossiping about us?"

"What do you mean, Sian! We Westons create situations; we don't bow down to what others decree! Now, what d'you think of a Friday evening? Saturday is such a common day on which to celebrate anything, don't you think?"

"With Islwyn in this state?" She whispered this, glancing towards the door to the hall. "How can you celebrate with Islwyn hiding like . . .?"

"A scared rabbit?"

"Mother!"

"The celebration will be for your father, not Islwyn and Ryan, and I'm sure you won't want to disappoint him, he deserves a show of our love and support."

Outside the door, Islywn listened, his expression hardening.

On Friday, Jack and Viv arrived at Montague Court on Jack's motorbike. Hurriedly arranging their clothes for a suitable entrance into the rather

39

elegant restaurant, Jack announced their booking. They were shown into a very large room which had been changed very little from the drawing room it had once been.

The Jenkiness were a family who could trace their ancestors back for many generations. The area had once been their estate and Montague Court the family home. The land had been sold and now supported families of people instead of cows and sheep, but the house remained in the family, only its use had changed. As an Inn, run by Mr and Mrs Leonard Montague Jenkins, it was still their home and also their business.

Gwennie Woodlas smiled at them from a corner and two of Arfon's friends nodded politely as they ate.

"Isn't that Edward Jenkins?" Viv asked after the waiter had taken their order for steak Montague, which wasn't steak at all, but sausage meat. "I remember being told about him at school."

"Shot during the war, see how he limps?" Jack whispered. "Good runner before that, now he helps with the family hotel with his sister Margaret. I heard about them from Terry, their cousin. We met in the army but I've lost touch now."

"If you know him why didn't he speak?" Viv demanded. "Stuck up, is he?"

When the waiter returned, Jack smiled and said hello, and asked if he heard from Terry.

"My cousin is in London, I believe," Edward replied, without looking directly at them. "Selling jewellery in some store. My grandfather writes to

40

him occasionally. He would have his address if you wish to get in touch."

"No, it's all right, we weren't close, I just thought, seeing you, that he might be living here too."

"A separate part of the family really, Mr – er—"

Unknown to either of them, Terry Jenkins was on his way to Pendragon Island, but he had no immediate plans to see either his grandfather or his cousin Edward. All he wanted was a place where he could hide.

In Sophie Street, life for the Lewises continued in its uneasy way. Dora no longer worked. She had given up her insurance round soon after she had discovered her husband's long-standing affair with Nia Martin who owned the corner sweet shop. Her husband Lewis Lewis was still living at home, although their marriage was nothing more than an act for the benefit of others.

Dora was frightened to the edge of panic several times each day and for much of each night. What would she do when Lewis left her? She was certain that one day he would. There was a limit to how long she could hold him with the threat of illness. It was Nia Martin he wanted, not her. Not any more.

With the children grown up and ready to leave the home she had provided for them for over twenty years, and no longer even having a job to make her get up and start the day, she was fighting the temptation to stay in bed and lose hours, day after day, in wallowing

41

self-pity. No one needed her any more. At forty-five she was of no further use.

She blamed Nia for much of the time and Lewis for a lot more but somehow it always turned around and became her fault. If she had been different. If she hadn't been so quick-tempered. If she had made something more of herself, built a career, made herself more attractive. The list was endless and in the end counting all her faults on her fingers achieved nothing. She was still going to lose him and she was still afraid. The rejection was so cruel. All the years of loving thrown on the rubbish heap like dead roses and rotten potatoes.

Lewis Lewis had lost his job selling freezers and frozen foods when revelations about his private life came to the attention of his employers, and he now had a lesser job selling sweets. Their daughter, Rhiannon, worked at the sweet shop owned by his mistress, Nia, and it was to Rhiannon he went now, at the end of his day, to see if she needed anything. Not that he needed to, it was a ploy to delay walking into number seven Sophie Street and seeing Dora's accusing and bitter face.

"Rhiannon, love, it's me." He stepped behind the counter and called up the stairs on realising the small shop was unattended.

Lewis Lewis was tall, slim and extremely well dressed. His shoes never needed a shine, his suit was immaculately pressed and his shirt so white it dazzled. His black hair was slicked back and his moustache was a perfectly trimmed thin black line emphasising his full and shapely lips. His dark eyes had a habit of staring just that moment too long and made every woman believe he saved that special look of admiration for her alone. He was a flirt, and to old and young he gave his special wink and loving smile.

"Coming, Dad." Carrying down a bowl of hot water, Rhiannon came into the shop and smiled a welcome. "I'm closing in a minute, I hope you haven't called for an order. It's Friday and I'm off out to see Eleri and Basil later. Invited for supper I am. Then I'm going to set Eleri's hair so she's tidy, in case – you know, in case the baby comes."

"Are you walking all the way over to the Griffithses' house in the dark? Across those fields? Pity she doesn't still live with us, in Sophie Street. It's funny, love, but I still think of Eleri as my daughter-in-law. She might be married to Basil Griffiths now, but to me she's still Mrs Lewis Lewis."

"I still think of her as my sister-in-law and I don't think that will change." Rhiannon began washing down the counters and tidying the jars of sweets. "There's sticky these jars get. All the children seem to have hands that have been dipped in treacle!"

Lewis looked around the shop. "It looks spotless to me, everything neat and shiny. I don't think Nia has any reason to complain. She's delighted with the way you run Temptations."

"You still see her then?"

Lewis nodded. "I still see her. I'm living at home with your Mam but my heart is with Nia. Sorry, Rhiannon but that's how it is. And always will be."

43

Rhiannon rubbed harder on the sides of the jar of pear drops. Her long brown hair falling and hiding her face from his sight. "No point saying you're sorry."

"I know I messed things for you all, but life isn't orderly and harmonious. It's a pack of cards shuffled and thrown wildly about and we just have to tidy them as best we can and play the hand we end up with."

"There's certainly more than one joker in my pack!"

"Don't hang on to Barry Martin, love. He's out of reach now and a bit of an old sobersides anyway. Best you start looking for someone who'll give you some fun. It gets harder to find the older you get, mind."

"You saying I'm getting past it, our Dad?" she teased and he caught hold of her chin and turned her to face him, her eyes so brown in her small face framed in the thick, dark hair.

"Beautiful you are, Rhiannon Lewis, and there are plenty of young men out there who'd be proud to have you on their arm, believe me. Younger and more handsome than Nia's son, too."

"I'm happy to wait for Barry," she said quietly, her eyes suddenly serious.

"You think he and Caroline Griffiths will divorce then?"

"For sure."

"I'll have a word if you like?"

"No need, Dad. Barry and I know exactly what we're doing."

"You don't take after your ol' dad then, do you love?"

44

"Different colour hair and no moustache," she laughed.

Lewis walked to number seven Sophie Street and took out his key. He didn't want to go inside. He never did these days. It was Nia with whom he wanted to spend his evenings. But although they met frequently and even spent the occasional night together, he was committed to spending much of his time with Dora. Just enough to give the impression of a close-knit family to those who were unaware of the truth. Playing happy families, he thought bitterly, looking down the dark road as if planning an escape.

The lamp opposite was broken. With a couple of houses missing, victims of a bomb more than twelve years before, the council probably didn't think it was worth replacing. Number ten in the terrace was standing with nothing on one side of it, shored up with lengths of wood, the roof a frill of uneven slates, the gutters askew. Buddleia and rosebay willow herb had colonised the empty space, making a glorious display in the summer but a heap of tangled and rotted foliage now, that even from this distance smelled of earthy dampness.

There was no light in number eight and he wondered if Maggie Wilpin even had a fire. He stared, half closing his eyes to pierce the gloom. He saw a movement that could have been an arm waving, and knew Maggie Wilpin was sitting in her doorway looking out, watching him, aware of everything that went on.

Three of her grandsons had been killed during the

war and her grandson-in-law Charlie Bevan, was in prison for housebreaking and burglaries including a break-in at Nia's sweet shop, Temptations. Her great-grandson lived with her, his mother having run away soon after her husband had been conscripted into the army.

Lewis walked across and handed her a shilling. "Give that to your Gwyn, will you?"

Maggie snatched the coin and put it jokingly into her toothless mouth. "A good one, is it, Lewis?"

"Time you went inside, Maggie. It's cold sitting there."

"The night is long enough without me locking myself away before necessary," she grumbled.

When Lewis went inside, Dora called from upstairs, "What did she want, old mother Wilpin?"

"Nothing. I gave her a few coppers for Gwyn, that's all. With his dad in prison he probably doesn't get much."

"I don't think he goes short of anything. What he doesn't get given he steals. Like father like son!"

"I'm going out, Dora," Lewis announced as he finished his meal. "Probably call in at The Railwayman's for a swift half." He had to shout because Dora was eating her meal in the kitchen as she always did when he was at home.

He was eating with Rhiannon at the table made to accommodate six. Viv was out with Jack. Dora never ate with him, preferring to eat alone in the back kitchen. He never understood why, but presumed that to sit beside him and share a meal was some sort of favour he had failed to earn the right to receive.

"Is Viv going to The Railwayman's later?" he asked his daughter.

"Might be. It's his twenty-first, remember, and he'll want to share it with his friends."

"Jack has to go to his grandparents' house tomorrow," Dora called from the kitchen. "Old Man Arfon and Gladys summoned the family to a meeting about something or other according to Viv, and Gladys – 'She who must be obeyed' – Weston, refuses to accept any excuse for them not to attend."

"I thought Jack was the rebel, the one who refused to be browbeaten into doing as his grandmother demanded?" Lewis queried.

"He used to be," Rhiannon told him. "But with the family in trouble I think he feels more obliged to support them."

"It's over now though."

"Still plenty for the local gossips to chew on," Rhiannon said bitterly.

"People will soon forget. We gave them plenty to talk about, didn't we? But it's blown over."

"Fat chance for the Westons being allowed to forget in a hurry," Dora called from the kitchen. "All their grand talk and fancy ways, people love seeing them come toppling down. The reporters are licking their lips ready for any further juicy details that might be revealed."

Lewis looked thoughtfully into the fire. "It's hard on the family though. If Basil Griffiths and our Viv had only burnt the letter they found instead of taking it to the police—"

"They did the right thing!" Dora came in and snatched the plate he had just cleared and took it into the kitchen.

"I suppose so," Lewis said doubtfully. "Old Man Arfon setting fire to his shop was a criminal offence and he shouldn't get away with it because it harms his family. And our Viv wasn't responsible for the police discovering that Islwyn Heath had been robbing the firm, was he? But it's still hard on them."

"They'll survive," said the voice from the kitchen between clattering the saucepans.

"Joan and Megan put a brave face on things and they still have a few friends, mostly those who, like them, enjoy the notoriety I suppose, but they must be scared of what will happen to them all now there's no money."

"Arfon and Gladys will have to sell their big house then, won't they?" Dora called. "Have to manage with a small one like the rest of us do. It won't fetch much, mind, being in an unfashionable area."

"Gladys won't have so much money to waste on the girls either," Lewis added. "It's there the Weston Girls will be hit, in their pockets and on their backs. I don't think the actual disgrace upsets them too much, they have too much confidence for that!"

"Confidence or good actors," Viv said later, when Rhiannon told him of the conversation. "I doubt if Joan and Megan are as brave as they pretend."

Chapter Three

When Gladys Weston had all her family around her she felt like a queen. They were so beautiful: her twin daughters, Sian and Sally, Sally's twin daughters Megan and Joan – her wonderful Weston Girls, and Sian's son Jack, her handsome if stubborn grandson. Her sons-in-law she ignored. They were not important apart from behaving, for most of the time, as befitting a member of the Weston family, and caring for her daughters in a manner which she accepted as moderately good.

When she had provided them all with thinly cut sandwiches and small cakes, and a cup of tea stood beside each one, she told them the reason for inviting them all.

"My dears, I do think it's time we started to plan something for the party. Now what suggestions do you have? I thought a rather grand affair to celebrate the end of our worries, hiring a hall and a good orchestra and, perhaps an entertainer. What d'you think?"

The men looked at each other stiff-faced and obviously dreading the whole thing, the girls grinned, thinking of new dresses being made, and Sian and

Sally glanced at their father wondering if he thought the idea of a party a bit ill-timed.

"Gladys, I think we ought to leave it for a while. At least until echoes of the court case have faded, and we are better fixed financially," Arfon said pompously. He didn't want to remind her that they were broke. Not now, in front of the family, when it would embarrass her. He whispered to Jack instead. "She won't face the fact that we haven't the money for a big party. God 'elp, I can't even afford to take you all out for a meal in a restaurant, unless it's a Joe's Caff."

"Let her talk about it, Grandfather, then we'll gradually cool the idea."

"So, what ideas do you have for an entertainer?" Gladys was asking.

Ryan coughed and said now was not the time to celebrate. Islwyn said nothing, staring at his cucumber sandwiches as he nibbled and shaped it, as if working on a sculpture that was causing problems.

"Oh, come on all of you, whatever has happened, it's over. Joan and Megan need an excuse to revive friendships and make new ones. Besides, it's time to show the town that the Westons are still showing others how to do things." She looked at their dull faces and sighed. "A party for my girls. How can we let anything spoil that?"

"No one will come," Sian said. "Most of my friends ignore me these days and I'm sure it's the same for Sally."

"All the more reason for having a party. My parties are always events no one would want to miss." Gladys

50

was talking louder, a clear indication things were not going well. "D'you remember how hesitant you all were when your father and I wanted to take you to France? That was a wonderful holiday wasn't it? Do I ever plan something that's less than perfect? *Do I?*" she demanded when she didn't hear the expected response.

"No, Grandmother," Joan said and beside her Megan muttered an echo.

"Forget your so-called friends, Sian, and let us make a list of the young people we can invite. Jack?" She raised a pen and waited for him to suggest names.

"What about Viv Lewis? Basil and Eleri Griffiths?"

"I didn't intend inviting people like the Griffithses, dear, as you well know."

"Frank and Ernie Griffiths are good fun, even better than Basil where parties are concerned, and they've never been known to refuse an invitation," Jack went on.

"Now I know you're teasing me, dear. They'd start a fight within the hour and end up in – in court again," she ended quietly, regretting her choice of word. "Now, shall we be sensible?"

"Viv, and Eleri and Basil," Joan said firmly. "If it's our party then we should be able to choose."

"At least they don't treat us like lepers!" Megan added.

"Very well, dear," Gladys scribbled on her pad. She could always forget to send the invitation.

When they had made a list of possibles and prob-ables, Jack said, "It was Viv's twenty-first yesterday;

we went to Montague Court. You know, the house the Jenkinses have made into an hotel. Very smart and very expensive. Gwennie Woodlas was there, Grandmother, you know, from Guinevere where you buy your frocks."

"Was she? Pots of money, that one, I suppose she has to spend it somehow!" She frowned, remembering. "The Jenkinses? I remember Edward, wasn't he a tennis player or something, Jack?"

After a brief discussion, Gladys wrote the name on her list with a star beside it. The Jenkins family had been rather grand at one time, but perhaps they might consider an invitation to her party now they had come down in the world.

Jack stood to leave and others followed suit but Arfon raised his hand and settled into the stance for speech-making.

"There's something I want to say while we're all here together. I know your grandmother doesn't want to talk about it, but our financial problems won't magically go away. I want you to promise me that you will look after each other, support each other if the worst happens and we lose the business. Viv Lewis is doing a remarkable job." He glared at Ryan and Islwyn as if daring them to disagree. "But we're balancing precariously and it only needs a slight change in fortune and down we go. In an attempt to lessen that chance, I have to sell this house."

There were embarrassed murmurs and Gladys wiped away a tear.

"This house is in the hands of the estate agent and

he thinks it will be sold within the month as he already has two couples interested in buying it. Now, wherever we live, your mother and me, it will be the family home and I want you to make up your mind to that and not start weeping about losing anything. It's a change of address, that's all, something we should have done years ago if your mother hadn't been so sentimental about this place, where she came as a bride."

"Pity you didn't move to one of the houses near the park, Grandmother," Joan said. "It would have been worth several hundred more."

"We've been happy here. I've never wanted to move to somewhere grander," Gladys said firmly.

The reason Gladys had never moved from the large old-fashioned house overlooking the docks was that here she stood out from her neighbours and was a person of importance. The local people looked up to her and it made her feel good. Up among the really wealthy, either around the beach or alongside the park she would have been struggling to keep up.

"I wouldn't mind living over the island, as long as its not too near the Pleasure Beach," she mused. "Perhaps near the Jenkins. If it's good enough for them, with all those houses clustered around them, we should be able to find something acceptable."

"A house in that area is out of the question, dear," Arfon said, holding back increasing irritability. "Why won't she face facts, just this once?" he muttered to Jack.

"Something small of course," Gladys went on. "But with a view across the sea."

The Island was not an island but a spit of land on which the popular Pleasure Beach was situated. Pendragon Island, the town was called, even though the place had been joined to the mainland for centuries.

"Yes," Gladys said. "I think a small house over the Island would be rather nice, don't you, Arfon, dear?" She glared around at her family and added firmly, "We are considering moving simply because we are getting older and no longer need this large house, the court case is not the reason, I hope you will make that known."

Having to leave the house was distressing but she tried to hide it from the others. It wouldn't help Arfon if she were to get weepy. Yet it was breaking her heart to think of moving. This house was the story of their marriage, filled with memories. Every room and every corner of the garden echoed with children's laughter.

It had seen her carried in as a bride, had seen their daughters born and watched them grow. The scars of their activities were clearly seen on the walls and the furniture; scratches on the woodwork from their tricycles, a worn part of the bedroom linoleum where the old rocking horse had taken them on rides of fantasy, the apple tree on which they had all scratched their shins.

She gathered up the teacups and forced a smile. "Yes, Arfon, dear, I think we will start looking for a house over the Island. But—" she paused and looked slowly around the room, "– but what on earth will we do with all this furniture? Now if you two girls were courting, planning to be married, how convenient that would be. I could give each of you enough to make a start and we wouldn't have to part with a thing."

Islwyn didn't join in the general conversation when Gladys left the room, pushing the trolley into the kitchen for Mair to deal with in the morning. He stood up and looked out of the window across at the docks which were barely visible in the darkness. Only lights on the ships and along the edges of the water gave outline to the scene. A mist had reduced some isolated lamps to pale lollypops. A ship's hooter made a mournful sound. The view and the melancholy sounds matched his mood.

A party! he thought irritably. How ridiculous. And how could they even think of inviting Viv Lewis, whose lack of loyalty had put them in this mess? He walked through the hallway and gathering his overcoat, stepped out into the dark night. He didn't tell his wife he was leaving, or call goodnight to the rest. At the gate he stopped. Someone was coming and he didn't want to talk to anyone, not even to exchange a polite greeting as they passed. For no particular reason he went around the house and into the garden where the apple tree stretched up like the ghostly hand of a giant, bare of leaves and lit by the glow from the house.

Through the window he saw the family beginning to rise. The 'royal audience' was over, he thought sneeringly. Arfon handed out coats and, in pairs, the party left the room, pausing at the doorway to kiss Gladys. Childishly, Islwyn stood out of sight behind a straggly forsythia and listened to the snatches of conversation.

"Poor Grandmother, she's so brave but she doesn't want to move."

"Perhaps they won't," Sally said. "Perhaps the house is advertised for sale but they won't actually sell."

"They'll have to," he heard Jack said firmly. "There are still debts to pay and money is needed to build up the business again. The house will have to go so they can use what little they gain to help the business. It's their only chance of keeping it, according to Grandfather and Viv."

"I hope Daddy will cope with it all, he looks so tired," his mother sighed.

The mutterings faded as the group reached the pavement and went their separate ways.

"No one wondered where I went," Islwyn muttered. "*Persona non grata*, that's me."

He didn't follow Sian, and their son Jack, instead he wandered around the lanes and roads until he found himself outside the Lewises' house in Sophie Street. Two bicycles were in the front garden. One a woman's, obviously Dora's. The other must belong to Viv. He picked it up and rode it through the docks' entrance and along the narrow road beside the still, dark water, where the huge bulk of ships occasionally darkened his route with their shadows. When he reached a disused dock, where experiments for the beginnings of the wartime Mulberry Harbour had been built, he pushed the bike into the water. The resulting splash wasn't loud but very satisfying.

In their bedroom in Glebe Lane, Joan and Megan were discussing their family's problems.

"Perhaps we should get a job?" Megan suggested.

"That's ridiculous!" Joan retorted. "That would make Grandmother feel a real failure if we had to go out and earn a weekly wage."

"Things have changed, we aren't the wealthy Weston Girls who shock with their fashions and lead with their ideas and extravagances. We probably won't have an allowance for much longer. We have to do something, Joan."

"I've agreed to help Viv with the book-keeping, just for an hour or two on Saturdays, so I am helping, aren't I?"

"What can I do?"

"Get married."

"Chance would be a fine thing! It's ages since we were invited out."

"That's what this party's all about, isn't it? We're twenty-one, Grandmother and our mother were married and settled by our age. They're making a desperate attempt to create a marriage market, with us as the top offers!"

"In that case, I'm not going!" Megan said firmly.

Joan laughed. "Why not? If the Griffithses really do come it should be entertaining. There's sure to be a fight!"

"Poor Grandmother." Megan began to read her current library book but looked up in surprise when she saw Joan taking her winter coat out of the wardrobe. "Joan? You aren't going out?"

"It's only just after nine, you'll cover for me won't you? Go down and make two cups of cocoa and tell Mummy we're having an early night. Please, Megan."

Hurrying through the darkness, she was afraid Viv would have given up and gone home and she needed to talk to him about the situation in the shop. Grandfather must be exaggerating. Things were never that bad. Viv would tell her the truth.

Although the area was pitch black, she took a short cut through the empty space where Philips Street had once been and down Goldings Street. A sound split the silence and halted her, made her press herself against the side wall of the house she was passing. The house was one of three of which the middle one was occupied by Victoria Jones's family, her grandmother's ex-maid. It was from there that the sound came. The sound of a woman crying and wailing, eerie on the night air.

Cautiously she stepped back onto the pavement and walked past the houses. The door of the middle one opened as she passed and a woman stepped out. Her clothes were torn and ragged, and her face looked like somebody's nightmare. Joan felt the urge to run, and to add her screams to those of the woman who blocked her way.

Then she heard a calm voice say, "It's all right,

Miss Fowler-Weston. It's me, Victoria. My mother's had an accident. Fell she did. I'm just taking her to the hospital."

"Victoria?" Joan said in disbelief. "This is your mother?" The woman, covering half her face with a white towel looked more like a grandmother. She was small, and very thin, and her face was dark, almost skull-like. "Do – do you need any help?" she asked.

"No, the children will be safe enough, locked in till we come back."

"No, you stay with your brothers and sisters, I'll go to the hospital with your mother."

Frightened without really knowing why, Joan walked with the small woman back up to the main road and, when Mrs Jones refused to take either a bus or a taxi, continued through the back streets to the hospital.

Once in the light she realised the darkness of her face was due to bruises. Her eye was partly closed and her nose looked a little out of true. There was blood on her scalp too and, shaking with distress and shock, the woman looked weak and dreadfully ill.

It was apparent she had been there before as the nurse who met them took her away at once, calling her by name and soothing her with comforting words. Joan sat there in the coldly tiled area wondering what to do.

"We'll be keeping her in this time," the nurse explained later. "Because of the baby you see."

"Oh, I'd better go and tell her husband—"

"I doubt you'll see him for a while! But yes, I think

you need to let Victoria know her mother's safe. Friend are you?" She looked at Joan curiously, taking in the expensive coat and shoes and the leather handbag.

"No, I just happened to be passing," Joan said, disapproval on her face at the suggestion she could be associated with the woman she had brought there.

Victoria didn't invite her inside, but accepted the message through a crack in the door and thanked her formally and with some embarrassment. Walking away from the tragic little house, Joan began to think more seriously of her grandfather's attempts to revive the family business. The prospect of being poor after the comfortable way they had lived was terrifying. Surely he didn't want Grandmother to live in a house like that one?

She went home, sobered with the thought that whether they wanted to or not, she and Megan might be forced into looking for work. "We have to do something. Earning our crust is better than ending up in a place like Goldings Street," she told her sister when they were settled in their warm, comfortable beds.

Enforced jollification was how Jack described Gladys's search for a new home. Each one of them in turn had to go with her to look at the few houses available in the area she had chosen, and each place seemed sadder and more derelict than the last.

"It's no use, Grandmother," Jack said on his third trek, this time to look at a terraced house that had promised a fascinating view and ample room for a family. "The only view is of the house across the street and the family would have to be mice!"

"We can at least look while we're here," Gladys insisted. "At least the knocker has been polished. That's always a good sign, dear."

To their surprise a maid wearing a black skirt and a crisp white apron opened the door and invited them to wait in the drawing room.

The owner was an elderly man and from his clothes he hadn't been shopping since before the war. A heavy tweed suit that looked several sizes too large had once fitted him, Gladys guessed, and his shirt, although clean, was in need of a trim around the collar and cuffs. The brogues on his feet had been repaired just once too often and the leather patches on his elbows were out of place revealing tattered holes.

Thick eyebrows sprouted like wings above sharply intelligent blue eyes. A stained moustache, together with the ash on his waistcoat, revealed him to be a pipe smoker. Wealthy once but now finding times hard, was her whispered assessment.

The house was far larger than they had imagined, it was on a corner and actually spread wider than three of the houses nearby. Previously hidden from their view was a walled garden and there was a garage that had once been home to horses and a carriage.

Jack nodded encouragement as they were shown room after room. Four bedrooms, three reception and a scullery that was nothing more than a barn but which would make a nice kitchen. Above the bedrooms was an attic bedroom with a view that made truth of the description they had been given.

A brief conversation revealed that the man was Mr Jenkins, the grandfather of Edward Jenkins and his sister Margaret of Montague Court. Immediately, Gladys wanted it.

Jack was reminded of Terry Jenkins again. "You must be Terry's grandfather," he said. "I knew him for a while in the army."

"Oh, yes, Terrence," the old man muttered without exploring the connection further.

Three days later, an offer had been made on the Westons' present home. Gladys took Arfon and her twin daughters to see the one she and Jack had found.

"Gladys, dear," Arfon said when they had been shown around once more, "you don't understand. This one is as expensive as our own. We have to move to somewhere cheaper and use what money we can save to pay my debts and develop the business."

"In that case we aren't moving!"

"But Gladys, we have to raise some money."

"We'll manage. Ryan and Islwyn must help. We've helped them many times when they were getting started and plenty of times since. Now they must help us."

"But—"

"I'm not arguing, Arfon, dear. I'm just not willing to reduce our standards. How will my girls find suitable husbands if we are reduced to living in some slum?"

"Not a slum, but a small, inexpensive house."

"With small, inexpensive neighbours! No, we owe

it to Joan and Megan to give them a chance of finding someone deserving of them."

Arfon tried every way to convince her but Gladys would not be budged. Her answer to anger, frustration, insults and downright pleading was always the same.

"We are Westons, and we are staying put!"

Gladys went on with her plans for the party amid continuing protestations that the money was needed for more important things.

"Damn it all, Gladys, I daren't even take a drink of whisky from my cupboard in case I can't afford to replace it!"

"We're talking about my money, I've saved it from the housekeeping for this occasion and I won't let the goings on of Islwyn Fowler ruin my plans!"

"My 'goings on' too dear," he reminded her.

Gladys blamed her son-in-law for cheating the family firm but her husband's dishonesty was never mentioned. "Islwyn might be married to our daughter, Arfon, but he doesn't run this family, we do."

"Do *we*? Then I say *we* have to sell up and *we* have to cancel this party!"

"Pass me that writing pad, dear, I must confirm the Jenkinses on my list of invitations. That old man we met in the house you refused to buy for me, he's a Jenkins. I think we can count that as an introduction and invite his grandchildren. I wonder about Jack's friend Terrence? Is he married, d'you know? Perhaps he'll be home for Christmas; those old families make much of togetherness on special occasions – as we do of course, dear. If I arrange this party as close to Christmas as I can, he might be home and able to come." She tapped her cheek with her pencil, her eyes seeing into the future to a magnificent and glittering affair. "I wonder if I could call and ask his grandfather for his address?"

Arfon opened his mouth time and again to complain, but he gave up and chuckled instead. Somehow they were going to get through this and it wouldn't be crawling shame-faced in the dust, but head held high. He kissed Gladys and poured himself a large whisky.

In the disused area of the docks, a man was staggering along with a head full of aggression and a stomach full of ale. He stopped to pee in the water of the dock where the hollow containers floated rusted and forgotten. It had been intended to float them across the channel as part of the invasion plans but better designs had been developed and they had been left to rust away.

The man looked at the odd shapes, remembering how it had been to sail with those first invaders to set foot on French soil. A brightness in the water below him caught his bleary eye and he bent down to investigate. It was a bike and a good one by the look of it. The stone-built edge of the dock sloped sharply but he crawled down and reached out for the handlebar.

Giving a grunt of satisfaction he grasped the chrome handle but the shock of the water and the amount he had drunk caused him to be sick and confused, he lost his balance but still pulled on the handlebars. Instead of hauling it up, he was dragged down as the bicycle was eased away from the jutting rock on which it had been resting and the man sank, still holding to the handlebar as if for grim life.

It was very early in the morning and the ships, with their gangs of dockers busily at work, lacked form in the misty late-October air. Jack walked aimlessly, looking down into the depths occasionally for a sight of the grey mullet that abounded in the greasy water. Perhaps he'd meet Viv Lewis later and try for a few. Mucky water or not, they made a tasty meal.

Reaching the end of the docks he began to make for the road that would take him back through the town and to the school on the hill where his class of six-year-olds were waiting for him. He paused at the abandoned dock and at once saw the man. His legs were visible in the shallow water and the wheel of a bicycle could be seen beside his upside-down form.

He began to go down and haul him out but a sight of the man's face made him realise it was far too late; better not risk falling in himself, but go for the docks' policeman, whose house was not far away.

Later that day, the body was identified as that of Steve Jones, the father of Victoria, who had been a maid at the Westons' house.

"It looks like he'd stolen Viv Lewis's bike and was too drunk to manage it," the sergeant told Jack when he enquired later that day.

"His daughter Victoria, was my grandmother's

maid for a few years but I'm ashamed to say I know nothing about her family."

"Rough they are," the policeman confided, "and between you and me I don't think Steve Jones will be much mourned. Gave 'em a hell of a life, he did."

It was still distressing to learn of the man's lonely death and Jack's plans to go fishing were forgotten. He was heading for The Railwayman's to tell Viv and the others the news when he changed direction and went instead to Goldings Street to see Victoria.

At first sight, Goldings Street looked like the remains of some battleground. Bombed during the early part of the war, it had been more or less left for the tenants to make of it what they could. Most had been allotted smart prefabs, but three families still survived in the ruinous collection of houses, having refused to move out.

The three houses at the end, with empty space behind them, where Philips Street had been taken down ready for new houses to be built, were in reasonable condition and, when Jack approached, he saw that clean net hung at the front windows and the doorsteps had the half-circle in front of them where regular scrubbing had left its mark.

The rest of the houses had been cleared away but sufficient rubble remained to give the place a derelict appearance and the road surface, although patched, was uneven. Jack knocked on the door of seventeen and Victoria opened the door. He was shocked by her appearance, the neat little maid in her black dress and white apron was

66

unrecognisable behind the unkempt person before him.

"Victoria?" he began. "I just wanted to know if you're all right and coping with things. It was I who found your father, you see, and, well, I'm very sorry about his death."

Victoria burst into tears, and at once he put an arm around her to comfort her. "Don't be sad, it must have been quick," he said, but she pulled away from him and almost shouted,

"Sad? Sorry? I'm not sorry! I wish he'd choked on drink months ago, before he got my Mam up the spout again!"

The outburst and the crude expression startled him and he didn't know what to say. He stared, trying to recognise in her the quiet, extremely polite and obedient maid, and failed.

"You might as well come in," Victoria said and she stood back watching him quizzically as he entered.

There were two rooms and a small scullery and they were practically empty. A fire of wood burned in the oven range and a sooty pan simmered on the hob.

"He sold everything," she explained. "All our furniture, anything he could carry or cart away. Mam's in hospital and the others are with a neighbour till she comes home. I'm trying to think of ways of getting a bed for when she's discharged."

"The others? How many are you?" Jack asked quietly.

"Five besides me and there's another one due soon after Christmas."

"Is your mother all right? Not in any danger?"

"Just the usual beating. He gets – got – wild when he was drunk you see, and it ended up with him punching Mam then—" she was about to say he takes her upstairs but held her tongue. Even in her present tense state, she couldn't say such things to someone like Jack Weston.

"I don't understand, when you worked for my Grandmother things weren't like this?"

"They were heading this way. Dad's been drinking for years but he didn't get really bad until just before I left Mrs Weston. That was the reason I didn't try and persuade her to keep me on. I thought I could earn more, not having money stopped for my meals."

"Wash your face, I'm taking you out for something to eat, I'm starving," he added to quell her protest, "and I hate eating alone."

He took her to a fish and chip shop where a few tables were available for those wanting to eat on the premises. His first impulse was to go to a smart restaurant but knew that she would not be comfortable, in her unsuitably thin dress and shabby coat. His heart ached as he watched her thin red hands as she ate, neatly but quickly, until the plate was empty. Poor little kid.

"Basil!" he said and she stared at him curiously. "Basil Griffiths is the man to find you some furniture cheaply. He has a mind sharp as a razor, remembering who has what for sale and how much he needs to offer. We'll go now and see him."

"I ought to get back," she protested, but her voice held no conviction.

She waited outside The Railwayman's as Jack hurried in and dragged Basil out, then they went to another cafe and drank tea while they discussed Victoria's needs.

"I don't have much money, only a few pounds," she said, "until I get my wages on Saturday. Four pounds and five shillings altogether I'll have then." But the two men hushed her and promised to deliver what they could gather, on the following Saturday morning. Jack saw her back to her empty, lonely home and it was the most difficult thing he had ever done, to walk away and leave her there.

On Saturday morning he met Basil as arranged and with a borrowed horse and cart they arrived at Goldings Street, tooting the horn and shouting as if they were the beginning of some celebratory procession, which, in a way they were. Following a few minutes later came Frank and Ernie, Basil's brother and cousin, pushing a handcart. Eleri, heavily pregnant walked beside it carrying a loaded shopping basket.

An hour later, most of the furniture was in place, three beds, chests of drawers and couch and three chairs and a table which gave Victoria a surprise.

"That was ours!" she said, pointing to letters that had been carved on the drawer.

"That's right, I bought if off your dad, not knowing he was robbing his own family, mind, or I wouldn't have given seven and six for it."

The pantry held a few stores plus a couple of rabbits, a clutch of eggs and a dish of apples which were a result of Basil's 'scrumping' in a nearby orchard.

By the time Viv had closed Weston's Wallpaper and Paint stores and ran around to Goldings Street, most of the work was done and the weary removal men were sitting on the floor on a rug scrounged from Gladys and Arfon, drinking tea.

"Talk about timing, crafty sod," groaned Basil. "Look at him Eleri, how's he got the cheek to hold out a hand for a cup of tea when he's done nothing, eh?"

His wife laughed and stirred the cup before handing it to Viv. "Well, he ran all the way, not his fault if we've finished."

"Finished? He's down for painting the walls!"

The good-natured banter went on for a while, then they all left to allow Victoria to get beds made up in preparation for her family's return. Only Jack stayed.

"There's something you haven't unpacked," he said after the others had gone. "My cousins sent a few clothes, just to help until you get on your feet again." He watched her hoping she wouldn't be offended, but as she removed each article from the shopping basket Eleri had carried from his cousin's house, he saw she was laughing.

She held up the frilly, low-necked dresses and the summer coats in pale coloured flimsy material and asked, "Where do they think I could wear these? And these?" she added, holding up a pair of high-heeled shoes in pale blue suede.

70

"I might have known," Jack groaned. "My cousins aren't over-blessed with common sense!"

"I'm sure they meant well."

"You work for Viv, don't you?" he said, remembering being told about the new cleaner at the shop. "It's a bit hard isn't it, doing two jobs?"

"It's only until Mam is well again. She does washing and ironing – or she did, until the dolly tub and the table went!"

"I'll have a word with Grandmother Weston," Jack told her as he prepared to leave. "It would be better than going out at seven in the winter mornings to clean a shop."

"I don't mind, it pays for extra food, and Mam needs building up."

"I mind," Jack said firmly. "Grandmother wasn't such a terrible employer, I'm sure."

"I liked working there," Victoria admitted.

"She'd like you to come back. Mair Gregory is all right but she isn't used to Grandmother's little ways. She compares Mair Gregory unfavourably with you all the time. She really does wish you were back."

"What? After me giving evidence to the police about what I heard your grandfather and Viv saying about the fire?"

"We were all angry at the time, specially with you and Viv, but things settle and she would be relieved for things to go back to as they were. Mair isn't so willing – or as tolerant! I think she'll agree to pay you more than before, she wants you that much. Think about it and I'll call and see you tomorrow," he said.

"OK," Victoria grudgingly agreed. "But I want you to promise me you'll say nothing about my family troubles. If she takes me back it's because she wants me, and not because I'm a charity case."

He talked to Gladys with an urgency and with such persuasion that she almost agreed. Jack so rarely asked her for anything, how could she refuse him? But she did!

She admired his eloquent skills then scolded him, complaining that he really should have listened to her and become a famous barrister.

"But you can't really expect me and your grandfather to have a traitor in the house, dear," she explained, her face full of regret. So Jack had to accept her decision, for the time being, until he could think of another way to talk his grandmother round, without going back on his word to Victoria.

Chapter Four

Dora had lived in Sophie Street since her marriage to Lewis Lewis almost twenty-three years before, Christmas 1930. The sweet shop had been on the corner, three doors down, even longer than that, although in the old lady's day it had been called Katie's Confections. Nia had taken over from her grandmother and changed the name to Temptations and now with a long-time love affair between Nia and her husband, the name had an ironic ring.

The fact of her daughter, Rhiannon working for Nia was something that Dora tried not to think about. It had been arranged when in a flippant moment she had said she didn't care, but she did. Every day she hoped that Rhiannon would come home and tell her she was leaving but if anything Rhiannon was happier now than when she had first started work there.

A further tie between the families threatened as Nia's son had fallen in love with Rhiannon. It seemed for a while that she was going to have Nia's son as a son-in-law but thankfully that had fizzled out and Barry was now married to Caroline, one of the Griffithses. The accident that had killed her son, Lewis-boy had also caused the death of Nia's older son. Joseph Martin had died only hours after Lewis-boy, another connection between two women who each wished the other a thousand miles away. And it was then that the double tragedy revealed that Lewis was in fact the father of Nia's son, Joseph, as well. It was a shock from which Dora had never quite recovered.

What a mix-up, she sighed as she chopped mint and mixed it into vinegar to add flavour to two sad-looking chops. Viv heard her sigh and asked if she was all right. She pointed to the meat. "They call it lamb but I bet this poor sheep died of old age," she said.

"I don't care if it committed suicide, Mam. I'm starving," Viv replied. He ran upstairs to change out of his work clothes and into something more comfortable. "Will it be long? I'm going to see Jack Weston, do a bit of fishing."

"I don't know what you two do on that river bank, Viv, but I don't see many fish!" Dora teased.

"Mullet you'll have tonight, we're going to try the docks."

"After pulling that drunken old man out? I don't fancy any of that!" Dora heard Lewis's car and tried to keep the conversation going. It was always easier if she were involved with Viv or Rhiannon when her husband walked in. There was always that moment of uneasiness, the unspoken question about whether he would go out or stay in, and, if he went out, whether he would explain where he was going or leave her to wonder if he was meeting Nia.

Tonight he seemed to be in a good mood. He smiled, sniffed appreciatively and said he was starving. She didn't have the heart to tell him that the delicious smell was mainly the result of Bisto gravy and mint sauce.

"Rhiannon won't be long," Lewis said. "I saw the shop was closed when I came past."

"Unless she's talking to that Barry Martin. He seems to forget he's married and with a small son."

"Give over, Mam, we all know Barry and Caroline Griffiths aren't really married. He gave her son his name because his real father died with our Lewis-boy."

"I don't want to talk about Lewis-boy and all that," Dora said sharply, her eyes threatening a row.

"They're living apart and have been ever since the wedding. You can't expect Rhiannon not to see him until the divorce is through."

"I do expect it!" Dora's red hair and bright blue eyes seemed to glow as her temper began to rise. "There's no future in our Rhiannon carrying on with a married man. He might say he and Caroline are planning to divorce but where's the proof?"

"Leave it, Mam," Viv pleaded, glancing at his father who seemed to be concentrating on his food.

The conversation was conducted, as usual, with Lewis and Viv in the living room and Dora eating alone in the kitchen.

"I just hope she sees sense before she gets too old and ends up on the shelf," Dora shouted and with a forkful heading towards her mouth, added, "And Barry's too

75

old for her anyway! Not that that stopped his mother from carrying on with your father, mind!"

Lewis tilted back his chair and turned the radio on. There was an announcement that thirty thousand houses had been completed that month and he wished he was in one of them, far away from Sophie Street and Dora's bitterness. He wasn't interested in the news and didn't take anything in but it was better than Dora with her thinly-veiled reminders about his continuing affair with Nia. He had intended to stay in and go through his order book, listing the customers he would call on the following week but he changed his mind. Like so often in the past, he came through the door with good intentions but ten minutes of Dora and he wanted to escape.

When Rhiannon came in the mood lightened as she began talking about her day at the sweet shop. Who did his tolerant and cheerful daughter take after Lewis wondered, looking at her smile that encompassed them all? Viv was like his mother, red-haired and quick-tempered enough to prove the old story about redheads being fiery. Poor Lewis-boy had looked like him: black hair and dark eyes, and he had tried so hard to resemble him in every other way. Rhiannon with her brown eyes and thick brown hair was like neither and she was definitely the peacekeeper among the Lewises. If seven Sophie Street was a potential time bomb, primed to blow up, it was Rhiannon who held firmly to the fuse.

"I'm going out tonight, Mam," Rhiannon said as the table was cleared. "I'm going to see Eleri. Fancy,

76

her baby is due in a couple of weeks, can you believe how quickly the time has gone?"

"There's a box in the corner, that crocheted blanket I've made, and some embroidered pillowcases for later on. Take them, will you?"

Viv gathered his fishing gear, Rhiannon picked up the gifts for Eleri and before Dora could ask the question he dreaded answering, Lewis collected his order books and darted out of the front door to the car.

Dora thought of his smile when he had first arrived and it cut her deep inside. The smile was shallow, his real smile, full of affection and love was reserved for Nia Martin. Realising she was alone once more and unable, or unwilling, to find a way to pass the lonely hours, Dora smashed Lewis's plates and cup and saucer and calmly washed and dried the rest.

"I don't like you walking through the fields in the dark to visit Eleri," Viv said as they walked down Sophie Street. "It'll be different once the baby's born and she and Basil are back in their own home. Trellis Street isn't far."

"I'll be all right, I know the way blindfolded and I've never met a soul in all the times I've been there."

"Carry a stick then, just in case you meet a drunk or something," Viv pleaded.

"It's all right, Viv," Rhiannon said quietly. "I think us Lewises have had our ration of bad luck." She counted on her gloved fingers. "Losing Lewis-boy in that stupid accident, me and Barry finishing before we got started, Dad found out carrying on with Nia Martin, Mam and Dad fighting like cats."

They parted near Goldings Street and Viv hurried on to where Jack lived with his parents. Although they were not the close friends they had once been, they had recovered sufficiently to enjoy an occasional hour's fishing. Conversation did not flow as freely, confidences were withheld, but neither had many close friends and in the brief absence they had missed each other.

Using bread as bait they caught five grey mullet and argued amiably about who should have the odd one. In fact they each went home empty-handed, as Jack suggested they left the five fish with Victoria to help her feed her brothers and sisters, and their mother, recently discharged from hospital.

The house was surprisingly cheerful. In a corner a shabby Chritmas tree stood and the children had draped it with strips of coloured paper cut from comics, and drawings of what Jack presumed was Father Christmas and snowmen. "A bit early, isn't it?" Jack laughed.

Victoria smiled and assured him it was "– only a practice."

Jack and Viv went into the scullery to clean and gut the fish. Victoria's mother was ironing the children's clothes ready for the morning.

Mrs Jones looked very different from when Jack had last seen her. She was still very thin, her eyes huge in the drawn face, but bright without the enlargement of tears. The bruises were still visible but considerably faded and she was neatly dressed, her late pregnancy hardly visible on the small frame.

"Sad to say, Viv," Jack said quietly as they prepared to leave, "but that Steve Jones isn't missed, is he? Better off without him they are."

When they were turning the corner of Goldings Street, they saw a small boy dart across the road and disappear into the wasteland that had been Philips Street.

"That was Gwyn Bevan wasn't it?" Viv said. "I wonder what trouble he's up to?"

"The sneaky way he hurried out of sight, he's up to no good for sure," Jack muttered. "He's practically given up on school although he's no more than eleven. Hardly ever there and the schoolboard man can't get any sense out of poor old Maggie Wilpin. Threatened her with court and all, but nothing makes any difference."

"Perhaps when his father's out of prison things will improve."

"And pigs might fly and we'll have to shoot for bacon," they said in unison.

Gwyn Bevan watched until the two men were out of sight then he hurried back the way he had come and retrieved the basket of potatoes he had hidden when they threatened to cross his path. He generally only stole food, or money to buy some. Vegetables from garden sheds was his regular night's work, even digging them from gardens when he was sure of not being seen. All to try and persuade his great-grandmother to eat. He smiled in the darkness, wiping his earthy hands down his jumper. She'd enjoyed the eggs he'd taken from Farmer Booker's hens. And the sweets he'd pinched from Temptations when Rhiannon was upstairs washing her hands.

Before Viv and Jack parted, Viv dared to ask Jack about his father.

"What will your old man do, now he's decided not to go back to your grandfather's shop? Try to get something similar or begin again with something new?"

"I've been trying to persuade him to go back to Weston's Wallpaper and Paint. It's all he knows."

"Wasting your time, Jack, he won't be going back there," Viv said, edging away, preparing for another row. "I won't let him and Old Man Arfon needs me more than he needs your father. Sorry I am, but he's sponged off the old man for years not doing any work." He stopped as Jack swung around to face him.

"Don't you think it's time you stopped interfering in our family, Viv Lewis?" Jack demanded. "Ruined us you did, and now you fancy yourself in the role of saviour!"

"Like it or not, I'm the one to save the business!" Viv shouted. "If you really want to help your father, tell him to forget about going back to Weston's. Persuade him to get a job, any job, just make damned sure it's somewhere where he'll have to work bloody hard. It'll be the first time in his life!"

Regretting his outburst, yet at the same time knowing he couldn't have answered any differently, Viv ran home.

Viv and Jack weren't the only people discussing Islwyn that evening. His wife Sian and her twin sister Sally were sitting in Sian's kitchen wondering how they could persuade their husbands to find themselves a job. Sian was decorating a cake for a friend's birthday, with crystallised violets and a thin dusting of sugar.

"It isn't easy for Islwyn," Sally said, "with the suspicions about his taking more from the firm than he was entitled to, but why doesn't my Ryan find something? It's been months, and our savings are going down at an alarming rate."

"Ours too," Sian sighed. "And now we have this party of Mother's to deal with. New dresses and shoes and heaven alone knows what else we'll have to pay for."

"I've tried talking to Ryan but he seems determined to reduce us to poverty to spite Daddy for not continuing to support us. Stopping his wages was a terrible blow to his pride."

"Hasn't he thought of looking for something?"

Sian laughed. "Oh yes. He offered to go to see if this rival firm would take him on. Can you imagine what Daddy would have said to that? His son-in-law working for the competition?"

Sally secretly thought Arfon would consider it an advantage for Weston's Wallpaper and Paint, if the lazy Ryan began to work for the enemy, but she said nothing.

"I'm going to have a strong word with Islwyn, make him see that he can't hide for the rest of his life," Sian said. "I really don't care what he does, as long as he does something. He can do anything at all, I won't be embarrassed."

"Anything?" Sally stressed.

"Absolutely anything!"

Rhiannon had walked uneventfully across the fields to where the Griffithses' house stood far from the rest. Lights shone from every window and as usual, doors and windows were open to the chilly night. The Griffithses were frowned upon by many, having no regular work yet seeming to lack very little. They even had a television which blared away in the background. And a three pound licence proudly displayed! They all had so much to say, so many stories to share, Rhiannon thought the only difference television had made to the household was to make them shout louder as they exchanged views and discussed their day.

Janet Griffiths was small, wiry and ruled them with quiet determination. Her husband, Hywel was stockily built, bearded and with a laugh that frightened the birds from the trees. Their three sons, Basil, Frank, and Ernie – who was in fact an orphaned nephew – were constantly in trouble with the local police. Basil for poaching and trespass, Frank, Ernie and on occasions their father, Hywel, for fighting.

Basil was like a brittle sapling, so tall and thin

82

he seemed unsafe in anything stronger than a light breeze. The only one with a job, he was packing the sandwiches Eleri had made, into an ex-army rucksack ready for work. He was a nightwatchman in a factory and since marrying Eleri had managed to keep his job and even been complimented on his reliability.

He missed the privacy of their flat in Trellis Street, but with the baby due so soon, and having to be out at night, Basil had persuaded Eleri to live with his parents until the birth.

"Mam knows about babies, you'll be safe with her," he told her now as he anxiously and reluctantly surrendered to the clock and walked to the door. "Take care of her, Mam," he called back – twice.

His sister Caroline laughed as she turned the clothes on the clothes horse in front of the fire. "Who'd have thought our Basil would have become such a caring husband, Mam?"

Janet smiled at Caroline then turned to Eleri and added affectionately, "So good for him you've been, Eleri. Loves you, our Basil does, and love can change a person quicker than the sun brings the day."

"One of your mother-in-law's sayings, Mam?" Caroline smiled.

Caroline held her hand up then and listened intently before slipping out of the overcrowded room and running up to attend to her son. Joseph Martin had woken and needed prompt attention.

*   *   *

Walking back through the dark fields held no terror for Rhiannon. She had lived in the area all her life and from a small child had gradually explored until she knew every path and every tree. She was humming to herself, occasionally singing the words to Frankie Laine's 'I Believe', when she heard the rustling. She wasn't worried, it would only be an animal foraging. She wished she could see what it was; it would be exciting to see a fox, or better still a badger as she once had on this very stretch of lane. But suddenly and alarmingly the sound increased, a shadow loomed up in front of her and seemed to engulf her before she was grabbed and shaken.

Taken unawares, she didn't struggle but flopped about like a rag doll as he shook and slapped her. He punched her shoulder and the side of her face before taking her bag and dropping her to the ground.

She lay there stunned, listening as he ran off, crashing through the undergrowth, until the sound faded. If it wasn't for the pain in the tops of her arms where he had held her and the stinging sensation on the side of her face, she might have thought she'd dreamed the whole thing.

She stood up slowly, as if from a deep sleep and, staggering at first, walked down the lane, hurrying as her strength and wits returned. She was afraid to look back but could imagine him following her, creeping behind her, preparing to pounce. The chill in her back was like an exposed target.

When she reached the street she almost knocked on the first door she came to but the need to put distance between herself and her attacker, plus the primitive need to be safe inside her own home, gave speed to her feet and she was almost running by the time she reached Sophie Street.

Barry was locking the door of the sweet shop and she called out to him and ran into his arms. Explanations were brief before he led her to her front door.

His impulse had been to take her to his flat above the shop but she needed to be home and he didn't argue. Either way, they needed to inform the police immediately.

"Not that it will do much good," Barry explained to Rhiannon and her mother. "Whoever it was will be long gone."

"Where was it?" Viv demanded. On being given directions he wanted to leave straight away to look for the man but Rhiannon asked him to stay.

"Was there much money in your bag?" Dora asked.

"Yes. About fifteen shillings. But he didn't have to hit me, I'd have given it without him shaking me and hitting me." She shuddered then began to cry. "I was so helpless, being held by him and shaken like that. It seemed to go on for ever. He didn't make a sound, and all I can remember is the smell of woodsmoke and earth."

"A tramp, for sure," Dora said. "Filthy creature, attacking someone for money instead of finding a job!"

The police interviewed her and spoke soothingly,

reassuring her that she needn't be afraid of going out, the chances of it happening again were unlikely.

"That young fellow-me-lad will be miles away by now," the constable told her.

"You know him?" Barry asked with a frown. "'Young fellow-me-lad', sounds as if you've met him before."

"No, not met him, but there are a few young men out of the forces and unsettled. They're opening more reception shelters to accommodate them, you know. Places where they can get a meal and a bath and a bed for a night or two. They have people they can talk to and the aim is to get them on their way again, get them a job and some hope for a better life."

"Help them? Help them? In the meantime, girls like my Rhiannon have to put up with being shaken like a terrier with a rat, and robbed of the money they've worked hard for? That's a fine thing!" Dora shouted.

"Most of us need help at some time or another," the constable said. "We're the lucky ones that have family and friends who love us. It's easy to forget there are hundreds who don't have a soul to support them through bad times. It's easy to blame them but harder to see their need and offer help," the policeman said gently.

Viv went out as soon as the policeman had gone and went to talk to Jack, their differences forgotten in the need to search for the man who attacked Rhiannon.

They found no one sleeping in the places they

had previously seen used as temporary homes, and towards one o'clock they gave up.

Viv had been feeling guilty ever since the policeman gave the pointed remark about helping rather than criticising and as they parted he said, "Jack, I'm sorry for what I said about your father. I don't go back on my words so far as having him back at the shop, mind. But I really do think I should stop griping."

"How kind you are!" Jack said, sarcasm twisting his face.

"Listen to me, I really want to help. He should get a job. He's slipping into the habit of avoiding people and that could ruin his life."

"What's it to you? He's a thief and not worth a moment's thought, isn't he?"

"I can't change what's happened or what I did, and I don't think I would if I could. I'm not one for pretending, but it's time he was coaxed out of it."

"You're so noble aren't you, Lord Pendragon Island!" Jack began, then he calmed down and agreed. "Oh, damn it all, you're right. He's got to be made to face up to himself and stop blaming you for his own failings."

"We'll have a chinwag with the others and see if we can come up with any ideas."

Their precarious friendship patched up once again, they went their separate ways.

Rhiannon went to bed and for a while, Barry sat with her, with Dora in and out, bristling like a guard dog.

87

"If you want to go and see Eleri, tell me and I'll go with you," Barry said. "It frightens me how easily you might have been harmed."

"I'll be all right. After a few days I'll be able to forget the fright. It won't happen again, the police were right, he's probably miles from Pendragon Island by now."

"You know I care for you, and I want to protect you from anything unpleasant. Please, Rhiannon, tell me when you're going and I'll go with you."

"Barry, how can I promise that? You might be working. Out of town. Anything. Photography isn't a nine to five job. Parties, office do's, weddings, they all take you out in the evenings. That's why we see so little of each other these days. Isn't it?"

Barry recognised the hint of censure and hugged her, releasing her quickly as Dora's footsteps approached once more.

"I don't like being away from you, love," he whispered. "I want to marry you, share my life with you, it's you who make excuses not to see me, afraid of gossip, mistrusting me, not taking my word that Caroline and I are going ahead with a divorce. We are, you know. The solicitor has it in hand and we both want to be separated as quickly as possible. Although even that's misleading, separation suggests we were once together and you know we never were, not for one night. The only kisses we have shared have been those of a family: affectionate and loving, not the kisses of lovers."

"All right, Rhiannon?" Dora asked, walking in and

glaring at Barry until he released Rhiannon's hand. "Time you tried to sleep, isn't it?"

"Five more minutes, Mam," Rhiannon pleaded and reluctantly Dora left them.

"Down the bottom of the stairs I'll be, Barry, listening for if she calls, or if she needs me for anything," she warned.

"You see a lot of Caroline, though, don't you?" Rhiannon said. "You go over to the Griffithses often. Eleri tells me."

"My work keeps me busy but I do get lonely sometimes. If you aren't around, I sometimes call and see Caroline and the baby. I surprise myself by enjoying little Joseph. It's so sad that his father isn't here to enjoy him. Joseph would have made such a good father, he had a sense of fun and he'd have been so patient as the little chap explored his world, don't you think?"

"You can't be a substitute, Barry, not if you're going to leave them. It wouldn't be fair for Joseph to have you around then for you to vanish."

"Hardly vanish, love. We'll still see them, won't we? Marrying you won't cancel the fact that Joseph is my nephew."

Aching from the attack, Rhiannon thought the ache in her heart was the greater. It was an ache caused by unreasonable jealousy. The look on Barry's face as he talked about Joseph and Caroline gave his words a distorting echo. It was easy for him to talk about divorcing Caroline but signing on the dotted line might be more difficult.

As his footsteps hurried down the stairs and out of the house she felt it was representative of their love for each other; slipping away, fading and dying.

Barry and Rhiannon had been in love and were talking about an engagement when the accident that killed her brother Lewis-boy and Barry's brother, Joseph, had changed everything. Revelations about her father had caused a rift and, as Caroline was expecting Joseph's child, Barry had married her so the baby could be born a Martin instead of a Griffiths. Too late, Rhiannon regretted saying goodbye to Barry and now they waited uneasily for a divorce.

Knowing Barry and Caroline were not truly married didn't prevent Rhiannon from feeling guilty at being seen with him. Going out with him while he was Caroline's husband might seem to condone her father's infidelity and that she couldn't accept. She knew that at this moment, while her mother sat alone, her father was with Barry's mother, finding happiness with Nia that he could no longer find with his wife.

Lewis sat for an hour in the flat working on his papers. It was a flat he had hoped to share with Nia but their plans had been aborted by Dora's illness and they only met there occasionally. Tonight he had tried to phone Nia but she was out. He made himself some tea, cursing the fact that the occasionally-used flat never contained milk, and was sitting day-dreaming about the day when everything would be right, he and Nia together, Dora quiescent, the family accepting the situation. One day, he thought, one day I'll be living the life I want. He sat up when he heard the sound of a key in the lock. "Nia?" he called as he ran to greet her.

"I was walking back from the pictures when I saw the car, my dear," she said. "I'm so glad you're here."

Two hours later, after driving Nia back to her house in Chestnut Road, Lewis put his key in the door, calling goodnight to Maggie Wilpin sitting in the darkness. He walked into his house to see Dora sitting waiting for him. Irritably he asked, "What is it, Dora. Why are you still up?"

"Our Rhiannon was attacked," she said with some satisfaction, knowing how shocked and guilty he would be. "You weren't here, but that's nothing new, is it? Never with your family when you're needed, are you Lewis Lewis?"

Gladys checked and re-checked the names on the list of invitations for her planned party. There weren't enough young men. She stared into space racking her brain for fresh ideas. She wanted to discuss it with Arfon, he would know people of importance from his business meetings and his club, but she daren't. She knew she ought not to be arranging such an expensive event, but the money had been saved by her for the girls' twenty-first birthday party and, since that hadn't happened, the money had lain there, waiting for her to think of a way of using it. A way that didn't include simply pouring it away, consigning it to the money they had already lost.

A party to which she would invite all the most eligible bachelors in the town, was an excellent way to use the money. Giving it to Arfon to pay off some of their debtors would be as useless as throwing it down the nearest drain. It would disappear and there would be nothing to show for it. Why couldn't Arfon understand that? Really, men were so stupid sometimes!

Today she intended to call on Mr Jenkins. Apologising for not buying his house after viewing it was a weak excuse but it was sufficient. She would call and tell him how sorry she was for wasting his time and stay to ask about his grandsons. Smiling at her own deviousness and skill, she rang for a taxi.

As before the maid opened the door and after a brief enquiry, Gladys was invited in. To her delight, Mr Jenkins was not alone. A young and extremely handsome man sprawled in an armchair but stood up as she entered and waited politely to be introduced.

The young man who looked about the same age as Jack, was dressed in what Gladys called casual elegance. Well fitting, obviously personally tailored trousers and shirt that spoke loudly of money. His jacket was of some age but obviously good quality. On his feet he wore hand-sewn shoes. He was handsome in a rather boyish, old-fashioned way, fair skinned and with light brown, straight hair. His hands were beautifully manicured and looked as if they had never done anything more exhausting than lift a pen. Classically handsome, was how she described him to herself.

"This is my grandson, Terrence Jenkins," Gladys was told and she began mentioning names in the hope of a mutual friend that would create a link. It was when she mentioned her grandson Jack Weston that she struck the spot.

"I know Jack," Terrence said. "Didn't he go to training college to become a teacher or something?"

"That's right. He was 'called' to work with children," Gladys explained. "He could have gone into his grandfather's business but he was 'called', you see."

As if the idea had only just occurred, she said brightly. "I'm organising a party for the young people, would you like to come? Bring your cousins too. You and Jack would enjoy catching up with each other's news, I'm sure, and you could meet my lovely granddaughters, 'the Weston Girls' they're called."

Dates were checked and as Terrence marked the date and time in his diary, Gladys knew she was making progress with her plan to see her girls settled before the end of the year.

"He uses a diary, my dear," she told Arfon that evening. "I do think that's a good sign, don't you?"

Jack was surprised when Terrence called on him the following day. "Terry! Where did you spring from? I thought you'd gone to Australia!"

"Changed my mind, I thought I'd give it a bit longer before giving up on the old country."

"What are you doing round here?"

"As little as possible, of course! Are you still moulding little minds?"

They talked for an hour then Jack took him to The Railwayman's to meet his friends.

93

Viv was there with Frank and Ernie Griffiths. They were playing darts and arguing as usual. They all looked with some suspicion at the newcomer, his accent and superior manner off-putting, but Terry soon relaxed them with stories of himself and Jack during their army days and when they parted two hours later, Frank and Ernie felt they had made a friend. Viv had disliked the man on sight and his dislike hardened as the evening wore on.

"What are you doing in Pendragon Island?" Jack asked. "I thought you lived and worked in London?"

"I do – did. But I needed a change of scene. Selling jewellery to old ladies with podgy hands or young men shackling themselves to eager young women, I couldn't take it any longer. Grandfather is going to help me find something else. My London sophistication and experience will help me find a job."

"What d'you mean, your London experience and sophistication?" Viv demanded rudely. "How can working in London be an asset for finding work here? D'you think we're stupid, and in desperate need of your expertise then?"

"If you're anything to go by, manners are at a premium for a start!" Terry retorted.

Jack sighed audibly. Viv and Terry had been in each other's company for a couple of hours and were clearly set to be enemies.

Islwyn Heath watched his son coming out of The Railwayman's and wished he could have gone in and joined the young people, had a drink, shared their fun for a while. Apart from Viv Lewis of course. He could never be civil to that young man.

He got into step with his son when he had left the others and said, "Come for a cup of tea, Jack. I feel the need for company and your mother is off round at your Auntie Sally's again. Never apart them two these days!"

"I can't say I blame them, Dad. You aren't exactly sparkling company, are you?"

"Don't be so impertinent, boy!"

"For that you can pay for the tea," Jack laughed. "Come on, Dad, face the facts. You skulk about in the dark, or sit in a corner sunk in a chair like a sick parrot, hardly saying a word. You can't blame Mam for seeking livelier company, can you?"

They turned off the sticky wet pavement into the artificial brightness of a cafe, where sad cakes and curled sandwiches lay under the protection of glass domes, but too near the oven to survive.

Islwyn pointed to a currant bun and asked for it to be spread with butter.

"Not allowed," the assistant said with obvious relish. "Only bread rolls can have butter. We're still rationed, you know."

Islwyn nodded to accept the dry, butterless bun and looked at his son.

"Pass!" Jack said firmly.

"Did you have supper tonight?" Jack asked, knowing his father had not touched a mouthful of the meal. "Lovely soup Mam made today. It's

95

amazing what she can make out of the small ration of meat."

"I wasn't hungry."

"Hungry? You must be desperate if you're going to eat that rock!" He watched as Islwyn cut the bun and chewed a small piece. "Dad, why don't you get a job?" he said. "You won't earn as much as Grandfather paid you, but you can't go drifting on like this. You'll be an old man by Christmas!"

"What could I do, boy? I only know about book-keeping and no one will employ me to do that, now, will they? Thanks to your friend, Viv Lewis," he added sharply.

"Go to the Labour Exchange and see what they have to offer."

"Waste of time, boy. Waste of time."

Jack argued and coaxed but a huge bite from the currant bun seemed to have silenced his father for at least the next ten minutes. He knew Viv was right though. The time for sympathy was gone, now was the time for some action. He took a deep breath and tried again. "Go down and take a job, any job, so long as it gets you out of the house and facing people before you've completely lost the knack, Dad."

"That's what your mother said this morning. Anything is better than nothing, she told me."

"And she's right," Jack said firmly.

Chapter Five

Islwyn Heath wandered along the lanes behind terraced houses, and headed gradually, by a convoluted
route, to the beach. In his melancholy state of mind, he
liked the closed-down funfair and the shops with their
shadowy reminders of hot, sun-filled days. Artificial
sticks of rock, plaster ice-cream cones, closed and
shabby cafes with the air still redolent of fish and
chips, the canvas-hooded fairground rides, all suited
his mood. He had made it one of his regular stops
on his nightly prowls.

He knew he was becoming more and more irritable.
His resentment was growing rather than lessening and
his wife was losing patience. Sian spent more and more
time with her twin sister and this exacerbated Islwyn's
feeling of isolation. It had reached the point at which
they rarely spoke without arguing.

He still spent most nights wandering the town, alone
and lonely, unable to break the pattern he had built of
hiding during the day and creeping out at night. Too
late he wished he had faced everyone when the news
broke, as his father-in-law had done.

Deep down he knew the problem was his to deal

with, that he couldn't depend on others to bail him out of his self-imposed ostracism, but he refused to admit it. Now even Jack, his amiable son, was finding it hard to be patient.

He was unaware that Jack had other things on his mind, the problem of how best to help a family with far greater problems than his own. Islwyn thought he had worn out his tolerance, as he had of others. He walked through the dark streets, a self-pitying sob building inside him, and wondered what he could do.

A car squealed to a halt at the corner then scorched past him as he stood undecided at the kerb, forcing him to jump back for fear of being knocked down. Perhaps it would have been as well, he thought, with an increase of melancholy welling up into a wail. His had been a wasted life so far, he admitted to himself. Marrying one of Arfon Weston's daughters and being given a job for life had seemed wonderful at the time, but now he was paying the price.

He had looked down on people like Viv Lewis and now he was depending on him to revive the family fortune and give him back his comfortable life being supported by his father-in-law. He cringed when he remembered how he had treated Viv before his treachery had been revealed. Acting all superior to a hard-working man like Viv, while robbing the family who had given him everything.

He ambled on through the empty streets, seeing nothing, hearing nothing – apart from the voices in his head; accusatory voices that berated him and forced him to see what he had become.

He hadn't gone home last night. He had walked to the gate but had been unable to go in. Like several times before he hadn't been able to face the family. The house was like a prison, the air frosty with mostly unspoken accusations. Sian glared but rarely spoke and Jack too had little time to talk to him. What was he going to do with the rest of his life?

Shaking his pocket to check he had a few coins he went into a phone box and dialled Ryan's number. Ryan had refused to go back to Weston's Wallpaper and Paint too, unable to accept working with Viv Lewis as his boss. Perhaps he would meet him for a cup of tea and a talk. There seemed to be no one else prepared to give him time.

Jack was sitting at the bus stop close to the park trying to work out how to persuade Victoria to ask for her job back and how to persuade Grandmother Weston to give in and accept her. The Jones family was much improved since the death of Steve, but Victoria was still undernourished and he guessed that the best of the food went into the bellies of the younger children. Grandmother would help in more ways then paying a wage once she knew the situation, but he'd promised not to say a thing. How could he persuade her? It was a miracle his grandfather had taken Viv Lewis back after Viv had exposed his secret. He didn't think the Weston family could manage a second miracle. Fortunately fate played into his hands.

It was on Friday, late in October, when he called at his grandmother's house to find her a little upset.

"What is it?" he asked. "No one ill, I hope?" With the strain his grandfather had been under, illness was a constant dread.

So it was relief he felt at first, then hope when Gladys said, "Mair Gregory has given me notice. What a nerve, giving up a good position like this. Not that she'll be much of a loss, but it will be an inconvenience, having to look for someone else. Since the war it hasn't been easy to find a willing girl, they all want such high wages these days."

"I know someone who would be excellent, Grandmother," Jack said, crossing his fingers superstitiously. "But you'd have to pay her more than you paid Mair, to persuade her to come."

"Your grandfather is being careful at the moment, dear," Gladys said primly.

"He wouldn't begrudge you a good, efficient and trustworthy maid, though, would he?"

"No, I think I could talk him round. Who is the girl?"

"Victoria." He raised a hand to ward off the protest "You know you'd love to have her back, Grandmother, why don't you think about it?"

"We've already discussed this Jack. Your grandfather would never agree."

"Are you telling me you can't persuade him?" he laughed. Suddenly Jack became serious. He knew now he'd have to tell Gladys the truth and break his promise to Victoria. He told her then of the difficulties the Jones family were facing, with the father dead, having wasted all the money and even

100

sold the furnishings to buy drink. Soft-hearted as he knew her to be, Gladys was in the mood to go at once with a parcel of food and clothing, but Jack stopped her.

"I know your intentions are good, Grandmother, but Victoria doesn't want charity from you, she wants the chance to earn money. I even promised her I wouldn't tell you about her problems. I know you'd make sure she had plenty of good food too, but it wouldn't be charity." He amused her by reporting on the Griffithses' deliveries of beds and other urgent needs but assured her that Victoria had pledged to pay them for it all.

"She isn't a scrounger, she's proud and independent and just wants the chance to work and be paid a fair wage," he insisted.

"I'll talk to your grandfather," Gladys promised and Jack hugged her, knowing the agreement was as good as made.

When Victoria was summoned to go and see her ex-employer, she was quaking. She had always found Gladys formidable and wondered what the woman could want, imagining complaints and racking her brain to wonder what she had done or failed to do. Her aprons had all been washed and returned, the wages had been correct to the last penny. What could she have done? Surely Jack hadn't been right and she was going to be offered her job back? That was too unlikely to consider! She entered the room where Gladys sat as if on a throne, preparing herself for an apology.

"Victoria," Gladys began, and to the girl's relief she began to smile. "I know you did wrong, helping Viv Lewis and Basil Griffiths to report Mr Weston to the police, but that's all behind us now and I think you should come back and work for me again."

"I couldn't—" Victoria gasped.

"Oh, I know you'll expect a little increase in your wages," Gladys frowned, "the shops can pay more than I, but that will be arranged. Mr Weston is a forgiving and generous man."

"But, I—"

"Give your notice this Friday and you can begin here a week later, on the Friday evening. I'm having a dinner party for the family and you will help. I will increase you wages by—" Here Gladys paused as if about to bestow a sweet on a favoured child, then said, "– four shillings and sixpence a week."

Still without having uttered a sentence, Victoria was dismissed.

She was still shaking when she let herself out of the kitchen door. She didn't go back home but walked instead to Somerset House where Jack lived with his parents. It was four o'clock and Jack should be home. Tentatively she knocked on the heavy front door and when it was opened by Jack's mother she asked if she could speak to him. Closing the door and leaving her standing on the step, Sian went to find her son.

"Victoria! Come in. Is everything all right, there's no problem?" Jack asked.

Remaining on the step, Victoria said, "Your grandmother, Mrs Weston, has told me to go back there to work."

"Told you? Not asked? Yes, that sounds like Grandmother. Do you want to?"

"I'm a bit nervous, like. Won't she still be angry with me?"

"She isn't as fierce as she tries to pretend."

"And, she's offered me four and sixpence more than before."

"You're worth more," Jack smiled. He had agreed six shillings with his grandmother. Trust her to cut it down. "Well, are you going to accept?"

"I didn't say more than a couple of words," Victoria said seriously, "but I think I have!"

Jack laughed and pulled the door shut behind him. "Come on, young lady, I'll walk you home."

They turned out of the drive and headed for Goldings Street. Jack felt good. He didn't analyse the feeling but just knew it felt more like happiness than he had experienced for a long time. Victoria was only sixteen, a shy little thing, dark-haired and with an expression of apology ever present on her small features. She barely reached his shoulder and he slowed his steps to allow her to walk beside him without having to run.

Before she went inside, she asked hesitantly and with a rosy hue revealing her embarrassment, "Did you, I mean, was it your idea? Was it you who suggested I went back to work for Mrs Weston? Like you said you would?"

"You don't need anyone to speak for you, Victoria," he said. "My grandmother wanted someone hard-working and helpful, there was no one better than you and she was sensible to put the past behind her and ask."

"Thank you, Mr – thanks."

"What for?"

"For—" Here words failed her and she went inside.

Walking home Jack felt suddenly bereft. He found himself thinking up excuses for future calls both on his grandmother and on the neat little house on Goldings Street.

Jack's father still wasn't at home. His parents had had a row, and his father hadn't been home the previous night, but he imagined he was back and once more slouched in his chair. He knew his mother had followed Islwyn when he had stormed out of the house, concerned more than angry. She had followed him around the streets, back to the house and saw him hesitate then leave again. Sian had only returned home when she had seen her husband installed in a small hotel on the road to the Pleasure Beach. She and Jack had telephoned the hotel when she got back home and they felt reassured enough to go to bed. A second call that morning had reassured her again, and now she was waiting for him to return.

Islwyn had mulled over his discussion with Ryan all through the night. Ryan had insisted they did nothing, just wait for Old Man Arfon to shake himself and sack Viv and offer them their jobs back. "Bound to happen," he assured Islwyn but Islwyn had not been convinced.

Going to Ryan for sympathy, their talk had had the opposite effect. He had left his brother-in-law feeling guilty of failing the man who had given him so much. Watching Ryan's face as he said smugly that the old man would soon climb down and realise that family had to come first, he wanted to slap it. Ryan was wrong, he was wrong, and it was time to do something about it. The question was, what? The following morning the answer came to him.

Just before Jack came back from walking Victoria home, Islwyn had slipped in through the back door and gone straight up to the bedroom. Hearing her husband come in, Sian followed and she closed the door and stared at him with anger softening as she waited for him to speak. He looked so old, and abandoned somehow. The words she had prepared, about worrying her and being inconsiderate quickly faded, and instead she said, "Islwyn, you have to find something to do."

"Yes," he surprised her by saying. "I agree. I've been to the Labour Exchange and they are sending me to see a Mr Brasen, at two-thirty."

"Mr Brasen? I don't know the name. Who is he? What business is he in? There isn't a wallpaper and paint business with that name, is there? I'll ask Daddy if he knows him."

"Mr Brasen wants someone to cook chips in the Fortune chip shop. I'll be working in his cafe over the beach in the summer."

"What? Islwyn, you can't!"

"I might not be suitable, I've never cooked anything since scout camp's burnt sausages, but I dare say it won't be difficult to learn."

All morning Sian pleaded, but Islwyn ignored her protests. At three o'clock he came back and told her he had the job. Jack was the second to be told and he thought it an excellent idea.

"Something different, and with no headaches or hangovers, I mean there'll be no worries to bring home. You finish your shift and forget it until the next day. Easy, relaxed and perfect."

"You are both completely mad!" Sian wailed.

"And there's something else," Islwyn said. "All these months I've been hating Viv Lewis, blaming him for the mess I've got myself into. Well, I've sorted all that. And I've been looking to your parents to rescue me, when I know I should have been trying to rescue them."

"How can you help my father? We haven't any money! Although," she looked at her husband, a steely expression in her eyes, "we do have the means of raising some, if you're serious about wanting to help."

"I am."

"Then I propose we sell this house – it's too big for us anyway. We could find a rented one, smaller and more convenient, and give the proceeds to Daddy to help clear his debts."

"Sian! He'd never agree!"

"Then we won't tell him until it's done."

Islwyn looked startled for a long moment then he relaxed and nodded. "All right, love, that's what we'll do."

Sian gave a huge sigh of relief. She had been thinking of the idea for days and had expected more opposition. "Right then. Now, Jack, where do we start looking for a house?"

The sweet shop on the corner of Sophie Street was full to the door and when Barry came home to change ready for an evening appointment he saw Rhiannon trying to cope and stayed to help serve.

"I can manage," she told him, between helping customers to choose their sweets and chocolates, thinking how wonderful it was not to have to cut out the tiny pieces of paper that rationing had meant.

"I know you can," he whispered back, "but I want to talk to you and we have to get rid of this lot first."

In a lull, Rhiannon went upstairs to make some tea and when she came back down the shop was again full to the door with people wanting to buy sweets. Most of the customers were children, some with their mothers, some clutching coins in hot hands while their mothers chatted outside. Barry was curious. "What's caused the rush?" he asked when once again the small shop had emptied.

"There's a new dance class opened in Gomer Hall. Children at four and five o'clock, and adults seven and nine. I thought we could join."

107

"No, I couldn't manage a regular attendance, Rhiannon. I have appointments in the evening."

"Not all that many," she protested.

"Enough. Besides, I don't think I'd enjoy learning to dance."

"They do all the usual ballroom dances including the rumba and tango," she coaxed. "It sounds like fun."

"Can't stop. I've been invited to tea at the Griffithses'. I've got some new photographs of little Joseph to show Caroline."

"Will you come to the dance class with me?"

"You go if you want to," Barry said generously, gathering his folders, which he had thrown behind the counter. "I won't mind."

Something in this exchange irritated Rhiannon. "You don't mind? How magnanimous! All right," she said in a voice that reminded her of her mother's. "All right. I will go. Better than sitting in night after night while you further your career and visit Caroline!"

Her first thought was, who could she go with? No point going without a partner, there was always a surplus of girls at dances and dance classes probably weren't any different. She asked Viv when she got home, but he said he'd go if he could persuade Joan Weston to go with him. She pleaded with Barry to reconsider when he called the next day, and, when she was about to give up the idea, Jimmy called.

Jimmy Herbert was a rep, selling sweets for Bottomley's, the same firm for which her father worked. He was handsome in a rather traditional way, tall and slim, curly fair hair and bright, cheeky blue eyes. He had a moustache. But unlike her father's pencil-thin line, Jimmy's seemed to take over his face and straggle rather wildly, refusing to accept the shape Jimmy chose.

"Rhiannon, I want you to come out with me tonight and I want an order. Which shall we discuss first?" he said, words coming fast. "I thought the pictures and then some supper. Nothing flash, mind, fish and chips and a glass of pop?"

"Give me a chance to speak!" she laughed.

Theatrically he slapped a hand across his mouth and widened his eyes.

"Um, no thanks, to the pictures. I went last night. And, yes to supper and what d'you think of joining the dance class at Gomer Hall?" She tried to speak as fast as he but failed.

"What about an order first?" he said then, and they both ended up laughing.

Barry came down the stairs then, and stood looking at the two of them, obviously friends, and with a flirting look on their faces. Stiffly, he said, "I'm off then. See you tomorrow, Rhiannon." He leaned forward to place a proprietory kiss on her cheek, she turned to say goodbye, and they bumped heads.

This too seemed funny and the young couple stifled their laughter only for as long as it took Barry to leave the shop.

Jimmy and she joined the dance class that evening, and they met once during the week, to walk around the town and have a coffee somewhere before walking some more. Although he had a reasonably good job, ten shillings a week was all he allowed himself for pocket money and his usual two trips to the pictures was reduced to one when he paid for Rhiannon.

His liking for her was growing and the dance class was a way of getting her used to being with him rather than Barry Martin who was married, even though he was getting a divorce. He mentally upped his pocket money by another seven and sixpence. No point skimping if he wanted Rhiannon to take him seriously.

Viv Lewis had no illusions about Joan Weston and a future with her. Arfon Weston might have forgiven his disloyalty and had even made him a partner, but he would never allow Joan to marry him. He also knew that for Joan, their occasional secret meetings were simply fun, a way of having an adventure without risk. And for himself he knew he would never be able to afford the sort of life Joan would expect. No, he wasn't involved. Their secret meetings were nothing more than a way of getting one over his employer.

He had tried to kiss her on more than one occasion and each attempt had resulted in having his face slapped. Yet Joan acted as if they were more than friends when they were in the company of her twin, or some of their friends who had been told in confidence of their 'secret love'. It was all nothing more than a joke, and a joke that was beginning to pall.

He wasn't tired of meeting her after dark and occasionally slipping into the back row of the cinema, and leaving just before the film ended to avoid being seen. But Joan was. She had never been warm towards him, but even in her icy manner there was a cooling off.

It saddened him, no matter how he told himself it was what he expected. In his heart there was a perverse spark of hope that one day they might openly start courting, although Joan had given him no encouragement in this.

He wondered idly and without much dismay, if he would be passed back to Megan.

"Why don't you come to the dance class?" Rhiannon asked when Jimmy called for her a week later.

"No partner," Viv replied.

"Plenty of girls looking for one," Jimmy told him. But Viv shook his head. He had arranged to meet Joan.

At eight o'clock he was still waiting for Joan to appear. Rain began to fall and quickly increased to a heavy downpour. He tilted his trilby and pulled up the collar of his mac, but the rain seeped in and he had the uncomfortable feeling of wetness around his neck. Still he waited.

He found himself singing the George Formby song, 'Leaning on the lamp post, at the corner of the street'. At half-past he began to fidget changing from one foot to the other in squelching shoes. Then he began walking up and down, and stretching to look along the street, and idly counting the remaining houses in Goldings Street.

"'I hope that she will get away, she doesn't always

get away and anyhow I know that she'll try'," he sang, wiping around his neck with a handkerchief. At nine-thirty, wet and dispirited, he headed back to Sophie Street.

The music coming from Gomer Hall was that of a tinny piano played badly. He chuckled, went to see what was happening and saw his sister and Jimmy standing with one foot raised, being taught the quarter turn of the quickstep. In the corner, as if part of the same tableau, the elderly pianist sat with her arms raised, waiting for the signal to thump the keys.

Standing by the desk at which someone waited for the entrance fees, he watched, with the intention of teasing them later and hardly noticed the rest of the couples, until a voice called, "Come on in, the water's fine!"

"Jack Weston! I never thought I'd see the day!"

Leaving the rest still struggling with the quarter turn, this time to a record of Roy Fox's Orchestra, Jack joined Viv with his partner, Joan. So that's why she couldn't come, he thought to himself.

Another couple came over once the music stopped, Joan's twin, Megan, and a man Viv recognised as Jack's friend from his army days, Terry Jenkins.

Viv nodded in an unfriendly manner, his second impression the same as the first: he wasn't going to like this man. He glanced at him, taking in the smart suit and neat evening shirt and bow tie. He was even wearing proper dance pumps. Terry was hard-eyed and over-confident, looking around him in a manner that suggested he was used to mixing with people far superior. He's worse than Gladys Weston, Viv thought. He doesn't have her soft centre. His hands were soft, though, feminine almost, and small, like his neatly-clad feet. Dislike spread from the man's face through his elegantly clothed body to his small feline feet and hands. The man was a bit of a pansy, never soiling his hands with honest work for sure. And as for dressing like that for a dance class in an old hall, God 'elp. A pansy for sure, but one with an eye for the girls, judging by the way he was admiring Megan.

The five of them left the dance hall at eleven o'clock and stood in a huddle outside the entrance with several others. Viv hoped for a word with Joan, guessing she had been put on the spot by her family. Although he couldn't imagine why the Weston Girls would go to such a shabby dance class when they'd had lessons at their private school and were excellent dancers.

"We only went in to get out of the rain," Megan said. "It was fun, though."

"Rhiannon's been trying to persuade me to join," Viv said. He turned to Jimmy and asked, "You will see her safe home, won't you? No leaving her at the stop where you get your bus, mind."

"I've got a car," Jimmy reminded him, "and I wouldn't leave her to walk home alone, would I? Not after the fright she had last week."

Leaving Rhiannon and Jimmy to stroll back to the house, Viv stayed and talked to Jack, the twins and Jack's friend, Terry Jenkins. Always outspoken to the point of rudeness, he waited for an opportunity and whispered to Jack, "What the 'ell's he doing round here then? Which slimy hole did he crawl out of?"

"Grandmother found him for me," Jack hissed back. "She went to visit the Jenkinses and I think she saw him as an extra eligible batchelor for this party she's planning. Don't you like him?"

"Not staying long, is he?"

"Looking for a job and somewhere to settle I understand."

"Don't encourage him, Jack."

"Looks as if Megan will though." He nodded to where Terry and Megan stood talking, Megan looking up at him in a way that even the low light from the lamp couldn't disguise. "It looks as if she's smitten."

"Lock her up 'til she's come to her senses!"

For a few days Viv heard nothing from Joan. When she arrived for work on Saturday she offered no explanation about not meeting him on the Monday evening, and there was no invitation for them to meet. He wasn't surprised. He had felt she was getting bored, but he hoped she wasn't getting mixed up with that Terry Jenkins.

Jack had brought Terry to The Railwayman's twice and each time the others had made an excuse to leave. With his casually spoken boasting and the way he had of belittling them, he dispersed the normally easy-going group in a few minutes.

"Don't know what it is with that bloke," Basil mused, "but there's something I don't quite like about him. He's always acting like he's a cut above the rest of us – like Pendragon Island is beneath him. I'd really love to knock a bit of sense into him!"

"I'd sign agreement to that," Viv said gloomily. "But how can I convince Joan and Megan that he's no good?"

With Eleri's baby due in a matter of days, Basil rarely stayed long with his friends, he contented himself with a half-pint on the way to work. On his night off, he and Eleri would go for a walk.

She was self-conscious about being so obviously due to give birth, and avoided the town. Even the pictures, where she had once worked as an usherette, no longer appealed. She preferred to walk through the dark lanes, listening to Basil telling her about the birds he had seen, showing her the den where the vixen had brought up her two cubs that year, and to sit with him patiently waiting for a sight of the beautiful barn owl as it set out on its twilight search for food.

"Basil, love," she whispered on his evening off as they sat and watched a family of badgers trotting off on their nightly foraging. "I don't think I could ever be happier than now."

"I'm glad. I was so afraid I'd let you down. I'm not as smart or as handsome as your Lewis-boy was."

"I wouldn't change anything about you. I feel so safe with you."

He didn't reply and she asked if there was anything worrying him.

"No, love, but I wish you hadn't said all that just now."

"Why?"

115

"Because I was going to ask if you'd mind if I went to see Viv and Jack."

Eleri laughed. "Of course I don't mind! Your Mam and Dad will be there if anything starts to happen with our baby. Although he isn't likely to arrive for a week yet. Go on you, and enjoy an hour with your mates. Which way will you walk home? I might come and meet you."

"No, don't do that. Stay back and I won't be long."

It was a rare occasion for Janet and Hywel Griffiths to be out, but they had gone with Caroline and Barry and the baby to see Nia. Uneasy in the isolated house on her own, Eleri began to think about the man who attacked Rhiannon.

The doors and windows of the cottage were always wide open and if she closed them the Griffithses would probably tease her. She wondered idly which was the strongest emotion, fear itself or the fear of being made to look silly. She decided on the latter and left the windows open.

The pains, when they began, were little more than a twinge in the small of her back. She rearranged her cushions and tried to concentrate on the television. A squeezing sensation alarmed her and she stood up, turned off the television and stood at the door waiting for someone to return. The Goon Show was on the radio at quarter past ten, she'd listen to that. A laugh would settle her nerves. Nerves was all it was, the baby wasn't due yet. It couldn't be the baby.

The pains became sharper and she leaned on the

back of a chair gasping, sweat pouring down her face. She had to get help. It normally took fifteen minutes to reach the edge of the town and she surely had time even if tonight it took her double. Babies took for ages to come, everyone knew that.

In Nia Martin's house in Chestnut Road, Janet and Hywel were standing ready to leave, coaxing their daughter Caroline to come with them. But Nia insisted on them having another drink. Flagons of beer, port and sherry bought for Christmas had been opened early and with some lemonade and a few sandwiches, a party had developed from the visit intended only for Nia to see her grandson.

Caroline and Barry were behaving like the proud parents, although the child was in fact Barry's nephew. When Joseph had died, Caroline had been in despair and with Rhiannon swearing she would never marry him, Barry had married Caroline, so the baby would have his father's name. Now, the pride on Barry's face could have been mistaken for paternal pride and Nia wondered if Caroline was becoming more important than Barry had intended.

Baby Joseph, who should have been in bed hours ago, was lively and entertaining, showing no sign of tiredness, so Janet and Hywel sat again and offered their glasses for, 'just a small one'.

Basil had intended to stay an hour at The Railwayman's then go back to Eleri, but the conversation

117

dwelt on the party Gladys Weston was planning and which Jack insisted they attended.

"She'll never invite us, man," Frank, Basil's brother said. "What, ask the Griffithses to mix with the likes of the Westons, and the Jenkinses, and all them fancy lot up at the park? Never."

"You know how much store Grandmother sets on having all the family together? Well, I've told her I won't be there if you aren't invited and she wrote your names down on the invitation list." Jack laughed ruefully. "She rubbed them out again too, mind. But I've added them and circled them with mine and the twins. They've told her you have to come. Poor Gladys, we lead her a terrible life."

Suddenly aware of the time, Basil jumped up and reached for his coat. "I'd better get back. Our Mam and Dad are there, but I don't like being away from Eleri for long with the baby due so soon."

The others laughed and teased him.

"It'll be weeks yet, man. We're still in October. It's November she's been told."

Viv didn't laugh, he was glad Basil cared so much for Eleri. "I'll walk with you part of the way," he said.

Outside the public house there was a knot of people, huddled against the cold weather and gradually drifting off. To Basil's alarm he recognised his parents. Who was with Eleri?

"We've just got off the bus. Barry is taking Caroline and the baby home. Eleri with you, is she?" Hywel said, cheerful from the pleasant evening and from the drink he had consumed.

"Damn it all, Mam! She's on her own."

"She'll be all right, love, the baby's a long way off due. But we'd better hurry in case she's nervous there on her own. I thought you were staying in?"

"I thought you'd be at home!" Each looking for someone to blame, they hurried through the dark street, and across the fields towards the cottage. Viv went with them.

Eleri was staggering by the time she crossed the field and reached the first stile, and as she rested on the wooden rail she heard sounds, muffled sounds as if someone was trying to be quiet. For a moment she thought it might be Basil checking his traps, but he didn't work this close to the house as a rule. She was about to call out. Whoever it was, they would surely help her; but something made her hold back.

There was a squeal and she knew it was a rabbit's death cry, and then another. Low, murmuring voices reached her and she tried to climb the stile, slipped and allowed a gasp to escape her lips and at once the sounds ceased. Poachers for sure, but not Basil.

She succeeded in clambering over the stile in a somewhat ungainly manner, fully aware she was being watched by invisible eyes. She wished she had stayed in the house – and locked the doors. Better to be teased than harmed. Janet and Hywel would surely not be long, and Basil was probably on his way home at this very moment. Memories of the attack on Rhiannon returned to add to her fears. Who knew who, or what, was out there, beyond her vision?

119

More voices, this time loud and accompanied by impatient footsteps crossing the field, it must be Basil and his parents. Thank goodness. She ran blindly towards the sounds and tripped and fell headlong.

What had she fallen over? It seemed like a body. Then figures rose to a crouch all around her and although the light was poor she saw a couple of dogs, held on short leads. The shadows crept further away and moved faster – right into the path of the others. She had fallen over the poachers who had dropped to the ground for concealment.

It seemed as if she were in the middle of a war. Voices threatening, the dull thud of blows and the grunts of the recipients. People running, calling in low voices for their partners to follow, then, at last the night's confusion subsided and there was Janet's voice calling for her echoed by the urgent exclamations of Basil.

Eleri answered with a sobbing, "I'm over here," she was held in strong arms, and the world of sanity returned.

Chapter Six

Eleri's child was born three hours later. The midwife arrived in time and the doctor admitted that he had hardly needed to be there as it was such a quick and straightforward birth. A little boy, they decided to christen him Ronald but call him Ronnie.

While Eleri was giving birth to Ronnie, the police were searching for the rest of the men she had interrupted at their night's work. Two had been held firmly by Frank and Ernie, and Basil and Hywel when the police came, but two more had run off. The policemen had spent some time at the cottage where Janet had given them tea and Hywel had sat sprawled on a chair as if giving an audience, refusing to get up and give one of them a seat, insisting he was "worn out, puffed out and fagged out".

The warren from which the men had been taking rabbits, with the aid of ferrets and a couple of dogs, was in a field belonging to local farmer, John Booker. He was someone from whom Basil and his father had taken many a pheasant, partridge, hare and rabbit, but Basil had never touched the large warren so near his home. John Booker had ferrets of his own and he killed a couple of hundred rabbits once a year and sold them in the local market. With such a small meat ration, many families who had previously refused to try rabbit had become fond of the dark, tasty meat. To Basil, with his odd sense of fair play, rabbits from that warren were the farmer's personal property, and he never touched them, unless one ran into one of his traps further afield, when he considered them fair game.

John Booker arrived before the police had gone, and he too stayed to drink tea and hear the full story of the capture of the men who had been robbing him. He was a burly man, over six feet tall and several stone heavier than Hywel and he looked flushed and puffy having been woken out of a deep sleep by the police.

"Give the man a seat by the fire, Hywel," Janet coaxed, giving her husband a push to encourage him but Hywel groaned and said he too had had a disturbed night.

"It's all right, Mrs Griffiths," the farmer said. "I wouldn't want to disturb you further, but I'll be back in the morning with a gift for the new baby. I owe him a debt, him having brought some of these damned poachers to justice, eh, Hywel?" There was a quizzical look on John's face as he smiled down at the sprawling Hywel, a look which he transferred to Basil: two of the men he had been trying to catch for years. "Yes, I'm grateful to the boy and his mother."

The police told them the men had come in a van and planned to fill it with stolen game and take it to London arriving in time for the markets. They had discovered the van hidden in some trees, already half filled with pheasants. Gleefully, Basil prepared to give evidence against the thieves, assuring the men in blue he had given up his previous bad ways now he had a wife and a child, and denying any knowledge of the traps found in the woods, three fields away.

"What a night, Mam," he said as, at five o'clock the following morning Janet and Hywel prepared to get a few hours sleep. "Me and our Dad helping the police. That's the second time I've been helpful. They won't be watching me so close now they believe I've become a respectable man who works with the police, will they? Damn me, our Dad, they'll be asking me to join up soon!"

"Not if they'd found these they wouldn't!" Hywel lifted the cushion on which he had been determinedly sitting throughout the police and the farmer's visit, and showed his son three squashed and very dead partridge.

Gladys Weston usually had to persuade her son-in-law Islwyn to visit, specially since what she referred to as 'his little lapse'. So when he arrived unannounced and during daylight hours, she at once expected a problem.

Victoria admitted him and called Gladys from where she was filling pages of a notebook with preparations for her party.

"Excuse me, Mrs Weston, but you have a visitor, Mr Islwyn Heath."

"Show him into the lounge, Victoria, and it's

123

Heath-Weston. Bring us a tray of tea, will you? Now I wonder what the trouble is? Does he look all right?"

"Smiling he is, Mrs Weston."

"Good heavens!"

Islwyn insisted on talking to both Arfon and Gladys, so she had to be patient until Arfon finished a phone call and joined them.

"Sian and I have sold the house, Mother-in-law," Islwyn announced.

"That is downright inconsiderate, Islwyn. Hasn't your family been through enough without you planning something so ill-considered? How can you think of moving just now? We haven't any money to spare, so you'll be looking at something worth far less that your present one. I'm sure Sian won't like that, and why should she?" Gladys said, before looking at Arfon for him to continue.

But Arfon didn't add to her blast of words, he simply asked, "Why?"

"We've agreed to rent a small house, just for the time being, until things have picked up, and we want you to have the money we make on the house."

"What?" Gladys and Arfon said in unison.

"I said we've rented—"

"We heard what you said! But why are you doing this?"

"We want to pay you back some of the money you lost because of me, and in future I'll keep Sian on what I can earn. It isn't much help, I know, but it's all I can do at present."

"Keep Sian? You'd have to get a job first!" Gladys said harshly.

"That's the second thing I wanted to tell you. I've got a job." He looked at Gladys with what Arfon thought was a smile, but which Gladys later described as a smirk. "I'm the new cook at the Fortune fish and chip shop by the beach."

When Islwyn left, he overheard Gladys say tearfully, "I knew this would happen, Arfon, dear. He's finally gone off his head."

Islwyn smiled widely. On the contrary, he felt more sane than at any time since he had married into the Weston family. Marrying Sian had ruined him. He had been offered a soft and easy life and had willingly accepted having to live life their way. He felt drunk with freedom as he walked to the Fortune fish and chip shop to begin his first lesson in cooking the best fish and chips in Pendragon Island.

After discussions lasting well into the night, Arfon decided he wouldn't, couldn't accept the money for the house. Early the following morning he and Gladys went to see their daughter, hoping Islwyn wouldn't be there. It was a Saturday so Jack was sitting reading the paper and commenting occasionally about Father Christmas coming as early as November the seventh, only two days after bonfire night, and there being live bears in the Swansea Pantomine, and yet more rumours that food rationing would end the following year.

When they were settled with coffee before them, Arfon explained the reason for their visit. "Your mother and I wish to thank you for your generous offer, Sian, my dear, but we cannot allow it."

"But you must, Daddy. I think it's important to Islwyn that you do." She didn't tell her parents it was she who first muted the idea. Better for Islwyn if they thought it had come from him.

"Tell him we refuse but we are grateful," Gladys said.

"I'm sorry Mummy, but you must agree. Making this decision was what brought him back from his withdrawn and depressed state, don't you agree, Jack?" she looked to her son to pull him into the conversation.

"Mam's right, Grandfather. It took a long time and a lot of guts for Dad to face the facts. Now, with Mam's help, he has. You mustn't throw his apology in his face."

"But where will you live?"

"We've signed the rental agreement on a house in Trellis Street," Sian told them. "We'll have to sell much of the furniture, it wouldn't fit anyway and that will be more off the debt he owes."

Gladys stared at her daughter, searching for regret or dismay and found none. "You are willing to accept this, dear?"

"Mummy, I'm so proud of him for this decision. You can't take it away from him without destroying him completely and I – wouldn't want that." She didn't add that the Westons had made him the way he was but she thought it. "It's a chance for him to find out who he really is," she ended.

Gladys glared at her. That was going too far.

"He is married to a Weston. That's who he is," she snapped.

Jack looked at his grandfather and winked.

"We accept and thank him most sincerely, Sian," Arfon said as he stood to leave. "You have a man with hidden depths in Islwyn and you may tell him I said so."

"Now . . ." Gladys said, rising and leaving the coffee she hated but thought smart to drink, ". . . about curtains . . ."

Jack and his grandfather exchanged a look and a silent groan. Gladys was off again.

In late November, Basil and Eleri took their baby back to the flat they rented in Trellis Street, where, a few days later, they watched Sian, Islwyn and Jack Heath-Weston move in.

Sian had been excited about the move, a feeling of sacrifice made her walk tall and the shame of her husband's stealing was fading fast. What Islwyn was doing was wonderful and it reduced the shame of his behaviour, which she in any case had explained away to her friends with a hushed mention of 'illness'.

The road was more shabby than she remembered, with a hazy November sun revealing the lack of paint and the scarred walls. She swallowed her qualms and told herself that it was going to be wonderful living among these poorer people and helping them to improve their lot by emulating their betters. A small child was chalking on the pavement, marking

127

out a hopscotch game. Sian frowned at her. "That," she said firmly, "will have to stop!

The furniture van was pulling up as Sian reached number forty-four. Standing outside their various homes were whole families, gathered preparing to be entertained. They made no attempt to hide their curiosity, but watched with interest and added a light-hearted commentary as the furniture was taken inside.

Sian hurried the men about their work, really she had never imagined such embarrassment. Why had Islwyn insisted on moving on a Saturday when the husbands and children were at home? To her shame the door opposite and to the right opened and the gangly form of Basil Griffiths appeared followed by his wife with the baby carried in a Welsh shawl. Sian almost ran up the pavement and into the house, colliding with one of the removal men, tilting him practically off-balance, then glaring at him until he apologised.

"Eleri wondered if you wanted any help," Basil said, leaning in, a hand on each side of the doorway.

"We're managing perfectly well, thank you. Now, if you would kindly move out of the way, the workmen will soon be finished. Goodbye."

Basil turned away and she saw him shrug in the direction of his wife. Sian wondered for the first time if she had made a terrible mistake. Neighbours she could cope with, they could simply be ignored, but one of those awful Griffithses living practically opposite and worse, offering to help? That was an onerous start.

128

"Islwyn?" she called. "Do hurry up with the curtains. I want them drawn as soon as possible!"

Determined to be a good neighbour and perhaps lessen the hostility Sian was already creating, Basil offered to clear and dig their garden. In unison, Sian said no, and Islwyn said yes. In his present mood of forgiveness, he was even willing to allow Basil to speak to him. But Sian's voice was the louder and she repeated her refusal of the offer firmly.

"Heaven's above, Islwyn, they'll be asking us to mind that baby as soon as we're unpacked! These people don't do anything for nothing you know!"

Megan and Terry had been out together several times and Gladys was pleased. He seemed such a mannerly young man, and with jewellery as his profession he must be used to the best. He was the type to make sure his wife received nothing but the best too. Such a touch of luck meeting poor old Mr Jenkins with his need for a bib, and then finding out that his grandson was a friend of dear Jack.

Gladys was putting the finishing touches to an orange cake. Made with farm butter Arfon had bought illegally from a customer, and decorated with shredded orange peel, it looked very festive.

Joan and Megan were coming to tea and bringing Terry and Jack with them. It seemed likely that Megan and Terry were going to make their friendship into something more serious. One of her grandchildren possibly settled and two more to deal with before the month was out. It no longer seemed an impossible task. This party would help, bringing together all the best of Pendragon Island's young people.

She telephoned one of her most loyal friends and asked about the Jenkinses. Not really for reassurance but to boast.

"My dear granddaughters are coming to tea today and bringing Terrence, one of the Jenkinses. Do you know of him?" she asked Gwennie Woodlas, who kept the exclusive gown shop, called Guinevere.

"Terry Jenkins, Gladys my dear? Wasn't he living in London or Bristol or somewhere like that? Selling something, I believe."

"Jewellery, my dear. And only the very best. He was in the army with my grandson. I know his grandfather, Mr Jenkins who lives over near the Pleasure Beach. Lovely family, aren't they?"

They chattered for a while, promised to meet soon and Gladys put down the phone reassured that although practically penniless and reduced to running what had been the family home as an hotel, the Jenkinses were a respectable family as near to upper class as the town could provide. She added a few drops of cointreau to the orange sponge. No point in being niggardly when someone like Terrence Jenkins was calling.

Terry and Megan were in Cardiff, having spent an hour looking around the splendid market, with Megan drooling over the puppies and other pets on the upper floor above the main stalls. They were intending to

130

do some Christmas shopping. At least, Megan was hoping Terry would buy something for her and make their friendship more permanent. She told him to turn away when she bought him a rather expensive cravat and pushed it into her shopping bag with a teasing warning for him not to try and guess what it was.

She was gratified when a little while later he told her to wait while he did a bit of shopping on his own. Waiting on a corner at the arcade she noted the shops within walking distance and wondered if he might be visiting a jewellers. He returned in less than ten minutes and told her not to be nosy, when she asked what he had bought. It was fun, flirting and getting to know someone who might be 'the one'.

They left Cardiff at three, not wanting to be late for Grandmother's tea party. When they went in and saw the spread she had managed to provide, which seemed to suggest that rationing was a myth and had never happened, Megan secretly pretended it was a celebration of her growing friendship with the handsome and charming Terrence.

"Where are you two young people going this evening?" Gladys asked as she cut up the last of the orange cake.

Megan looked at Terry for confirmation before saying, "We thought we'd go to the dance class."

"Again, dear? What can you want with a place like that after the private lessons I paid for all those years?"

"Joan enjoys it and it is fun, Grandmother."

They went to Gomer Hall, with Joan, Jack,

Rhiannon, Jimmy and Viv, but they left after half an hour. Terry had whispered in her ear that there was a more interesting way to spend the next couple of hours and taking their coats from the attendant, they slipped out into the crisp darkness.

The park wasn't far away and with ease, Terry found a place at which they could climb through the hedge and find precious privacy. Almost at once he began disturbing her clothes and alarmed, she pulled away from him.

"Come on, Megan, you know you want it. You've been giving me the 'glad eye' all day."

"I want you to hold me and kiss me but not like this," she said, a sob distorting her voice.

He released her then and collapsed forward with his head almost on his knees. In a muffled voice he said, "Don't you know what you're doing to me? Teasing me like this?"

"Teasing? but—"

"Yes, teasing, tormenting me, saying 'love me' then 'don't touch'. You don't know how hard it is for me, loving you so desperately and being afraid of frightening you away."

She only heard the words she wanted to hear, the rest made no sense and she put her arms around him and pulled him to face her.

"You love me?" she said in awe.

"Of course I do, you silly little thing."

"Oh, Terry, I'm sorry. I didn't mean to tease. I didn't know you felt anything more than liking, you see."

He touched her face gently, allowing a sob to

132

escape his trembling lips until she stilled them with her own. Almost without realising it she was engulfed in a dreamlike sensation that made her unaware of anything except their two bodies and the love that had until then, been something read about, dreamed about, but not real. This time she made no effort to still his wandering hands. She had never been kissed so thoroughly before and she was starry-eyed when they returned to the hall to walk sedately home with Joan and her cousin, Jack.

Joan and Viv still saw each other at the dance and found their steps matched as if they had rehearsed for years. But through the last days of November, when Megan and Terry were out every evening, visiting friends and becoming accepted as a couple, she was lonely. She began to call at the Wallpaper and Paint store during the afternoons to give Viv a little help by entering the goods in and out, keeping the stock control system up to date. Viv was grateful but a little uneasy. He had asked her to meet him on several occasions but she refused.

The day after the dance class, when her sister's sparkling eyes had told of her discovery of love, she surprised him by saying she would be at her Auntie Sian and Uncle Islwyn's the following evening, and why didn't he come.

"What? Me call on your Uncle Islwyn? No fear! He hates the sight of me and can I really blame him? Damn it all, Joan. I daren't even call for Jack. We have to meet on the corner like shy lovebirds! I couldn't go visiting, specially not now, with them living in that little terraced house after leaving the posh place they had. No matter how I twist it round, it is down to me, isn't it?"

"He's changed, Viv. I'd like you to see how he's changed. Come on Monday then, instead of the dance, see what you think."

"You'll tell him I'm coming?"

"I promise there won't be any trouble."

"If there is, I can go across and see Basil and Eleri." He was thinking aloud. "All right then. Meet me tonight and we'll discuss it."

Joan smiled. He did have the most wonderfully blue eyes. "All right, Viv. Tonight."

Telling her mother she was going to the dance class again, she went to the corner of Goldings Street and Trellis Street and waited for Viv. Unfortunately, Gladys had been gathering children's clothes which she intended to take to Victoria for her younger brothers and sister. They met as Viv ran up and hugged Joan before walking off, arm in arm, in the direction of Sian and Islwyn's house.

"Joan? Is that you?"

"Grandmother!"

"Mrs Weston?"

Neither knew what to say and it was Joan who gathered her wits first. "Viv and I are just going to call for Jack. He's probably forgotten and it leaves us short of a man."

Gladys knew it wasn't done to start an argument

134

in the street, so said, "I will see you tomorrow morning."

Leaving the young couple hesitating about what to do, Gladys knocked on the door in Goldings Street and it was answered, not by Victoria but by her grandson, Jack, jacket off acting as if he lived there! The world has gone completely mad, she thought in alarm.

"Hello, Grandmother, I just called to deliver a new table for Victoria and her mother. Basil's here too, we got it from Mam and Dad, there were one or two pieces they couldn't find room for or sell. Want to see?"

Shaken and anxious to get home, Gladys shook her head and handed the bag of clothes to Victoria. "Your family might find a use for these," she said as if telling the girl off for some misdemeanour, adding, "Don't be late in the morning."

"I don't want you mixing with the likes of Vivian Lewis, dear," she said when Megan and Joan were in her sitting room the following morning eating 'Teisien Lap' spread with the last of the farm butter. "We are grateful to the young man, for supporting your grandfather in his efforts to rebuild the business, but that doesn't mean you can be friends. It's quite enough that we have to be grateful!"

"We only talk shop talk, Grandmother," Joan said, knowing how it angered her grandmother to hear the business referred to as the shop. When her sister was out of hearing, fetching a fresh pot of coffee, she added that it was Megan who Viv was soft on anyway.

"You mustn't encourage him to be 'soft' on either of you. How will you find a good husband if you're seen with people like the Lewis family? Look at Megan, she's found herself a handsome young man and so must you, dear."

With everyone accepting them as a courting couple, Megan should have been happy, but there was something about Terry that made her uneasy. He was charming and attentive and the look of admiration and love in his eyes made her weak at the knees, but just occasionally she sensed a lack of sincerity. His flattery came out too pat, as if it had been said many times before.

She had tried questioning Jack, but he seemed to know less about him than Terry implied, she had the impression that although they had been in the army together, Jack didn't actually know very much about the man.

"Shall we go to the pictures this evening, Joan?" she asked.

"Without Terry you mean?"

"Yes, I want a chat, and with you in the shop helping Viv most afternoons, I miss you," Megan said.

"Hasn't Terry asked you out this evening, dear?" Gladys asked refilling their teacups.

"Yes, but I said I wanted to stay in and wash my hair, Grandmother," Megan replied.

"Ring him up and say you've changed your mind. I'll pay for you to have your hair washed and set. It looks so lovely when it goes in that under-roll."

136

"No thanks Grandmother, I'd really like an evening in with Joan."

"Nonsense, go and telephone now and you can bring him for supper after the film, you know how he loves my cottage pie."

Megan agreed, but with a sense of being pushed in a direction she hadn't decided whether or not to take. The knowledge that she was being pushed into a closer relationship with Terry excited her but at the same time she knew she was moving too fast, she needed more time to gradually get to know him. Grandmother was pushing her and Terry was pushing her and Joan wouldn't discuss it. She had an uneasy feeling of loneliness.

"We won't ever drift apart, will we, Joan?" she said as they were walking home.

"Don't be ridiculous! But we do have to move away and accept that we have a life of our own, if that's what you're trying to tell me. Mummy and Auntie Sian managed to stay close but build their own lives. I don't mind – about you and Terry, I mean. I really don't feel jealous or pushed out."

But I do, Megan thought sadly.

At the cinema they found themselves sitting next to Rhiannon and Jimmy. Megan and Rhiannon were wary of each other. Through Joan, Megan knew a lot more about Rhiannon and the Lewises than she would be expected to know and she was on her guard, afraid of revealing her sister's involvement with Viv. For her part, besides being aware of Viv's occasional meetings with Joan, Rhiannon only knew the Weston twins as the prickly granddaughters of Viv's boss. They met at the dance class but Rhiannon didn't trust either of them to be friends. Any misbehaviour on her part would be reported back to Mr Weston.

She and Jimmy often brought a sandwich with them to save time when the shop closed late. Tonight she didn't want to do anything that might be criticised. She sat as far away from Jimmy as was possible and refused the ham roll he had brought for her.

"What have I done?" Jimmy demanded in a hissing whisper, her being so far away from him.

"Nothing. I'll tell you later," she hissed back.

Viv and Joan were working on an idea he had first mentioned the night he and Jack and Basil had delivered furniture to Victoria Jones's sad little home in Goldings Street. He had wandered around with a deep frown on his face until Joan had demanded to know what he was thinking about.

"The shop next door to the store is empty," he began in the hushed tone of a conspirator. "Now then, if we could rent it and knock the two into one, we could supply all people's furnishing needs under one roof."

"What are you talking about, Viv? Furnish a house? With paint and paper?"

He explained further in a reverential whisper, the idea growing like a spiritual painting in his mind.

"Utility furniture, dockets for this, coupons for that and the other, people have had enough of it all,

138

and with the new ideas of contemporary furnishings, and this bright carpeting that can be cut as easily as cardboard, people could transform their homes. The beauty of this new carpet is I don't have to buy expensive stock. We have pieces in the full range of colours and take orders, see? It's brilliant." He frowned then and added more soberly, "I'd need you to be my adviser, mind. In fact, you could go to college and learn more about interior design. How does that grab you?"

"Don't be ridiculous. I've had all the education I need and the thought of returning for more makes me shudder, so you can forget it! But, tell me more about you idea. Isn't it too costly?"

"Ask Old Man Arfon. He'll tell you that there are times to take chances and times to stand still. This is a time to grab opportunity and force the business upward and outward."

"Really, Viv, you're sounding like a politician now!"

"Carpets and a few small items of furniture at first, but moving on to bedroom suites and dining suites and three-piece suites and—" He hugged her and made their one remaining assistant look away in embarrassment. "Joan love, let's go and see your grandfather now this minute, or as soon as we close the shop."

"Don't call me love or the idea will be finished before you've even started to explain."

"You are my love, though, even if you don't yet

know it!" he said, boldly hugging her again. "My love and my inspiration."

"Don't be ridiculous," she said again, but she was smiling. And this time she didn't slap his face.

Chapter Seven

Joan and Megan, the Weston Girls, were similar in appearance, although with the tiny scar on Megan's cheek – a result of the accident in which Lewis-boy Lewis and Joseph Martin had died, most could tell them apart. But their characters were different. Joan was the leader, the forceful one, born first and four minutes older than her twin. Of the older twins, their mother Sally was the quiet one like Megan, their Auntie Sian the one most like Joan.

Sian and Sally had chosen different husbands, to match their disparate personalities and Sian had married the outwardly easy-going, but quietly resentful Islwyn. For the gentle Sally, her husband Ryan was the stronger of the two brothers-in-law. He was basically a lazy man and when the illegal behaviour of Old Arfon and Islwyn became known he had thankfully refused to consider going back to work at the Wallpaper and Paint store.

With finances becoming a worry, Sally tried again to persuade him to go back to her father and ask for his job back.

"You have had so much experience, Ryan, Daddy

needs you to rebuild what he's lost. I'm sure you can persuade him to take you back. We really do need to stop using our savings."

"Mix my name with all that dishonesty? I have to accept being called a 'Weston' when my name is Fowler, but I don't want people to think I'm like them. To be honest," Ryan complained, "I don't want to associate with them at all! But as we are family I owe them some loyalty."

Untypically angry, Sally said quietly, "Oh yes, you put up with them don't you, out of loyalty? And sitting around hoping my father will continue to support us isn't anything to do with it?"

"He owes it to me for having to face all the disgrace."

"Perhaps he thinks you owe him something for all the years he's helped support us."

"I'll get a job, I'm just considering the options. There's no rush. I will not go back to the shop, though, so forget that. Can you really imaging me having to do what that jumped-up Viv Lewis tells me? I'll get something."

"When?"

"Soon! And stop going on at me, woman! You're becoming a real nag!"

Sally left the room with a swish of her skirt and returned seconds later with a bank book which she placed before him.

"Just look at how much we've spent since this happened and tell me how long we can last without

142

having to do what Sian and Islwyn have done, and sell the house."

"They didn't have to move. Islwyn wanted to get rid of the guilt he'd been feeling. I've done nothing. It's different altogether."

"How long, Ryan?"

"Stop your fussing. Your father wouldn't see us in real difficulties."

"My father works his way through difficulties, perhaps he thinks it's time you did the same."

Ryan shook out his newspaper and held it up, a barrier between them and an end to the futile discussion. Couldn't Sally see how impossible it was for him to go and beg someone for a job? No, he'd wait until one was offered. If nothing turned up, well, Arfon would help. He and Gladys wouldn't allow their precious daughter's standards to drop. Gladys was too much of a snob for that. Thank goodness.

Sally met her sister that afternoon with the intention of getting started on Christmas shopping.

"Although," she explained to Sian, "I can't see how I can buy anything more than tuppenny-ha'penny gifts this year, what with Ryan not working and Daddy unable to help us."

"Why should he?" Sian demanded. "Why expect Daddy to bail him out? Why doesn't Ryan get back to work?"

"I've tried to persuade him, but all he does is tell me not to nag."

"Cowardly argument that is, Sally! A retort from the defeated!"

They went around the town, gathering items, some of which would be delivered later, then Sian suggested they went to the Rose Tree Cafe near the lake. They had once been regular customers but since the notoriety of the police investigation, their friends had been less than welcoming. Today, Sian decided it was time they returned to their normal routine and call in for a coffee and a chat after shopping.

The small tables were full and it was with some hesitation that one of their acquaintances moved up to allow them to sit.

Ignoring the clientele who were determinedly showing their indifference, they continued with their conversation quietly, their words muffled by the hum of a dozen conversations going on around them. Probably *about* them, they surmised.

"We can't go on without money coming in for much longer," Sally whispered. "I think I'll have to look for something myself. It isn't as if I have that much to do, now the girls are grown-up."

"It's certainly time *they* started earning!"

"It's hard for them, brought up indulged by a doting Grandmother who convinced them they would go from being kept by us, to being kept by their husbands, with the transition nothing more than a mild disturbance."

"A decade ago it might have worked, but things have changed. No one demands that women stay home any more. They have a choice, but in the case of the Weston family, now, in 1953, the choice is work or starve. Don't your three realise that?"

144

Sally shrugged, then she smiled at her twin. "Remember the fuss when your Jack came out of the army and announced he was going to train as a teacher? Without a word to anyone he applied for that one-year scheme the government cooked up to increase the fallen numbers of teachers."

"Mummy thought the teaching profession rather low down on the scale of things," Sian smiled. "Unless he were to teach Latin or Ancient Greek at one of the better universities, of course! Islwyn and I were no more keen than Gladys at the time, but Jack is good at what he does. Working with youngsters was one of his better decisions."

Rose Tree Cafe was a little way out of town, not far from the lake and the pebbly beach, but it was popular with the women who didn't work and who had a few hours on their hands each afternoon. They would come in twos and threes, spread their shopping bags to colonise briefly one of the blue cloth-covered tables. News would be exchanged then the huddles would break up, mix again and the knots of expensively dressed women would share a few minutes with an assortment of different people before waving brightly to all and leaving.

On this afternoon, Sian and Sally did not expect to be a part of the usual exchanges. A few smiled nervously and there were one or two doubtful nods of recognition. People who had once been their friends did not know how to behave. Sally and Sian sat and ignored them all. They had too many important worries on their minds to concern themselves about the antics of the idle wealthy.

Sally was worried and although Sian spoke harshly at times, she knew she spoke sense. Ryan needed to get a job, and with some urgency. Their money was running out at an alarming rate and she needed someone to tell her what to do. With her husband refusing to listen, Sian was the only other person she could turn to. Mummy would simply take out her purse and try to soothe the situation with a pound or two – "For a little treat to cheer you up . . ."

It was as they stood to leave that Gwennie Woodlas came over and sat down, determined not to be discouraged.

"You don't know anyone who could give accommodation to a couple of reps working for a motor car accessories manufacturers, I suppose?" she asked loudly.

"Hardly!" Sian laughed. "Islwyn, Jack and me in that tiny terrace? There's hardly room for us!"

Gwennie's eyes swivelled around to Sally. "What about you, Sally, dear? Great big house and only the four of you. Those extra bedrooms could make you a bit of money."

"She doesn't need money," Sian defended swiftly.

"Oh, I thought, being as though you haven't been to order anything special for Christmas parties and dances, you might be still recovering from bad old Arfon's bit of trouble."

Until recently Sian and Sally had been regular customers at Guinevere, Gwennie Woodlas's dress shop.

"We manage, we just won't be celebrating much this year," Sally said.

"Think about it, the summer visitors pay well for bed and a good breakfast, and they say rationing will be finished for definite before next season. Practise on a couple of reps and you could make a packet come the summer, mind."

"Just out of curiosity, how much do they pay?"

"Big posh house like yours, Sally love, and you could ask fifteen shillings bed and breakfast. Each! Two to a room. Fill up their plates with fried bread and fried potatoes so they go out feeling full to bursting and they'll come again and recommend you to all their friends. Worth thinking about, isn't it?" She lowered her voice and said to Sian, "Little house like yours, so near the bomb sites, you'd be lucky to get seven and six pence, mind. Pity you moved, eh? Big mistake that was, gel. Always look prosperous, Sian, even when you got nothing in your purse except dead moths."

"Wicked old busybody," Sian muttered as the large, impressive form of Gwennie waved to them all and went to where a taxi waited. "Wealthiest widow in Pendragon Island and she'd skin a flea."

"It is worth thinking about though," Sally said thoughtfully. "But there, Ryan would never agree, not for a minute."

"Then don't ask!" Sian said firmly. "If he won't get off his backside he can't complain if you find a way of earning money, can he? If it will give you an extra couple of pounds in your purse, why not?" She gestured toward the departing taxi

147

and added, "Better than a couple of emaciated moths!"

"It isn't as if food would be a problem, only having breakfast to get. I'm not as good a cook as you, Sian, but I'll manage that," Sally mused. "And it wouldn't inconvenience Ryan all that much, would it?"

"Pity. It might make him get out and find a job!" Sian retorted and Sally couldn't help but smile.

"Specially if I told him he had to do the washing up," she added.

Leaving the cafe, with its blue and white table cloths, artificial roses and groups of gossiping women, they went back to the main road and called to see Gwennie Woodlas.

"Definitely not, Sally. I don't know what you're thinking of. Can you imagine your mother's face if you told her we were taking in lodgers!"

"Summer visitors, Ryan, for about eight weeks in the summer that's all."

"Summer visitors, boarders, paying guests, lodgers, it's all the same, demeaning yourself and waiting on people who won't have any manners – or understand how to use a bathroom. Rough they'll be."

"All of them?"

"Yes!"

"Pity you aren't enthusiastic, Ryan," Sally said quietly, as she cleared the last of the dishes from the table, "because I have two motor trade reps arriving on Friday, looking for somewhere permanent. If I like the look of them, I might offer to take them

148

here." She glanced at his face as she left the room, assessing his reaction. Only hours earlier she would have said, 'if we' – and not – 'if I'.

His reply was lost as she closed the kitchen door and burst into giggles with Joan and Megan, who had been supporting her, waiting in the kitchen while she broke the news.

"Come on, Mummy, leave the rest of the dishes, we're taking you to the pictures to celebrate," Joan said. "Megan, you and me."

"On the way, we'll have to stop and explain to Grandmother and Grandfather. The Westons are really on the way – 'down', aren't they?" she laughed. "Poor Mummy, after all her efforts to make us into the most important family in the town, too. But d'you know, I think I'm going to enjoy the next few months, I really do."

Once it had been explained exactly what Sally was going to do, Gladys accepted it with reasonable good grace. "After all, if it's good enough for the Jenkinses, it's good enough for the Westons, I suppose," she said with a forced smile.

The smile remained as she waved them off but as the door closed it was wiped off as if by magic and she went to the telephone and demanded that Ryan call to see her at once.

"Are you really going to allow your wife to demean herself, cleaning up after other people, Ryan?" she demanded as he took off his coat. She glared at Victoria who was waiting to hang it up and snapped, "Go and fetch the tea, Victoria.

149

Mr Ryan can hang up his own coat, he isn't helpless."

When they were seated beside a glowing wood fire, Gladys shot a few whispered comments towards her son-in-law but didn't begin the real onslaught until Victoria had delivered the tea and left the room. She took a deep breath but Ryan stopped her with a raised hand.

"Don't waste your breath, Mother-in-law, I've given up any hope of changing Sally's mind. The two reps arrive on Friday and the room is ready for them. She won't even discuss it. She can be very stubborn you know."

"And you aren't? Months it is since you earned any money and my daughter is showing you how! She's capable enough to do something about the situation if you aren't."

"I can't go back to the business and work for that Viv Lewis character, I'm sorry Mother-in-law, I'd do anything for Sally but I can't do that."

"No one is asking you to. There isn't a job for you there if you begged! There are other jobs though and you haven't even been looking."

Ryan was saved from further criticism by the fortuitous arrival of Terry.

"I'm sorry Terry, dear, but Megan isn't here. She and Joan have taken their mother to the pictures."

She invited him in and when he sat, Ryan stood. "Sorry, but I have to go, I want to hear The Archers."

"Can you tell me which cinema they went to?

I can meet them and walk them home," Terry said.

"No need," Ryan said ungraciously. "It isn't far and hardly dangerous."

"Thank you, dear," Gladys said, and glared at her son-in-law. "You might have forgotten the attack on Rhiannon Lewis, but I have not!"

Gladys offered Terry a drink and he sat with her and Arfon, relaxed and comfortable. He flattered Gladys by admiring the room and congratulating her on her excellent taste. "There's such a skill in home-making, Mrs Weston," he said. "So few really create a room where people can feel truly relaxed."

"My girls have that skill too," she said at once. "Even in that poky little house on Trellis Street, and temporarily being out of funds, my daughter has made a little haven for herself and her family."

"It isn't money, it's flair," Terry agreed.

Gladys took out her lists of party arrangements and asked his advice about music entertainment and Arfon slipped away, leaving them to it. With one eye on the clock, Terry began to offer suggestions and admire her organising skills. If he were to succeed with Megan, he needed Gladys on his side. Specially now, where there was danger of his previous life coming to light.

That damned letter had followed him through several changes of address and finally caught up with him at Montague Court.

It had been so unfortunate that Basil Griffiths had been there when the letter had arrived. Basil was talking to Edward and Margaret about their order

151

for chickens and pheasants for the Christmas period. The letter was handed to him by the postman Henry Thomas and they had looked at him curiously as it had been re-addressed more than once and was tattered by its travels.

He had been unable to hide his shock and dismay at his whereabouts being known. Although his cousins had politely turned away, Basil had watched his face with undisguised curiosity. He had better think up a good story before Megan had suspicions roused by that interfering Griffiths. He'd better leave early and wait outside the cinema. He didn't want to miss her.

Megan was more and more uneasy with Terry Jenkins. He attracted her and excited her but there was something that wasn't right. It wasn't something she could put into words and discuss with her sister, just a less than comfortable state of mind. His kisses were exciting and she knew her body was developing a need for love, but his strength frightened her making her aware of his impatience, instead of making her feel safe. Grandmother was so enthusiastic and her friends envied her new and handsome escort, so why wasn't everything perfect?

It must be the strangeness of having someone special for the first time in her life, such a change from Joan's and her brief flirtations which had always ended in their derisory laughter, leaving the boy feeling gauche and less than worthy of them.

Being with Terry so much of the time and only

he, and being half in love and half afraid to let it happen, was like a barrier that she had to climb or push her way through to something wonderful that was waiting on the other side. She was half in love with him and she did want to let go and enjoy being one of a couple, yet something was holding her back from complete surrender.

It was nothing more than insecurity, a fear of depending on one person for her happiness and of someone driving a wedge between herself and Joan.

When she came out of the cinema with her mother and her sister she was unable to control the slight groan of disappointment that escaped her lips on seeing Terrence waiting for her. She didn't want to talk to him. Not tonight when she was so confused about how she felt about him.

Sharp where her twin was concerned, Joan pulled her away on the pretext of looking at next week's posters as soon as they had greeted each other.

"Are you getting fed up with him?" she asked in a whisper.

"No, I'm not! So don't think you can muscle in," Megan retorted.

"Wouldn't dream of it, but why did you groan when you saw him waiting for you?"

"It's late and I wanted to go home and get to bed."

Unconvinced, Joan walked with her back to where Terry and Sally waited. She walked with her mother, leaving Megan and Terry to follow them.

"Your grandmother told me where you were and

153

I offered to see you safely home," Terry explained, stealing a shy kiss.

"Thank you, but do you mind if I don't ask you in? It's late and Mummy's had a busy day."

"Only if we can lose the other two for a few moments," Terry whispered and at once she was filled with excitement, imagining his deeper, longer kisses when they were alone.

Without waiting for Megan's agreement, he called to Sally and explained they were going by a different route. "There's something I want to show Megan in a shop window," he said by way of an excuse.

"No, I don't think so," Sally said. "If you've waited so long to escort us home, then we should stay together."

Late on the following day he called and invited Megan to go for a walk. The weather was a typical December day, cold and damp, with a chill seeping up from the ground and stiffening the muscles of the poorly clad. Megan, dressed in a fur coat and thick leather boots was cosy. She wore a bright blue scarf at her throat and expensive fur-lined gloves with a hat to match. Her face glowed, her eyes were clear and shining with good health and she knew she looked her best.

To her surprise they didn't walk to the shops but instead, Terry led her through an alleyway and stopped where a bend concealed them from the sight of people passing. A tantalisingly brief kiss then he led her on to where a churchyard gate stood open. Another tormenting kiss and on again to where a seat and a porch offered privacy. There at last he stopped and after looking down into her eyes for a long moment, he gave a low groan and uttered her name.

"Megan. Lovely Megan, I love you."

Gathering her into his arms he kissed her slowly, eased her coat away from her and held her tightly against him so she was aware of his growing desire.

All fears forgotten she relaxed in his arms and drifted into a dream of such joy she wondered why she had ever been afraid.

Then he began sliding his hands over her most intimate places. His lips drifted lower and lower, touching her taut breasts through her thin blouse, his fingers reaching inside her skirt, and the fear came back.

"No, Terry. Please take me home."

He pleaded and begged, then, with his breath still ragged, he moved away.

"I can't stand much more of this, my darling," he said as they walked away from the tempting silence of the cold churchyard. "Seeing you, being so close to you, wanting you and being unable to have you." He put an arm around her shoulder, feeling the slight movement of rejection with some dismay. "I've loved you from the first moment we met."

Why did that sound so insincere? she wondered with sudden alarm. Such a well-used sentence, how could anyone believe it? They walked home in silence, side by side but separate.

When she went inside she looked at Joan and shared a frown. They would talk later. She had to talk to someone, however difficult it was. Terry had woken her body to love but not her heart. She just wasn't ready to put her life in his hands.

Gladys Weston looked at her daughter with horror. "You mean Gwennie Woodlas hinted that we couldn't afford new clothes for the Christmas season? How dare she? I hope you put her right, Sian?"

"I said we weren't in the mood for celebrating and that our Christmas would be a quiet one," Sian replied.

"And there's me organising a party and Gwennie knowing all about it? Good heavens, child, she must think we'll be buying from the chain stores!"

"Does it matter what Gwennie Woodlas thinks, Mummy?"

"Her clientele includes everyone who is anyone in Pendragon Island. Of course it matters! Come on, find Sally and the girls and we'll go at once and order dresses for the party."

"But Sally and I haven't enough money," Sian protested.

"Neither have I according to your father, dear, but why should that stop us? Come on, call your sister. Five party dresses for a start. That will stop her spreading rumours about the Westons!"

Having arranged to meet her daughters and grand-daughters at two, Gladys made another phone call, this time to Terrence Jenkins.

"We're going to choose our dresses for the party," she told him. "Perhaps you'd like to come and help

Megan pick one that makes her look her best." Terry agreed and persuaded his uncle's maid to press his suit for the occasion. He needed to look his best too if he were to persuade Megan into a night of passion. Things were not looking very good. Megan had cooled towards him and he hated to think he'd been wasting his time, staying put in this small town and risking the writer of that letter finding him, all for nothing.

Rhiannon Lewis was not looking forward to Christmas with her usual enthusiasm. With her relationship with Barry the cause for gossip and Jimmy hoping to make their friendship into something more she was in a turmoil.

Barry saw no reason for Rhiannon and himself not to be seen together as often as they wished, but he was married, albeit in name only, to Caroline Griffiths, and Rhiannon felt it was wrong. Her mother agreed.

"I understand how you feel, Rhiannon, love. With your father playing home and away, it makes everyone expect the worst of us Lewises and we don't want your life spoilt by more gossip."

Rhiannon and Barry knew that with Barry being the son of her father's 'other woman' there was no possibility of any sympathy for their plight from Dora. She had never openly demanded that they stopped seeing each other, but she did encourage Jimmy Herbert, inviting him to tea, and for an evening of cards or Monopoly, making him feel he could call any time, specially as he was a rep and often far from home. "Your second home this is, Jimmy and don't be afraid to knock at the door any time you want a cup of tea," she frequently said, and Jimmy, in his pursuit of Rhiannon often did.

One Wednesday afternoon, Rhiannon and her mother were sorting through the tattered decorations, survivors of many Christmases and countless repair sessions. There was a knock at the door and the cheerful voice of Jimmy called, "It's only me, can I come in?"

"If you do you'll have to help us untangle this little lot," Dora replied.

"A cup-a-tea first then I'll show you how it's done," Jimmy laughed, shedding his navy overcoat and hurrying over to warm his hands against the roaring fire.

"What are you doing here, Jimmy?" Rhiannon asked. "It's halfday closing so you can't expect any business."

"No, I came down special. I want to ask you if you'll come to a party with me on December the eighteenth. It promises to be a posh do, mind, so you'll have to dress up and do me proud."

"Cheek!"

"Funny really, I don't know why I've been invited. It's them Westons, you know, the lot your Viv works for. I only know Megan and Joan through meeting them at the dance class with you and Viv, so why they invited me I can't think. But will you come?"

"I couldn't! I don't like the Weston Girls for a start, and they wouldn't want the likes of me there.

158

They'll be asking the wealthy families not the scruffs of Sophie Street."

Jimmy put on a superior look and nodded. "Yes, I realised I'd be slumming asking someone like you, Rhiannon. Best if I take someone else, eh, Mrs Lewis?"

"After court cases and all the rest of it, I don't think the Westons are wealthy any more."

"But that won't stop them acting like they are," Jimmy frowned. "So, why ask me?"

"Short of men," Viv said coming from the kitchen where he had been cleaning his shoes. "Joan asked me for a few suggestions for eligible young men. I suggested you. Mind, I also suggested the Griffithses and so did Jack, but I don't think that went down too well!"

"They don't have as many friends as before the trouble," Dora said. "But you go, Rhiannon, and get a nice frock and show them how lovely you are compared with them Weston Girls with their haughty ways, long noses and short skirts."

"Thanks, Jimmy, I'd love to come," Rhiannon smiled. "I'll see if Eleri will come shopping and help me choose a dress."

The following morning, when she went to open the shop, Barry arrived and invited her to go the party with him.

"I'm sorry, Barry. I'd have loved to go with you, if only I'd known. Now it's too late, I'm already going with Jimmy Herbert," she said. After commiserations she suggested, "Why don't you invite Caroline? She

159

doesn't go out much and I'm sure she'd enjoy it?" She expected him to refuse, to say it wouldn't be right, or fair, and she would regretfully have to tell Jimmy she had changed her mind and was going with Barry.

She was sadly mistaken.

"That's a good idea! You're right, Rhiannon, it would be a real treat for her, and we would still see each other there, wouldn't we?"

Dora was very fond of Eleri. Although she was no longer her daughter-in-law, since the death of Lewis-boy, she still treated her as if she were. Now Eleri was married to Basil Griffiths and had borne him a son, she went to the flat in Trellis Street regularly to take small gifts, including clothes she had knitted for the baby.

On the afternoon following the discussion about Gladys Weston's party, she took out her bicycle on which she had collected insurance for many years, and, waving to her daughter Rhiannon as she passed the sweet shop, she went up to the main road to collect her rations. On the way back she stopped to spend an hour with Eleri and Basil and the baby.

It was a pleasant day, a winter sun forcing its way through the morning mist and creating a brief spell of brightness that belied the shortness of the day. In an hour it would be dark, but for the moment it was easy to imagine there was time to wander over to the beach and relax on the sand with other families. People she passed had opened their coats, enjoying the brief hint of warmer weather. The crowds looking in the shops moved at a more leisurely pace and Dora felt happy and more relaxed than of late.

Eleri was preparing supper, which Basil would eat at seven, before going for a pint at The Railwayman's then on, to work throughout the night.

"Mam! There's a lovely surprise." Eleri took Dora's coat and ushered her to a chair close to the fire. "Wait now while I finish grating this old bit of cheese into the pie and we'll have a nice cup of tea."

The baby began to bleat a warning that he wouldn't be ignored for long and Dora looked at Eleri. "Can I pick him up, love?"

"Of course you can. I'll be glad if you can amuse him for five minutes while I finish making this pie. Thanks Mam."

With a new mother-in-law, Janet Griffiths, Eleri's name for Dora hadn't changed from 'Mam'. Eleri saw no reason to change the name she had used for so long, and Dora loved it.

"What about if I finish the pie and you cuddle little Ronnie?" Dora suggested. She looked at the small piece of meat that Eleri had chopped to stretch into a meal for them and dug around in the food cupboard for inspiration. Lentils and an oxo were added, mashed potato to cover instead of the sad-looking pastry and the hard, stale cheese grated onto the top to make it more attractive. While it cooked she stayed with Ronnie while Eleri and Basil went to do some shopping.

When the pie came out of the oven an hour and a half later brown and shiny, Eleri hugged Dora and said, "Mam, you are a marvel. You can make a meal out of nothing and make it look great."

"Eleri's learning fast," Basil said proudly, "but she'll be glad when this damned rationing's finished."

"Won't we all!"

They chatted about the baby's progress and then about their arrangements for Christmas.

"We're all going over to the Griffithses as you'd guess," Eleri laughed. "The smallest house and the largest number of people. I don't know how they fit them in, do you?"

"No, but I wouldn't mind trying," Dora said sadly. "Rattles round in the house I do. And when Rhiannon and Viv leave, as they surely will one of these days, well it'll get worse won't it, not better."

"Why don't you come too?" Eleri suggested. "Your Viv and Rhiannon are coming in the evening and I know Janet and Hywel would love to see you too."

"And Lewis? Is he coming, with his fancy woman?"

"I don't know. Perhaps." She frowned then added apologetically, "Yes, Nia probably will come now she has a grandson there, won't she? Sorry, Mam. I wasn't thinking." Realising her mistake she quickly changed the subject. "Mam, it's not my business but why don't you get yourself a job again? You've been home for a while now and it seems such a waste, you being so clever with figures and not using your skills."

"It's a cook you ought to be," Basil said, sniffing the pie appreciatively.

"There's plenty to do in the house and garden." Dora's blue eyes brightened and her voice was sharp.

Undeterred, Eleri said softly, "Do all that standing on your head, you would, so fast you work. It would be good for you to have some interest outside the house, mind. Why don't you make that your New Year's Resolution?"

"Perhaps."

There was a slight uneasiness between them and anxious to clear it, Eleri took the baby she had been feeding and said pleadingly, "Cuddle him off to sleep Mam, you know he always relaxes with you."

"Bad habits we're giving him."

"And lots of love too," she smiled, kissing Dora's pale cheek affectionately.

As Dora cycled home, rain began to fall. Soft and clean onto the leaf-filled gutters. It stung her hands and she wished she'd remembered gloves. But she was soon distracted from the cold by her thoughts. She did need something to fill her time. No, not fill it, use it. She had to stop this hanging around hoping that Nia would leave Lewis and he would come back to her.

Perhaps she should buy herself a pet. A dog would be best, she could take him on walks. Or should she find a job? Perhaps Eleri was right and she needed to get out, meet people and stop hiding in shame. She needed more than just walking a dog. Nothing strenuous, but something that really interested her.

She smiled in the darkness thinking of Gladys Weston having to face the fact that her son-in-law

163

was working in a chip shop. What a laugh. She'd do better than that. The Lewises knew how to get on.

Her son Viv was running the Weston's business for them and bringing it round from disaster. Her daughter Rhiannon was managing that Nia Martin's sweet shop, and there was Gladys's son-in-law Islwyn Heath, cooking chips!

What a funny world it was when things could go so topsy-turvy. She began to sing as she turned the corner into Sophie Street, "How Much Is That Doggie In the Window, Woof Woof—"

Chapter Eight

Gladys Weston was in despair, her plans for her party were in complete disarray. She stared at the two lists she had made of possible guests, and frowned. On the first were the people she had met socially on a regular basis before their little bit of trouble, as she referred to police investigations. Most of these people had refused. Politely for the most part, but firmly.

The second list was longer and most of the people on it she did not want to meet at all. This list had been made up by her grandchildren. Jack had added the Griffithses and at first she thought he had been teasing her but no, he insisted that if she wanted a jolly party with young people having fun, then Frank and Ernie were necessary to its success.

Then there was Viv Lewis, who was an employee and since when did decent families like the Westons invite their staff to a social event? Now she had been told the girls wanted Eleri and Basil, plus Rhiannon and some salesman called Jimmy Herbert.

It wouldn't do at all. What would Terrence Jenkins think of them?

Unless the party were to consist of only the immediate family, she would have to be more persuasive. If a few more of Terrence's relations were to accept her invitation, others might be convinced that it would be a wise social move to accept too. She hadn't actually met Terrence's cousins but if they were Jenkins they must be acceptable, and she had been able to confirm that neither Edward nor Margaret were married.

Putting on her best felt hat and fur coat, she set off to visit the Jenkinses at their hotel, Montague Court.

It was not considered polite to arrive for a social call unannounced, so she telephoned and arranged a table for afternoon tea for two. Easy to explain that her friend had forgotten to come.

The room in which tea was served was furnished simply with tables and chairs, but the carpet was rich and the walls were covered with a pleasing array of oil paintings in wide, gold-painted frames. A fire burned in a large grate and on the mantleshelf an ormolu clock marked the quarter hours in subdued precision. There were a few highly polished shelves on which glass and china ornaments stood to add to the room's air of homely luxury.

A waiter came limping over to take her coat and lead her to a small table in which a folded card bearing the word 'Reserved' stood on a silver frame. Allowing herself time to look around, Gladys explained that she was waiting for a friend to join her. After ten minutes during which she had decided that the Jenkins family would be suitably fertile ground in which to look for a wife for Jack and a husband for Joan, she sighed gracefully and announced that her friend must have been unavoidably detained, and ordered.

She looked around for a sign that members of the family were present. She had learned from old Mr Jenkins that the place was run by his daughter Dorothy assisted by her son, Edward and her daughter Margaret. Although she stretched her neck to look around the various doorways, she saw only the waiter. He was about twenty-six or twenty-seven she decided, tall, slim and very efficient. The Jenkinses would know about training staff, she thought with approval. The telephone was near her and when it rang she saw the waiter answer and was startled to hear him say, "Edward Jenkins speaking. Yes, my sister Margaret is in the kitchen, one moment please, while I fetch her."

While pretending to struggle with a crumbled scone which tipped its jam onto her hand, Gladys listened and watched as a woman in her early thirties came out of swing doors wearing a white overall and hat, and spoke into the phone.

"Margaret Jenkins speaking, who is this?" the woman demanded in an imperious voice and after a few moments, she replaced the receiver, scribbled something in a notebook, whispered something to the water before returning to the kitchen. Edward and Margaret, Gladys was startled to realise were the grandchildren of the old man Jenkins, cousins of Terrence. She took out two of her printed invitations and sat with a fountain pen poised.

"Are you related to the gentleman who lives

in Channel View Terrace?" she asked when the waiter returned to pour more tea. "I believe he has grandchildren about your age."

"He's our grandfather, yes. This house was the family home when he was younger. I suppose it still is," he smiled. "Although we run it as an hotel, we've tried to keep the homelike atmosphere."

"Charming," Gladys smiled back.

"Of course most of the property has gone now, the gardens were sold to educate the new generation and are now covered with prefabs."

Gladys gave a sympathetic shudder. "My husband and I considered buying his house you know, but in the end we decided to stay put."

"You were right not to buy it I think. Rather a dark old place I've always thought."

"Would Terrence Jenkins be a cousin?" Glady went on, barely registering the look of disapproval that crossed the young man's face as he heard the name.

"I don't know cousin Terry all that well. He's lived in London for years, and before that I was away at boarding school, so we only met on the usual family occasions, Christmas and summer hols, you know the sort of thing. I've heard he is seeing some young woman from the docks area."

"Hardly the docks! You will have heard of the Westons?"

"Oh, I've heard of the Westons," Edward Jenkins began to smile, thinking of the notoriety the family had experienced. "Everyone must have heard of the Westons and their family embarrassments." Then, seeing her stricken face he added quickly, "Oh, you are Mrs Weston, aren't you? I'm sorry. Don't let a bit of gossip worry you, Mrs Weston. My ancestors acquired such wealth that they must have done a great deal more than burn down a small shop." He could see this had made things worse and he added, "Aren't your granddaughters called the Weston Girls? I've heard they are charming."

Unable to do more than nod, reminded of just how badly her name had been affected, Gladys paid her bill and left.

Edward Jenkins called after her noticing she had dropped something but hesitated when he saw that it was a printed invitation to the Westons' party.

Calming down as she sank into the soft leather of the taxi seat, she glared back at the fading lights as the hotel disappeared into the gloom of the early evening. Only innkeepers they were – innkeepers for all their swank. A girl from the docks area indeed! Her beautiful Megan! How dare they smirk at the Westons?

Back home, she looked again at her lists. Her wonderful party, planned with such excitement was doomed. She liked the word, and repeated it in her head: Doomed. She put the phone number of the caterers on top of the pile and thought seriously of cancelling. Would her embarrassment be worse by doing so, or by continuing and having people know she couldn't raise the support without stooping to inviting the dreadful Griffithses?

If something didn't happen soon, she would be

forced to accept the Griffithses or fall so short of guests they could hold it in her own living room. So far she had definite acceptances from only twenty people and she had envisaged at least fifty. She picked up the caterer's phone number but put it down again. Anger swelled in her against her stupid son-in-law Islwyn, and briefly against Arfon too. She shredded the list in agitated hands. Between them they had brought her to this.

Jack left school as the last pupils drifted homeward and, taking his cycle from the staff shed, rode through the town past the brightly lit shops with their Christmas displays, until, leaving the town behind, he travelled along the empty stretch towards the beach. It was the Pleasure Beach in the summer but now, as winter slowly crept in, he saw it as a silently waiting, shrouded giant.

A mother and a group of children stood near the edge of the tide in the Old Harbour busily throwing stones into the water. He wondered, not for the first time, what it was about water that made people of all ages do just that. And why he was tempted to dismount and join them.

He left the bicycle near the fish pond and walked along the prom to the slope leading to the sands. The wind seemed stronger here and from the look of the empty bay had driven even the most hardy of walkers back to their homes. The sky was already darkening with the approach of evening as if a watering can had poured a fine mist, emptying it over the day to end its business and forcing everything to slow down and take on the mantle of the night.

The sea was barely seen, but by concentrating he could make out the slight difference in the shades of grey as it moved in and out, its white frilly edges becoming clearer as he stared. Their regular in and out began making him restless, an irritability coming and going in his stomach with the ebb and flow.

Jack was normally a man at ease with the world. He loved his job, he had a few good friends, a casual but pleasant social life and books to tax him intellectually. Women were only a vague need to be fulfilled one day, so he had no thought to complain at being permanently placed in the role of chaperone to his cousins, the Weston Girls. He desired nothing that was even remotely out of his reach, expected little to change in his humdrum life. Yet of late, something was disturbing his contentment and he couldn't quite understand what it was. He only knew that he was poised, waiting for something to happen, something he couldn't begin to describe.

Coldness settled, dropping down from the clouds of night and making him shiver. He ran to where he had left the bicycle and rode slowly home. As he turned into the front garden of forty-four Trellis Street he changed his mind and instead of going in, he walked on and around the corner into Goldings Street and knocked on the door of Victoria Jones. Too late he realised that she would still be working at his grandmother's house.

Victoria's mother opened the door and smilingly

invited him in. He was startled by Mrs Jones's appearance. Used to seeing a shabby, exhausted-looking woman, he now saw a mother-to-be glowing with health and with a relaxed expression in her clear blue eyes. Her dress wasn't new but freshly ironed and it was as if she had been replaced with a better cared-for twin, he thought foolishly.

"Victoria isn't home yet, but if you'd like to wait? We could have a cup of tea, if you don't mind the lack of saucers?"

"No, I won't disturb you, you're probably about to eat."

Mrs Jones laughed and shook her head. "Not on Fridays. We have to wait for Victoria to bring home fish and chips." She waved an arm to point out the pile of chipped and damaged plates warming on the brass fender, the top one bearing the legend, '*Property of The Great Western Railway*'. "It's our regular weekly treat. It's pay day," she added when he didn't seem to understand.

"Oh, I see," he said as a bubble of laughter began to rise. "I was just thinking that perhaps my father is at this moment cooking them!"

Embarrassed at first, Mrs Jones soon joined in his laughter at the incongruity of the situation.

"I like Fridays," he said as he sipped his tea from a cracked cup once belonging to an hotel. "There's a smell of freedom about Fridays." He gave a mock frown. "Not that there isn't work to do at weekends. On Saturday morning I sometimes have to help with the school football team and

172

there's always something to prepare for class for the following week."

"My father was a teacher," Mrs Jones said surprising him again. "He taught piano, but he died of consumption when he was only twenty-two, so I don't remember him. I've often wondered if I might have been talented that way. No chance of ever finding out." She didn't complain, just stated the facts.

He looked at her as she sat near him, a small woman, who wore a gentle expression that belied her turbulent past.

"I know this might be impertinent, Mrs Jones, but you really can't be so advanced in years that you can consider all hope for the future is gone."

"I have all these children to care for, and if you think there's time for music in that future you must be crazy. Oh, I'm sorry, I didn't mean to be rude!"

Jack laughed, throwing back his head and enjoying the relaxed sensation and the humour which still had an edge from the idea of his father cooking Victoria's supper. "It's me who should apologise! Can you imagine, I was thinking you had plenty of room for a piano against that wall and plenty of people prepared to have lessons. How simple other people's problems are, aren't they?"

Victoria came in an hour later with a steaming newspaper-wrapped parcel, and found Jack on all fours giving rides to the two smallest children, with the other three laughing at their shrieks of delight.

"I called to see how you were," Jack explained hurriedly brushing his knees and straightening his

173

tie, "but I'll leave you to enjoy your meal and call again."

"Called to see how I am?" Victoria frowned after the door had closed behind him. "When he can see me any time he visits his grandmother?"

Jack walked slowly home, still reluctant to go inside. The restlessness had returned and he found himself wishing he could have stayed and shared their fish and chip supper on cracked china and bent cutlery that could only be described as eclectic. As he opened the door of number forty-four and called to tell his mother he was home, he wondered if Basil Griffiths knew of a piano going cheap.

Rhiannon looked up and smiled when Nia Martin entered the shop. As usual, Nia raised a hand and assured her she was not coming to 'snoop'. "The place is in your very capable hands, Rhiannon. I've just called to see how you are and whether there's anything you need."

"I need to order more Christmas chocolates and small gifts, unless you think it's too late? I still have plenty but they are selling fast and I'd hate to miss sales. They promise to deliver within a few days but I'm a bit nervous of placing an order, in case we're left with something that won't sell after December the twenty-fifth."

"Good heavens, Rhiannon, of course you must re-order. If we see some lines sticking we'll drop the price a little and they will surely sell then. Can I see what you're ordering and perhaps, if you wish, I can make a few suggestions."

They were pouring over the confectioner's lists when Barry's van pulled up outside. He still lived above the shop so Rhiannon was hardly surprised to see him but she hadn't expected the extra company. Caroline was with him, and her small son Joseph trotted towards the shop door without being told, stepped inside and pointed to his favourite penny chocolate bars.

"There's no doubt he's been here before," Nia laughed. "Did you notice that he went straight for the Cadbury's penny bars? Caroline thinks that size is quite enough for a child."

Rhiannon had noticed and wondered when Joseph had become so familiar with the shop. He didn't come while she was there. Barry must be seeing a lot more of his wife than he told her. She forced herself to return to the ordering.

"We'll have a dozen of the Lovells beakers then, and some Blue Bird's six-ounce pictorial tins?" she said to distract Nia from cooing over the little boy.

"Yes, dear, then if you would like to give the order to Jimmy Herbert?"

"Why him?" Barry asked, staring at Rhiannon as if noticing her for the first time. "Why don't you give the order to your father? He works for the same firm, doesn't he?"

"Yes, but this is really Jimmy's patch so we take it in turns," Rhiannon said, with a glint of trouble in her eye. Reminding him he hadn't greeted her properly, she said, "Hello, Barry!"

175

"Rhiannon, I'm sorry. I was watching Joseph. How are you?"

Rhiannon turned away and wondered whether it was jealousy she felt or just pique at being ignored. She wondered also, which category Barry's remark against Jimmy fitted. Were they jealous or had they drifted too far apart for that to be possible?

Caroline came over with her son in her arms, his face covered in chocolate. "Rhiannon, have you been invited to the Westons' party? Poor Mrs Weston must be hard up for guests if she's inviting the dreaded Griffithses, she's even asked my brothers!"

"Are you going?" Rhiannon asked. "I haven't made up my mind."

"If Mam will look after Joseph I might go for an hour, although parties aren't my thing really."

"It will do you good to get out and meet people," Barry said and Caroline laughed.

"I see plenty of people in the wool shop! Although I do admit the conversation might be more varied at the Westons' party!"

To Rhiannon's horror, the door opened and her father came in. He said, "Hello Rhiannon, love," but he was staring at Nia.

"I'll just pop up to the flat and get a cloth to wipe Joseph's face, shall I?" Rhiannon said and quickly left the shop.

Knowing her father and Nia Martin were lovers was something she could cope with most of the time, and certainly when she saw them individually, but being in the same room as them, watching the way they looked

176

at each other gave her an uneasy feeling. It was as if she were eavesdropping on strangers, or looking through someone's window at something that it was not her business to see.

She stood at the bathroom sink and looked at the flannel, letting the tap run, then she heard footsteps and saw that Barry, Caroline and the baby had followed her up.

"Easier to clean him up up here," Caroline smiled.

"Making it easy for those two to have their intimate talk, you mean," Rhiannon retorted.

"All right, Rhiannon, Caroline was trying to be diplomatic!" Barry snapped and at once Rhiannon turned to reply but she held back her words. She was on one side of the small bathroom and grouped together on the other, were Barry, Caroline and the little boy. She didn't belong. Barry had clearly decided where he wanted to be.

She pushed past them, shoving Barry as hard as she could as she squeezed through. "You deal with it then. I'm obviously not needed here." Running down the stairs she was in time to catch the final movement as her father and Nia separated from what had obviously been a kiss. "Oh, I hate this place when it's crowded!" she shouted and went to stand on the step.

Lewis was the first to leave and then Barry helped Caroline and Joseph into the van and drove off with a briefly muttered 'cheerio'.

"Sorry, I felt crowded all of a sudden," she said to Nia who stood near the counter, glancing once more through the order book.

"What if we ask Jimmy Herbert to call before we make the final decision? There might be some special offers."

It was a perfectly normal remark but in her state of jealousy, or pique, Rhiannon distorted it and said, "You don't have to try and tell me to forget Barry and find solace with Jimmy. I'd already worked out for myself that Barry is more interested in Caroline."

"It isn't Caroline, my dear. It's the baby who interests Barry," his mother said quietly. "I believe he's saddened by how long you and he will have to wait before you can have one of your own."

Rhiannon believed her. It was little Joseph whom he spoke about and showed such a delight in. He hadn't changed his mind about divorcing Caroline – his wife in name only she forced herself to remember. She would ring Jimmy and tell him Barry was taking her to the Westons' party, and they would revive their feelings for each other, set the mood for the holiday and the New Year to come. Meanwhile, she would look for a Christmas present for Joseph, that would please Caroline and Barry as well.

Viv was sitting in the empty building looking down on the shop floor as he thought about his plans for the development of the business. He still hadn't discussed his ideas with Old Man Arfon, but things were becoming clearer after talking his ideas through with Joan.

He wondered idly what Joan might have achieved if she hadn't been born to be the pampered pet of her grandmother Gladys Weston. Still outrageous in her dress, choosing colours that to everyone else's mind clashed, and insisting on fabrics and styles that were unfashionable but which others soon copied, she was frowned upon by some and admired by others, but, as she so frequently told him, she was never ignored. Unable to spend so much at Gwennie Woodlas's shop, she had found a dressmaker to alter garments of which she had tired, and still managed to look outstandingly and boldly fashionable.

To outward appearances, the shortage of money hadn't affected her. And he realised with admiration that no matter what her circumstances were, she would always uphold her standards. A remarkable young woman who had the ability to really make her mark but who would probably drift along until she found someone to marry. He felt sick that it could never be him.

He closed the ledgers where he had been checking the outstanding amounts due to suppliers and stood up. Things were beginning to look good. It was time to make a forward step he decided, as he stretched and reached for his coat. Tomorrow was Saturday and Joan would be coming to help with the books. After the shop had closed, they would go together to talk to Old Man Arfon.

They stood at the door for a moment and crossed their fingers before ringing the bell. The door was opened by Victoria who backed away to allow them to enter. She didn't have to announce Joan and she knew Viv would refuse to wait for her to tell Mr Weston he had called.

Arfon was at his most pompous having dressed to go to his club where he was chairman of the committee. Tonight he had to give a speech about the Christmas appeal and he had already put his loud voice in the correct mode.

"Joan, my dear," he bent to kiss his granddaughter's cheek and Viv ducked as if avoiding the same. "Come in and sit down," Arfon chuckled. "Now what is it you want to discuss, is there a problem?"

"I want us to make plans to expand," Viv began and smiled at the old man's startled expression.

"You don't think it's a bit soon, Viv? After all, we're hardly out of the wood regarding our debts yet. We have to be careful for a while."

"Careful yes, but afraid to take our chances, no."

"The sales are good but increasing our stock wouldn't make that much difference, would it? I mean, we don't turn people away by failing to give them what they need.

"Carpets. That ought to be our next step. People no longer want the traditional safe colours and 'practical' is becoming a dirty word. Plain carpets are available that can be cut and fitted easily by the ordinary man in the street and I think we ought to get a slice of the market. Preferably before too many others do."

"Can we afford it?"

"Can we afford not to?" Joan said.

"What do you know about business, dear?" Arfon smiled affectionately.

180

"I know the percentages offered are generous! And with six weeks allowed for payment, and ordering direct from the factory without having to hold stock, and with a range of colours to suit everyone, it's too good to pass up!" Joan snapped and again Viv chuckled at the surprised expression on the old man's face.

"You two have been discussing this, haven't you?"

"For a couple of weeks, Grandfather."

Viv opened the bag he had brought and placed sheets of papers before Arfon. "Can I leave them with you to look through? Then if we could meet after the weekend to discuss it further?" he asked.

"You're getting polite all of a sudden aren't you?" Arfon said gruffly.

"Only because Joan's here," Viv grinned. "And I want her there when we talk it through. All right?"

"You really think we can do this?"

"With that new decorator's supplies business up and running and searching for ways to steal our trade we haven't any choice."

"Carpets, eh?"

"And furniture later on," Joan added, "just to let you know we don't mean to sit back and take it easy."

"Be careful, Viv. If we go under now we'll never come up again."

"Don't worry, I won't let you down."

"– a second time!" Arfon couldn't resist adding.

"You and Grandfather get on really well don't you?" Joan said as he walked her to Glebe Lane.

"I'm fond of him. I think he's a remarkable old man. He was almost battered into the ground by the revelations about his bonfire and your thieving uncle Islwyn, but instead of hiding away embarrassed and humiliated, he tackled the business by taking on the only one who could save it, me, the one who caused the downfall in the first place. On top of that he stands for chairman at his club – and gets elected. Different from your father and your uncle, eh? More guts."

"Grandmother tried the same strategy but it hasn't worked."

"Yet!"

"Perhaps my mother and Auntie Sian are the strong ones. At least they're doing something. Auntie Sian selling the house to give money to Grandfather, my mother taking in boarders, or Paying Guests as she insists on calling them."

"And you? Are you willing to take on the challenge of expanding the Wallpaper and Paint and building it into a store where people can furnish their homes under one roof?"

She turned and stared at him, her eyes deep pools glinting slightly in the lamplight. "You can't be serious, Viv."

"Never more so. I can't do it alone, but if you committed yourself to getting this new idea off the ground, well, we can accomplish anything."

"You expect me to work for you? Treat it as a real job?"

"If we undertake this new line, I'll need more than one assistant and the business won't stand an increased wages bill. You could do it, Joan. At least until the business catches up on itself. You'd be good at helping people to choose colours and styles. Will you?"

"It's going to be the Weston Women who are going to pull Grandfather out of his present difficulties, isn't it?"

Risking a slap, Viv kissed her and said, "Yes, with you and me at the helm." Dramatically, he shouted, "Viv Lewis and the Weston Women, for ever!"

Gladys was sitting staring disconsolately at her various lists. One was of hair appointments and dress fittings, another was notes for the caterers. The third, of people she had hoped would be guests had more crossings off than names.

When Victoria entered and told her that a Mr Jenkins wished to see her, she perked up, straightened her hair and dabbed some powder on her nose then sat back expecting to see Old Mr Jenkins with an apology for the ill manners of his grandson. But it was Edward Jenkins who came in limping badly, and offered his hand.

"Mrs Weston, please forgive me for not recognising you yesterday. I was extremely rude and I'm sorry," he said. "When I told Grandfather what had happened he insisted that rather than write, I should call to make my apology."

Flattered and cheered, Gladys rang the bell for

183

Victoria and said, "I understand, Edward. I should be used to it, after all."

"You dropped this," Edward said, handing her the envelope containing the invitations."

"Oh, I hadn't missed them. Er—" she hesitated, then once Victoria had been dispatched to bring coffee, she added, "Perhaps you and your sister would like to come?"

"Thank you. Is it a Christmas Party? Or a birthday?"

Warmed by the man's pleasant manner, she said with a chuckle, "More in the way of a defiance party. I want to show people that we aren't hiding away in shame, but facing the criticism head on."

"Congratulations. Nil desperandum."

"Er—?"

"Roughly translated as 'Don't let the buggers grind you down'," he whispered and Gladys laughed delightedly.

She was enjoying her unexpected visitor, and loudly criticising Islwyn for his part in their situation, when Victoria announced more visitors and Megan and Terrence entered, followed to her dismay, by Islwyn.

Introductions followed and this time Gladys did not miss the obvious dislike between Edward and his cousin, Terrence. Gladys was embarrassed at the presence of Islwyn, specially after the way she had been discussing him with Edward. To cover her unease she was rude to him, ignoring any remark he made, or disagreeing when he added a word and generally

184

making it clear to Edward and Terrence that she had not forgiven him for his treachery.

Islwyn was furious having heard something of what had been said. He sat down near the table on which Gladys's lists were spread and, seeing the list with the name and phone number of the caterers, he memorised it. Later, he rang them to inform them the party was cancelled and that their services would not be required.

The visit from Edward Jenkins cheered Gladys enormously and she began to make plans for her granddaughter Joan to meet him. He was handsome enough and certainly well connected. A bit old perhaps but, she thought with a smile, sufficiently unconventional and outspoken to appeal to her wayward Joan. She wondered if his sister Margaret would suit her grandson? It really was time Jack settled down and produced a child.

In Goldings Street, Jack was helping Victoria to hang some curtains and thinking the same thing.

Chapter Nine

Gwennie Woodlas's gown shop had its regular clientele and although it was usually busy, on occasions Gwennie would decide she needed a break and would close the shop and head by taxi to the Rose Tree Cafe near the lake.

When Gladys and her granddaughters arrived to choose dresses for the party, they had telephoned first to be sure they wouldn't have a wasted journey, but when they tried the door it was locked. Giving a very ladylike snort of irritation, Gladys herded them to an hotel and ordered afternoon tea.

"Really, I don't know why we patronise the woman," Gladys complained as their teas were poured. "We could just as easily go into Cardiff and find what we want in one of the finer stores."

Joan and Megan glanced at each other. They knew why. It was so everyone of any importance – and that meant most of Gwennie's clients – would know they had been shopping and had bought expensive dresses.

When they left the hotel and made their way back to the gown shop, Gwennie was serving one of Gladys's ex-friends. Gladys amused herself by make caustic comments on the unsuitability of the garments the woman selected to try on.

When the customer had gone, Gwennie locked the door and told them she was 'theirs' until they were satisfied. At fifty-eight, Gwennie Woodlas was a very wealthy widow. Her husband had given her the money to start a small shop and once she had flattered her way into the confidence of the wealthy women of the town, she hadn't looked back. She did have a secret that she did not disclose: she was related to the Griffithses.

"Was it a little number in black for you, Gladys dear?" Gwennie asked.

"Good heavens, Gwennie, dear, it's for a party not a wake!"

Gwennie pulled out three dresses, each one more expensive than the last and hurriedly pulled the price label and size off each one.

"Size thirty-six bust that one is. Get into that with ease you will," she said, screwing up the label which clearly stated size thirty-eight.

The session went on, each of the Weston women being flattered and scolded and admired until Gladys had chosen a blue velvet and the girls in their usual way had decided on something more suitable for a summer fête than a winter dance. A *diamanté* hair ornament on Gladys was echoed with feathered hair ornaments on the twins chosen from the bridesmaids selection.

Gwennie gathered up forty pounds in crisp white fivers and handed them the change, sighing with

187

contentment. She had shifted the blue velvet she thought would never go, and convinced Gladys she'd had a bargain. As for the twins, really they were just pig-headed, and easy to persuade to buy the blue and yellow dresses left over from summer by telling them they were model previews for the spring collection.

She sorted through and decided on the ones she might offer to Sian and Sally when they came. It might be worth going to the warehouse again. They sometimes chose to dress in identical clothes and if she found a pair in their favourite blue to match their mother she could give them some false psychic drivel about a united front in adversity and 'seeing' the colour was right. Sally usually fell for that although Sian was more sceptical.

Covering the railful of long dresses in the white wraps, she closed the shop and sat in the small back room to decide where she would eat. Perhaps the Ship Hotel, or that new French style restaurant on the main road. She sighed contentedly. Really, life was remarkably good compared with her expectations as a young woman. But no doubt she had earned it.

Rhiannon emptied the last few sweets from a jar of mixed boiled, and put the empty jar aside. Now the contents had been sold, in two ounce and four ounce portions, it meant another four shillings and twopence profit. The business was improving week by week.

Her decision to fill the small shop with as many varieties as she could fit on the shelves had paid off. Although it meant keeping a very close watch on the stock and more than the usual number of orders each month. Space was precious and without the support of her suppliers she wouldn't have succeeded.

More and more people used Temptations for their weekly treats and the Christmas sales were unbelievably good. She had made a success of the shop after years of the limitations of rationing and she knew Nia was pleased with her. If only Barry were more demonstrative and showed her how proud he was of her, life would have been sweeter than the sweets she sold.

She looked up at a customer and smiled politely. It was that newcomer, Terry Jenkins again. He was looking at the larger boxes of chocolates and she stepped forward to help him.

"For a young lady?" she asked. "Or for a mother or aunt perhaps?"

"A young lady. So tell me, Rhiannon, which of these boxes would you like to be given?"

"You know my name," she said curiously.

"Oh, I haven't been back long but I've sussed out the prettiest ladies in Pendragon Island," he smiled. "You're the sister of Viv Lewis and a close friend of Basil Griffiths's wife Eleri. Right?"

"You have done your homework."

He choose a two-pound box with a picture of kittens on the cover and winked as he gave her the money. "This should soften her up, don't you think?"

As he left, Rhiannon's smile slipped. He was charming, and handsome in a rather obvious way but she sensed in him an undercurrent of something akin to irritation and knew that she wouldn't like to be the one receiving the chocolates. Barry was hardly the most attentive of men, but at least she trusted him and felt safe with him. She didn't think she'd feel the same with Terry Jenkins.

Perhaps that was what Viv felt too. He made no secret of his dislike for Terry and he hated the idea of Megan seeing him. She shrugged impatiently. Viv was an idiot worrying, but he had always felt protective towards those silly Weston Girls.

She adjusted the display of Christmas cards which she had stocked for the first time this year. An addition to the selection of birthday cards, they had moved surprisingly well.

Christmas was fast approaching but before that there was the party which everyone except Gladys Weston referred to as the Weston's Christmas Party. She had decided not to phone Jimmy and tell him she would go with Barry. Jimmy's car would be better than getting her taffeta dress crunched up in Barry's van. And he was sure to expect her to sit in the back amid the tripods!

Gladys crossed off 'Buy Party Dresses' from her list and turned to the next item. With less than a fortnight to go, she was at the stage of checking every arrangement in the hope of avoiding last minute disasters. Picking up the phone she rang to check a few things with the caterers. That was her first shock of the day. The caterers were very sorry but they had obviously made a mistake and they were already fully booked for that day.

Arguing and pleading had no effect. Nor did talking to the manager.

"I'm very sorry, madam. But you did cancel after making the booking and now it's too late. This is a busy time for us, you know."

"Cancelled? But I haven't spoken to you since I first arranged the date and venue." She began to feel angry. "Really, you should listen when people speak to you! I am Mrs Arfon Weston. I have arranged for you to cater for my party on December eighteenth."

"And I'm sorry, Madam, but you cancelled over a week ago!" The phone was replaced and Gladys gasped as if it had hit her.

Someone must have made a mistake. Or deliberately tried to ruin her party. Hurt and angered by that possibility she thumbed through the telephone book desperately trying to find a firm to deal with the buffet. Everywhere was fully booked. There was only Montague Court left to try and she could hardly expect two of her guests to change into caterers. Besides, the food at Montague Court was too expensive and she had firmly booked the hall anyway. In a panic she rang to confirm that arrangement was safe.

Her second shock of the day was when she asked Terrence Jenkins to call and see her. When she put it to him in what she thought was a subtle way that it was time to declare his intentions, he broke down and looked close to tears.

"Mrs Weston, I an strongly attracted to your

granddaughter. I think she's beautiful and charming and—"

"And—?"

"Well, I don't think she cares for me. Not in the same way. We get on well, we laugh at the same things, share opinions on most subjects, but she holds back from loving me. I think she's waiting for your approval. She thinks a lot of you, Mrs Weston, it's much more than a grandmother-granddaughter relationship. She'd never do anything you wouldn't like. Perhaps I'd better get out of her life before I make a fool of myself."

At once Gladys was filled with sympathy and promised to talk to Megan, try to discover what it was that was preventing her from accepting this personable and well connected young man.

Before he left, she asked, "What are your plans for the future, Terrence? You haven't found employment yet?"

"No, I've been so wrapped up in your lovely Megan I can't think straight. I've decided to continue with what I do best though, and look for a position in a jewellers. There are some excellent showrooms in Cardiff."

Gladys smiled approval. A jewellery showroom sounded so much better than a shop. She was smiling contentedly when Victoria came to removed the tea tray but the smile dropped away as she remembered the problem of finding caterers.

Victoria was not averse to eavesdropping so Jack

knew about his grandmother's difficulty with caterers before Gladys had told anyone. At The Railwayman's that evening he mentioned it to Viv, who in turn told his mother. Dora at once decided she would offer to help.

"It can't be difficult," she said to Eleri the morning after Gladys's devastating blow. "You and I could make a hundred pasties easy. They'd be mostly potato mind, with oxo and a bit of onion for flavour. And plates of sandwiches shouldn't be difficult to fill. Cakes will be a problem, mind. We'll have to buy them from a cake shop because of rationing, but we could make a few sponges if Gladys will hand over some of the butter she denies getting from the local farm. I bet them Griffithses of yours would find us something illegal. What d'you say, Eleri, give it a try? Dab hand I am at pastry."

They discussed it for a while and Eleri was pleased at the prospect of earning some extra money before Christmas. Then Dora went home and phoned Gladys, who asked them to call and see her on the following day.

"No tomatoes," Gladys said firmly before they had opened their mouths. "And definitely no beetroot, they are death to party frocks and everyone will be in their best."

They assured her there would be no tomatoes and not a beetroot in sight.

"It won't look – er – shoddy, will it?" she asked, when they had decided what they could supply. "You not having done anything like this before, I mean."

"I don't put anything but the best in front of my family! Eleri will tell you that. We both have the highest standards."

Eleri hurriedly agreed, afraid that Dora's quick temper would lose them the chance of earning some extra money.

So Gladys rather doubtfully put her faith in another of the Lewises. "Who," she complained to Arfon later, "seem determined to force their way into our lives one way and another. Where will it end?"

"If you're thinking of Viv marrying Joan, forget it," Arfon said. "Even Viv knows just how far he can go with me."

"Oh, no, I'm not worried about Joan, I have plans for her." Gladys smiled as she thought of the mannerly and unmarried Edward.

Joan and Viv were in a huddle, measuring out how much of the present shop area they could allot to carpets. Joan was crawling on the floor with a measuring tape in her mouth and a long length of 2″ × 2″ wood in her hand. "This is crazy," she muttered. "How can we imagine what it would look like with a length of wood and a few chalk marks?"

"Don't talk with your mouth full," Viv said. "And keep that bit of wood straight or I can't get a proper line."

They struggled on for a while, then Viv reached down to haul Joan to her feet. She resisted and instead she lay on the floor and he knelt beside her. The shop lights were on but they were hidden from sight by the partitions errected to represent rooms. "Tired?" Viv asked solicitously.

"D'you think Grandfather really will allow this expansion, Viv?"

"I'll keep on at him until he does. I always get what I want in the end."

"You do, do you?" she looked up at him provocatively. "Always?"

He pinned her arms at her side and lowered his head until their lips were less than an inch apart. "Sometimes I bully, sometimes I plead, and then there are times when I just wait," he said. Her eyes looked huge and he wanted to let go and submit to the temptation they offered, but he didn't. "Come on, love, let's get you home before your mam and dad send out a search party."

"They don't worry about us all that much," Joan said as she shrugged on her coat. "Too busy looking after the lodgers."

"Then they should. Lovely you are, Joan Weston. Lovely, desirable and terribly, terribly tempting and they shouldn't let you out of their sight."

"I'm safe enough with you," she said. "They should look after Megan, though."

"She's with the handsome and well-connected Terry I suppose?"

"Yes."

"And they think he'd be some catch, him being a Jenkins?"

"Background but no money! I can't bear the man."

"I always knew you were the clever one," Viv said. "Smarmy sod is what he is."

"Megan thinks he's wonderful but – I know this sounds stupid but I think she's a little afraid of him."

"Want me to have a word?"

She shook her head before fixing a scarf around her hair. "I'll try and get Megan to talk to me. That's part of the worry. We've always talked to each other, there's never been any secrets, but since Terry's been on the scene she clams up."

Later that evening, Megan was leaving the house in Glebe Lane with Terry. The house was empty apart from Joan, and she was dressing ready to meet Viv at her grandparents to discuss further the plans for the extended showroom. Megan and Terry intended going to the pictures but at the end of the road he pulled her to face him. "Megan love, d'you really want to go to the pictures?"

"Well, Dean Martin and Jerry Lewis are on at The Plaza. And the second film is Sidney Taffler in *The Saint's Return*. It's a good programme."

"I think we need to talk."

Excitement struck in the depths of her. She knew he meant finding somewhere private and indulging in some petting. She wanted to say yes, but she held back. She knew she wanted it too much. Would she stop him when he led her too far? Each time it was harder to resist.

"Come on, Megan my darling. I don't want to spend

the evening trying to steal the occasional kiss when the film is exciting enough to keep people's eyes on the screen."

He took her hand and without allowing further argument, led her back to her parents' house.

Megan was remembering Gladys's flustered attempt to tell her there was a time to be strong and a time to allow the defences to ease. "Never submit to what is wrong, my dear," the old lady had said, trying desperately to warn her granddaughter not to send Terrence away by her coldness yet to hang on to her virginity until after the wedding.

With desire making Terry's presence a blissful danger, Megan's barriers slipped in a way her grandmother would not have approved. She loosened her grip on his hand and leaned against him, her head against his shoulder, so his arms came around her and held her tightly. At the gate she hesitated, aware that from this point, there might not be any turning back. Her father was out with friends and her mother was visiting her Auntie Sian, in Trellis Street. They would be alone and without fear of interruption for a couple of hours. Two hours that might change her life.

"Come on, love," Terry pleaded. "We have the place to ourselves. Why waste an opportunity like this?" They stood in the garden and watched as Joan left the house, and then they let themselves inside.

Terry's hand stopped her as she reached for the light switch. "No, darling, wait, in case Joan has forgotten something."

"Terry, you're so clever, you must have done this sort of thing before."

"Only in my dreams, darling."

Standing in the darkened room, silent, listening for the returning footsteps was making the very air sizzle. She was bewitched by the closeness of Terry, the way his body moved and touched hers. Slowly his hands began to caress her and her emotions went haywire and she was filled with an urgent and desperate struggle to achieve something her body demanded.

The romantic dream was shattered the moment she relaxed against him and he had coaxed her to the floor. He began to hold her firmly and for a moment she panicked. Desire left her in brief panic, only to return with greater intensity. Instead of the gentle loving of which she had so often dreamed, her body was demanding and selfish. Terry's hands were rough and impatient and as she struggled to ease her own aching desire she forgot all warnings and struggled to achieve release.

As they lay relaxed and confused by the urgency and the suddenness of its ending, fear returned. What had she done? Frightened now, she fought against him trying to free herself from his powerful arms. His voice whispered soothingly, telling her it was what they both wanted, and that she was a woman now, a wonderful fulfilled woman. All she could think of was that the last few minutes had probably ruined her life. She no longer found Terry charming, his face close to hers had been distorted and ugly, and she hated him almost as much as she hated herself.

Forcing back tears she pushed him away and climbed the stairs to the bathroom. Locking herself in, she began to wash her body.

In the darkened living room, Terry sat for a while utterly ashamed and angry with himself. All the weeks of waiting for his patience and control to snap like that. He was nothing more than an animal. Tears seeped through his lashes and he made no effort to brush them away.

After half an hour he went up and knocked on the bathroom door, but a whispered, "Go away," was all the response he had. Promising to see her in the morning, he crept out of the house feeling like a criminal.

In the Westons' large house overlooking the docks, Viv and Joan were making plans for the changes to the Wallpaper and Paint Store.

"The samples are already available and I've sent for them," Viv told Old Man Arfon. "Six plain colours and two patterned, and there'll be more later. We thought we'd open the new department some time in January 1954, ready for the spring cleaning craze a couple of months later. But we can start accepting orders straight away."

"Before the new store gets the same idea. It's important to be the first if we want the new business to continue, people are surprisingly loyal," Joan said.

Old Man Arfon was cautious. "Best we wait, get Christmas and the sales over first. Plenty of time to decide on this move in the spring. Around Easter perhaps, we'll have a better idea of how things are going by then. The debts will be down and the banks will look more kindly on the project."

"Damn the banks! I've negotiated a good deal here! We'll be getting the money before we have to pay for the goods. Taking orders we'll be, not filling the place with stock we have to pay for. There'll be no money standing idle with these carpets. Not like the paint and wallpaper. Can't you see?" Viv's temper made further persuasion impossible.

"You've been thinking this out for weeks," Old Man Arfon said pompously. "Please allow me an extra hour or two at least."

"We ought to do this, Grandfather," Joan said. "And now, not next Easter. By then others will have taken the best of the business and we'll be left behind."

"What d'you know about business?" her grandfather said grumpily.

Viv stretched forward to retort but was held back by Joan.

"I'll think about it and tell you my decision next week," Arfon said and stood to indicate the interview was over.

"Tomorrow. I want to know tomorrow," Viv said firmly. "We can't let this chance go."

"All right, tomorrow, you ill-mannered tyrant!" Arfon said with a tight smile. "I'll look over your ideas and tell you tomorrow. Now go away before I thump some manners into that red head of yours!"

With their discussions complete, Viv walked Joan

home, arm in arm, strolling casually, like the good friends they were. The house was empty and Viv waited with her, until first Sally, then Ryan returned. They talked for a while about the expansion to the family business.

Although Ryan contributed nothing to the conversation, he listened carefully to all that was said. Bitterness filled his heart. This young upstart running the business that had been his. Carpets indeed. What a stupid idea for a paint and wallpaper shop. Arfon should never have re-employed him. He hoped every day that the boy would fail. Yet here he was, sitting in his living room and talking about his plans for expanding the business, comfortable and relaxed as if he were a family friend, and walking his daughter home like her equal. And he and Sally had to take in lodgers. It wasn't right.

Megan came in later, having waited until Terry had gone then walked around the town to ease her distress. She had held back tears of self-pity by the expedient of remembering how impossible it was to hide their effect.

She told her sister she was tired and escaped to bed. When Joan came up an hour later she pretended to be asleep but her thoughts were racing. She might have a baby. She might be forced to marry Terry and she wasn't sure she loved him. He wasn't open about his life before he'd returned to Pendragon Island. There was a secrecy about him that she didn't like. If he didn't trust her with his past she didn't think they could have a future.

She was sure about one thing, she didn't want to marry him – or anyone else at the moment. By morning she hadn't slept but her plans were made. She would not be able to prevent a baby, but she could avoid marrying Terry Jenkins.

Over breakfast, she told her parents that she and Terry wouldn't be seeing each other any more.

"Oh, Megan, I'm sorry," her mother said. "What went wrong?"

"We just don't want to go on with something that won't work."

"I'm glad. I didn't like him," Joan said, "and Viv calls him a smarmy sod – sorry Mam," Joan grinned. Sally began to berate her for copying someone like Viv Lewis, her father joined in, and Megan was glad her sister had taken the focus away from her.

"What happened?" Joan asked her sister when they were alone but Megan shook her head.

"Nothing. We just decided we wouldn't see each other any more."

"Poor Grandmother. I think she was hoping for an engagement to announce at this party of hers."

"Well it won't be mine! I don't think I'll ever marry. But we needn't tell her just yet. I don't want an inquest on what happened."

Joan looked at her sister's sorrowful expression and asked again, "Tell me, Megan. What happened? I know something upset you, that was why I tried to take the heat off you at breakfast."

But Megan refused to discuss it, she was too distressed. She had committed the ultimate shame.

202

Giving in to a man before they were wed was something she had never imagined herself doing. She could be expecting a baby. How could she tell her sister that?

Viv was walking to work on Friday morning a week before Gladys's party. He was in a bad mood. Arfon had still not given him permission to go ahead with the carpets. He and Joan had spent hours mapping out their displays but Arfon was still insisting they waited until Easter. On impulse, Viv changed his route and walked past the new wallpaper shop down a side road near the Church. He sometimes looked in their windows to see if there were any new ideas which he could emulate, although, he thought smugly, they usually copied him.

He glanced in as he strolled passed but was shocked into stopping and staring. Apart from the back wall of the window, there were no rolls of wallpaper or tins of paint on display. It was filled with carpet samples.

Squares of several colours formed a pattern and in the centre was a sign stating that it was the introduction of the newest do-it-your-self carpets.

"Damnation!" he said aloud. "How could they have got on to it so quick? And why has Old Man Arfon dragged his heels and allowed it to happen?"

He ran to the shop and telephoned Arfon and told him to go and look at the new wallpaper shop. "You and your waiting for the right time," he moaned. "Lost your nerve you have. And now they've made us second best."

"Never, boy. First we are. I'll have a look at their prices. If we're careful and keep our prices down we can beat them yet."

"But we haven't even got the window display yet and it's Christmas in two weeks! Head start they'll have and I know I had the idea first. They copy us with window displays and even copied my idea about setting out areas as rooms right down to the bedside lamps! There's no way he'd have thought about it first. No way."

"She, not he. It's a Miss Franklin who runs the shop and I think she's a friend of Sally and Ryan's."

"Now there's a thought! I bet your precious Ryan had something to do with this!" Furiously, Viv rang the carpet suppliers and demanded that the samples were delivered that day.

To appease what was likely to be a good outlet, the samples arrived and they were more than Viv had anticipated. Rolls in the various widths and every colour in the two designs. Joan was there when they arrived and Viv said to her, "We'll spend the weekend getting the display in place and show that tinpot firm round the corner how it should be done."

"Are you asking or telling me?" Joan glared at him dangerously.

"Sorry, but I'm so flaming mad. We tried to persuade Old Man Arfon to do something before Christmas, didn't we? And he was too cautious." He calmed down and said quietly, "Will you help me, Joan? I can't do it on my own and besides, I need your flair. This one has got to be good. We don't have to stock it, just take orders and post them on to the manufacturers. But we do have to make it look tempting."

"I wanted to spend the weekend with Megan. I think she's upset, Viv."

"That smarmy sod Terry has upset her, hasn't he? I'll sort him if he has, mind."

"They aren't seeing each other any more."

"Hoo-bloody-ray! Best news I've had all week. Saw sense, did she?"

"I don't know what happened but I do know she was upset and what's worse, she won't talk about it."

"Ask her to come and help us. She might open out if she's away from home."

"That's an idea. But you won't press her, will you? And don't call Terry a smarmy sod. It might have been he who decided to end it and she could still be wanting them to get back together."

"You're right. This is a time for saying as little as possible. But if he's harmed her—"

"All right, we know you and your gang would love to sort him out," she smiled.

"Me and the Griffithses strike fear into the hearts of the ungodly!" He looked at the samples again and added, "And who ever told Miss Franklin about the carpets had better look out too!"

Chapter Ten

With a combination of pleading and blackmail, Dora and Eleri had managed to find sufficient food for the buffet at Gladys's party but there was a serious shortage of meat.

"Pasties made with onions and oddments of crusty old cheese scrounged from the grocers, and one tin of corned beef having to make thirty, the guests aren't going to be sick from a sudden increase in meat, are they?" Dora sighed as the ingredients were gathered on her kitchen table.

"We haven't tried the Griffithses, Mam. I mean apart from Basil's rabbits and the offer of a pheasant."

"Basil's promise of a pheasant and a couple of rabbits is wonderful but they won't do for a buffet. Who's ever heard of rabbit sandwiches? No, what we need is something like ham and where are we going to get that?"

"I'll ask Basil," Eleri spoke with utter confidence. If something could be found, her husband was the one to find it.

"God 'elp, girl, you can't expect even Basil to go out and shoot a pig!"

Eleri smiled mysteriously and said," You've never seen the Griffithses' back shed, have you?"

"Where Frank and Ernie sleep you mean? Two men sleeping there, it's bound to be a pig sty, but how does that help us?"

"Behind that shed there's another one, the back shed. Come up with me this afternoon and we'll try a bit more blackmail."

"A couple of chickens? That would be a help, goes down well a bit of chicken."

"Wait and see," Eleri chuckled.

The Griffithses lived almost independently of the village, brought back to the ways of the previous century by rationing and the sheer joy of it. They were practically self-sufficient and Hywel felt the occasional twinge of dismay at the thought of food rationing ending and there being no further need for his prowess as a provider.

The building behind the shed which had been converted into a bedroom for Frank and Ernie was small, and it was used for the purpose for which Hywel's grandfather had built it, curing bacon and ham by smoking.

Outside the family, not many knew of its existence as few ventured outside into the untidy yard apart from a visit to the lavatory. Oddments gathered over the years including an assortment of bicycles in various stages of decrepitude, the large bath, and the mangle used on washing day, had become a jungle through which only Hywel and Basil knew the safe way.

The brick-built pigsty was empty – Hywel had been reported for keeping a pig illegally and the animal had been confiscated. But the smoke house was in use. Slow-burning sawdust was issuing smoke through the small hole in its roof and beside it, a large barrel released tempting smells through its bung. Suspended inside both shed and barrel were joints of ham and bacon, being smoke-cured for bartering and for the family's winter breakfasts.

When Eleri and Dora arrived with baby Ronnie, Eleri explained at once what they were looking for. "Some ham, for a few sandwiches so we can charge Gladys Weston top price for our services," she said.

"It'll be a bit fatty," warned Janet. "The best has gone and the new won't be ready until after Christmas."

"Ham? Ready after Christmas? What are you talking about?" Dora asked. And Hywel showed her, under the promise of secrecy, the home curing in progress.

"I smoke fish too. And if you haven't tasted wild duck smoked over oak chippings, well, you have a treat in store," Hywel told Dora, licking his lips at the thought.

"I want this buffet to be a real success, see. If this one goes well we might be asked to do a few more. Only as favours, mind, nothing official, but later on, well, you never know."

"I might not be able to help for long, Mam. Basil and I want another baby before Ronnie's two, mind."

"No matter, love. I'll be glad of your help for as

long as you can give it, then I'll find someone else, don't be worried."

"So either way, this first one's got to be good, make your name," Janet said. "Right then. Tell me what you've got already and we'll see what we can do."

An hour later Eleri and a bemused Dora left, having been promised smoked ham, some streaky bacon for crispy bacon rolls, sausages, and some freshly baked bread rolls.

"We haven't started yet and already we've got a useful contact!" Dora said excitedly. "This first one will be expensive, aimed to impress. We won't expect to make much, but once rationing ends we should be able to make a tidy little profit on do's like this."

Eleri agreed. "I think we should be bold, appear confident, look ahead and make plans for the next, Mam."

"You and me working together, Eleri. Wonderful!"

"Only for a while, Mam."

"Oh, I love you calling me Mam." The excitement in Dora's eyes could have been mistaken for anger, but in fact she was happier than she had been for a very long time. She had something to think about instead of sitting waiting for Lewis.

On Saturday evening, Rhiannon stepped out at the dark street and felt the chill wind before locking the shop door and hurrying home three doors away. It was too cold to stand and stare out over the distant sea as she once had. That was before she had started

209

work at Temptations, when she had run the home while her mother went out to work.

Although the wind was whipping along the street like a knife, she saw that old Maggie Wilpin was sitting in her doorway, wrapped in a blanket and waiting. But for what, no one really knew.

Her mother was out, there was a note for her to find herself something to eat. Barry had an appointment to take photographs at some function, Viv was at a dance with his friends, she had the house to herself. But instead of staying in and enjoying the rare peace and solitude, she ate a sandwich and went back to the shop. There were several jobs needed doing. At this time of year, Mondays weren't quiet enough to allow time for other than routine cleaning.

Letting herself into the shop which, with its window blind down and the door locked, looked small and friendly, she leaned through the door leading to the stairs and listened, wondering if Barry was up there getting what he needed for his evening's work. All was quiet.

She began cleaning the top shelves and bringing down the spare boxes of sweets stacked there. Changing the displays took longer than she expected and it was almost half-past eight when she turned off the light to leave. She stood for a moment and felt the comforting thought of it being her own domain. She was only twenty but responsible for running the shop, making a profit and keeping the books in order. She smiled in the darkness. When she and Barry eventually married there wouldn't be need to change a thing. She was building it up for their future.

Thoughts of being married to Barry held her a moment longer as she day-dreamed about them sharing their lives completely. A car pulled up outside and she unlocked the door before realising that footsteps were heading towards her. She saw Barry's van then, and she pulled the door wider and stepped forward to greet him. He hardly acknowledged her presence as he pushed past to go up to the flat. Hurt rapidly changed to anger. Now was a good opportunity to remind him they were supposed to be engaged. He was sure to have forgotten she was going with Jimmy.

"Barry. I'm glad I caught you. What time will you call for me on Friday?" she said sweetly.

"Friday?" he asked. "What's happening on Friday?"

"The Weston's party of course. Really Barry, you're getting absent-minded!"

"But I can't, at least I can, but—"

"Don't say you've forgotten you asked me? You have! You've arranged an appointment haven't you?"

"No, but I've promised to take Caroline. You can come as well," he added as she began to take a deep breath to complain. "I thought we could all go."

"You didn't think anything of the sort, Barry!"

She hadn't altered her arrangement to go with Jimmy, but she didn't intend to let him off the hook by telling him. "So, you're letting me down again, Barry Martin. What am I supposed to do, catch a bus there and walk home?" she shouted. "You didn't think

211

of me at all! You'd forgotten all about me. You didn't even *think* of taking me! I cancelled my arrangement to go with Jimmy and you've forgotten me!" The lie, she felt, was a justifiable addition to her anger.

"Caroline needs a break, Rhiannon. She rarely goes out and it took a lot of persuading for her to agree. Joseph goes to bed without trouble and her mother will look after him. She needs a bit of fun in her life."

"Pity for her! And what about me then?"

"You'll be with us, I just thought she'd enjoy a night out. Her brothers will be there and——"

Pushing him aside, Rhiannon shouted more insults mainly on the subject of his peculiar attitude to a woman whom he was supposed to be divorcing, and ran back to the house.

Across the road, in her doorway, Maggie Wilpin pulled the coat tighter about her shoulders and watched with interest. From the open door behind her, music on the radio announced the end of The Archer's Omnibus.

On Sunday Rhiannon telephoned Jimmy to check that he was still taking her to the party. Uneasy with the thought that she was leading him on unfairly, she showed irritation when Barry called as she was helping to set out their midday meal.

"I wondered if you'd like to come with me to the Griffithses' later, to see Caroline and young Joseph. About seven? He's usually allowed to stay up later on Sundays when everyone calls."

"No, I'm too busy," she said ungraciously. "Now go away, I'm listening to Billy Cotton's Band Show."

"If he's more important than talking to me," Barry retorted.

"He is!"

"Well, I'll be leaving about seven if you change your mind. Basil and Eleri will be there, they always go over on a Sunday evening and Basil leaves there to go straight to work."

She showed him out and immediately wished she had been less rude. "I'll go down at seven and start the evening off well by apologising to him," she told Viv, Lewis, and Dora – who had been listening in the kitchen.

"Best for you, you bad-tempered idiot," Viv said. "You're always glad to see Eleri and baby Ronnie aren't you? And Joseph is a nice little chap."

"If he had asked me to go and see Eleri, I wouldn't have been so angry."

"You like Caroline, don't you?"

"I did, until Barry began to make it clear he prefers her company to mine!"

"Rubbish," Viv snorted.

But Rhiannon wasn't so sure.

She went to a lot of trouble over her appearance and went down to the sweet shop at seven, but the place was in darkness, no light shone from the flat above. She even unlocked the shop door and called up the stairs to the flat, but Barry had gone. She debated whether to walk over to the Griffithses' lonely house or go back home to sulk. Remembering the attack on her a few weeks before she decided that sulking might be childish but would certainly be safer and more comfortable than a walk across the fields on a December night with the cold already nipping at her feet.

At the Westons' house, Viv had arranged to meet Jack. Victoria wasn't there to answer the door, which was opened by Jack himself. Putting on a squeaky voice Jack asked for the callers name and told him, "Please to wait in the 'all while I finds the master." Shoving him good-naturedly out of the way, Viv went in.

Their task that evening was to climb into the loft and seek out the Christmas decorations. Jack was the tallest by several inches so he climbed onto Viv's shoulders and heaved himself into the roof space. Handing down boxes to Viv, they found all they needed and began to plan how they would use them to make the hall Gladys had rented for the party look its festive best. Most were old having been bought pre-war and repaired several times.

"Don't worry, there'll be plenty of bunting," Gladys told them. "Victoria is making some at this moment."

"Where is she?" Jack demanded.

"In the attic dear, using my old sewing machine."

When Gladys had gone to make some tea, they went up the short flight of stairs which led to a room over the front of the house and found Victoria cutting triangles from old clothes and sewing them on to tape to make bunting.

"This is breaking Grandmother's heart, all this economy," Jack said after greeting Victoria. "Before all this trouble she would simply have arranged for someone to do it all and sat back waiting for the day to arrive."

"That's what she's doing now," chuckled Victoria. "I'm making the bunting, Viv's mother is doing the food, and you are putting up the tables and decorations in the hall. All your grandmother did was write the invitations."

"She's right, Jack," Viv said. "So get on with it, sort out them trimmings and take a deep breath for blowing up all them balloons."

"We haven't got to do that, have we?"

"We? Not me, mate. Your name is on every one."

Jack began handing Victoria the flags for her to fix on the tape. "I'd forgotten this old sewing machine."

"They're very handy. One would save Mam a lot of time, the boys are always through the seat of their pants, and making cot sheets from old ones takes a long time."

"I'll ask Basil if he can get one."

"No, Jack. We haven't paid for the other furniture yet. We can't afford one."

"A gift," he pleaded.

"No," she said firmly. "Thank you for your kind thought, but no."

"I want to buy her things, Viv," Jack said when they were walking home a few hours later, having seen Victoria safely back to Goldings Street. "She has so little and it costs hardly anything to get her the things she needs. Everyone is in a spate of chucking out old stuff and buying new these days. After so many years being unable to buy anything new, most want a change. You ask Basil, there are dozens of bargains to be had. I reckon I could furnish a house for fifty pounds. Good quality items too."

"Thinking of setting up home then, are you? Who's the lucky woman?"

"Don't be soft, man. I was thinking of people like Mrs Jones."

"There's one way you could persuade her to accept what you offer her," Viv said. "Marry the girl."

"Don't be soft," Jack repeated.

"Oh, I see. Not grand enough I suppose."

"It isn't that. I'm far too old for her! She's only sixteen."

"Not too grand, but too old? Now there's a thing. I wonder what she'd think of that." He looked thoughtful for a moment then said, "My father and Nia Martin wanted to marry each other years ago but thought the age difference was too great a hurdle. Look where that bit of stupidity has led us."

It was just after eight o'clock and Viv was pleased with the way he had casually left at just the right time to meet Joan. She had made the excuse of visiting a friend and was waiting at the bus stop near the park. The night was cold and frost glistened on the fence posts and made the occasional stretch of pavements slippery. Pleased with the excuse to hold Joan close, Viv suggested they went to the beach.

"In December? In the dark?" she laughed.

"Only fools would do such a thing so we're unlikely to be seen," he said. "Most people are indoors watching the Sunday night play on the television."

If there was a moon, dark clouds had hidden it from view and the darkness was only broken by the faint light on the edge of the waves. If anything it was colder at the sea's edge and they ran across the deep sands to warm themselves. Finding a sheltered spot where they could sit for a while, Viv was allowed to put his arms around Joan.

"Only to keep ourselves warm," she warned in her acerbic manner. "No ideas, mind."

"You can't stop me having ideas, Joan love. Not even the Westons can do that." He pressed her against him and was content to breath in her special scent and feel her heart beating close to his own.

They were later than usual and he watched as she went indoors to tiptoe up the stairs and hope her parents didn't hear.

He didn't hurry home and it was just after eleven as he turned into Sophie Street and saw Barry.

"Hi, Barry. Our Rhiannon was looking for you earlier. Dressed up sharp as sharp she was, mind, so I hope you didn't forget a date."

"Oh God. She didn't change her mind and call for me, did she?"

"About seven it would have been."

"Look, Viv, do me a favour will you? Tell her you saw me but at nine o'clock, not past eleven?"

"What have you been up to then?"

217

"Nothing, but if she knows I stayed this late with Caroline she'll think I have been. I'll tell her I came home at nine, sounds a lot better than eleven."

Viv shrugged amiably. "If you like. It's no skin off my nose."

They stood and talked for a while outside Temptations then calling goodnight they each went home. Viv to number seven and Barry to the flat above his mother's shop.

Since breaking up with Terrence, Megan found time hanging heavily. The time she had been spending with him seemed to leave great gaps in her day that defied all efforts to fill.

On that Sunday evening before her grandmother's party she was with the Griffithses. Using a casual request from her grandmother as an excuse, she had called to ask what time Eleri and Dora wanted to have the key to begin their display of food the following Friday.

As usual, the place seemed to be having a party of its own, with Basil, Eleri and the baby, Caroline and Barry and baby Joseph. With The Railwayman's closed, it being Sunday, Hywel, Frank and Ernie were there as well. The place was crowded and filled with lively chatter. The cheerful company had the effect of reminding her how alone she was and filled with that melancholy thought, there was tension for what she was about to do.

She was close to tears and holding them back made her appear even more than usually stand-offish, refusing even to laugh at the nonsense coming from Frank and Ernie and Hywel. Baby Ronnie she kept well way from, frowning disapprovingly at his dribbling smile. There were whispered remarks about her haughty manner but when she said she was leaving, Frank stood and offered to walk her home. She refused briskly and rudely, and left about nine-thirty to walk alone down the dark, silent lanes.

Stopping while still some distance from the houses on the edge of the town, and making sure no one had seen her, she scratched her long nails across her chest and hit the top of her arms with a heavy stick. She tugged at her clothes until they were torn, and, removing her knickers, hid them under a bush before scratching herself some more. It hurt. She hadn't thought about how much it would hurt and the tears in her eyes were real. She ran home, pulling her hair out of its tidy style, and as she reached the back door, screamed for help. It was Jack who answered the door, and Joan who took her in her arms, leading her into her mother's care. Her sobs were genuine as she gasped out the story of an attack and screamed hysterically for them not to call the police. Between getting her into a bath and trying to get details of what had happened, she was asked why she had been walking home alone.

"Viv—" she began, before another spate of sobbing stiffled her words. She had been about to say 'Viv is usually there', but the single word remained in the air, a reproach, an accusation.

219

Joan's eyes widened in shock and she stared in disbelief at her cousin Jack. "No," she whispered. "Not Viv, there's some mistake!" She didn't tell them Viv had been with her. Better to wait until Megan cleared it up tomorrow.

Sally gestured silently, stopping further questions. Now was not the time. "We have to reassure her and make her comfortable. If she refuses to talk to the police there's nothing more we can do tonight." She turned to her other daughter and asked, "Go with her, Joan, love. Try to make her talk."

Sitting outside the bathroom until Megan was dressed in a clean crisp nightdress, Joan whispered soothingly, assuring her it would be all right. It wasn't until much later than Megan told her she had been attacked sexually. A lie, but at least if she were to have a baby no one would know it was Terry's. No one would try and persuade her to marry him.

Jack didn't go into school the following day. He spent the morning making enquiries, first about the whereabouts of Terry, who told him he hadn't seen Megan since a quarrel a few days ago. At lunchtime he went to find Viv.

The shop was about to close for lunch and Viv was thankfully alone when Jack walked in. Without a word, he punched him so powerfully Viv fell to the floor and slithered several yards, where he lay wondering what had happened. A pencil, fallen from his pocket rolled across the floor, the rattling sound loud in the silent aftermath of violence.

He shook his head and stared in surprise at the blood on his hands and clothes. When he spoke his voice sounded as if it came from a long way off. "Jack?" he frowned.

"That's for Megan."

"Megan? What the hell you on about, you mad sod?"

"Not satisfied with carrying on with Joan you have to have Megan as well. Oh yes," he said as Viv was about to deny it. "I know all about your little meetings at the shop and at the bus stop near the park. My father has seen you there and so have I!"

"Never had you down for a Peeping Tom, Jack," Viv muttered, still bemused by the blow.

Slowly, absentmindedly, still unclear of what had happened, Viv scrambled up and when Jack ran at him again, he bent down to retrieve the pencil. He rose after picking up the pencil, so the velocity of the attempted blow sent Jack completely off balance. He found himself flying over the smaller man's shoulder.

"Damn it all, Viv, you aren't bad for a little 'un," he said grudgingly as he picked himself up.

"What's this all about, Jack?" Viv asked, trying to staunch the blood from his nose.

"What time did you get home last night?"

Viv hesitated, remembering Barry's request for an alibi. "Nine o'clock or thereabouts. Why?"

"Megan was attacked last night on her way home from the Griffithses'."

"What?"

To Jack, his friend's dismay and anger appeared

genuine. After showing his concern by asking how she was, Viv demanded, "Where was Terry? What was he doing letting her walk home alone in the dark? Our Rhiannon was attacked along that path remember! Where was he?"

"He's gone from the scene. More to the point, where were you? The poor kid arrived in one hell of a state and the only name she uttered was yours."

"I didn't see her last night. Dammit, I was with you!"

"Not all evening!.."

"Well, I walked about a bit, 'til nine. That's when I got home."

"Maggie Wilpin says different. She told me you and Barry walked up together and were talking outside the shop at eleven o'clock."

"Well, that's right, but I promised Barry I'd say nine so he won't get a row from Rhiannon."

"Oh yeh?"

"It's true, Jack!"

Later that day, while Viv was trying to avoid being seen, hiding his bruised face behind ledgers and staying in the office above the shop floor, Jack returned. He ran up the stairs and Viv prepared himself for another blow.

"Before you start. I didn't harm her," he almost shouted. To his relief Jack held out a hand.

"Sorry, Viv, I was too angry to wait for a reason. I had to swipe someone. Sorry. Megan has assured us she didn't recognise the man who attacked her."

222

"Could it have been that Terry Jenkins?"

"Megan denies it. She insists she didn't know the man and wants to forget it. She doesn't want to go to the police and she refuses to see a doctor."

"D'you think I can see her?"

"Looking like that you'd be a revival of her worse nightmares. Wait till your chops are less lumpy and the colour of your eye has toned down a bit, eh?"

"You did this!" Viv said angrily. "Used me for a punchball you did, to ease your anger. Damn it all, Jack. I should be going to the police and sueing you!"

"I've said I'm sorry haven't I? What more d'you want?"

"This!" Viv curled a punch that landed on Jack's mouth and they both danced around in pain.

Honour satisfied, they went to The Railwaymen's for a pint and as many explanations for the bruises as they could invent.

Megan made Joan promise to tell no one about her fears of a pregnancy and although her sister pleaded with her, Megan said she would not see a doctor.

"I'll just wait a while and see what happens. If there's nothing wrong then I'd regret mentioning it to anyone. Besides, the doctor might been honour-bound to tell Mummy if I ask for a pregnancy test."

"All right, but if you think there's even the slightest chance that you're expecting a baby you'll tell me and we'll go together. All right? Promise?"

Megan hugged Joan but she avoided making the

promise. She would see this through herself. She would be strong, and cope with all the decisions and make sure she wasn't forced into taking an action she would later regret.

Chapter Eleven

The anniversary of the accident that killed Lewis-Boy Lewis and Joseph Martin was so near Christmas it made a mockery of mourning. Lewis went to the cemetery with Nia and again with Dora, Viv and Rhiannon keeping a secret from both women of his other visit. While crowds of people filled the florists ordering door wreaths as part of the preparations for Christmas, Lewis went twice to buy flowers for his sons' graves.

He and Dora's son, Lewis-boy, had been killed in an accident in which Nia Martin's son, Joseph, had also died. During the horror and grief of the deaths, Lewis had told his wife he was the father of both boys: Nia Martin had borne him a son at the same time as he and Dora had been celebrating the birth of Lewis-boy.

The deaths of the two young men had changed everything. From that time he had no longer been able to keep the parallel elements of his life apart. He couldn't end the long-standing affair with Nia and Dora was unable to accept his double life. Even now, standing beside their son's grave, Dora's blue eyes glared as if with anger, hiding the sadness of the death that had coincided with the end of her marriage.

For Nia, that Christmas-time – which brought back painful memories of the tragedy – there was the addition of a birthday to consider. On the day of Gladys Weston's party, she would be fifty. A time when she should be settled, instead of hovering on the edge of change.

Thankfully, her name had not been included on what she considered to be a very peculiar guest list. It included people with whom Gladys Weston would normally never share a room. Perhaps that dreadful business with her husband accused of arson and her son-in-law of fraud had turned her mind. Why else would she invite the Griffiths boys? She was unlikely to allow them to dance with her precious granddaughters!

The reason she was pleased not to have been included was that Lewis Lewis wasn't going either and, as his wife was responsible for the evening's food, she dared to hope they would be free to spend the evening together. Of all the people she loved, Lewis Lewis was the one whom she would choose to share it. She was fifty. She said it aloud and it had a doleful ring.

It was a sobering reminder of how far she had travelled along the allotted route to old age. It was no longer a day to be celebrated, but simply another milestone and best forgotten. Widowed from Carl

Martin, she had been Lewis Lewis's lover for well over twenty years and had given him a child, who had died exactly a year ago. Then moving to London and marrying poor dear Laurence Davies when Dora discovered their secret. Laurence was a hasty marriage, certainly repented at leisure. He had left her after a few months, unable to compete with the physically absent yet ever-present Lewis.

With just over a week to go before Christmas Day, her birthday was the end of a year and the end of the time in which she could consider herself young enough to forget about old age. At fifty she had to decide where she was going and who – if anyone – would travel with her.

She telephoned Lewis's office and left a message that 'Temptations' needed him to call. Pointless really to indulge in the transparent subterfuge; everyone in the office knew about them and Temptations was in the area covered by Jimmy Herbert. The office girl was polite as she took the message but Nia thought sadly that once the receiver was replaced stifled giggles would pass from desk to desk. At fifty, the young girls would think her too old for more than a chaste kiss, she thought with increasing gloom.

That evening, after the Lewis family had eaten, Lewis made his excuses and went out. Dora didn't even look up and certainly didn't ask what time to expect him. She was poring over lists and prices, working out what to charge Mrs Weston for the food they were supplying. Lewis would have been a help with the estimations but this was something she needed to do for herself.

Thankful to have escaped without a row, Lewis drove to the flat for which he still paid rent, and joined Nia.

"It's my birthday on Friday," she told him.

"I know, you can't catch me like that, my love. Have I ever forgotten?"

"I'm fifty."

"I know that too. That's why I've arranged a special celebration."

"What is there to celebrate? Fifty is old," she said sadly.

"We're none of us children," he laughed. "I'll be forty-four next year. What does it matter? If we had two birthdays a year you'd be a hundred and I'd be eighty-eight! And you'd still be beautiful."

"Idiot." She smiled.

"Good of the Westons to have their party on the same day, isn't it? With Dora doing the food we'll be free."

"Never free, darling."

"Oh dear, we are melancholy tonight. Wait till I tell you what I've arranged."

"Tell me."

"I'm taking you up to London. I've booked an hotel and the theatre, and we won't come back until Sunday evening."

"We can't! What will you tell Dora and the others?"

"I did think of making up some story about a

228

conference. A number of firms are arranging these now, sharing ideas and encouraging their salesmen, it's the latest thing. If we aren't careful we'll be having courses on Pressure Selling like they have in America."

"But you aren't telling them there's a conference?"

"No. I'm telling Dora that you and I will be going to London. It's up to her what she tells Rhiannon and Viv."

"That isn't very wise, Lewis. We don't want a recurrence of her illness."

"I don't think that will happen, not when I tell you the rest."

"You want to do what?" Dora shouted when Lewis told her the rest.

"I want to make this house completely over to you, and go and live with Nia. Just now no one is happy; if I do this at least two of us will be." He looked at her to see the effect of his words but she seemed hardly to have heard him. Her eyes were staring into a future he was unable to see. "Naturally I'll pay you an agreed sum each week."

"All right." Dora stared up at him, her bright blue eyes challenging. "If you agree to one more thing."

"And that is—?" Lewis asked, expecting the impossible.

"Instead of a weekly sum, give me enough money to build a professional kitchen here."

"Dora, you can't just start catering, you have to

know what you're doing. You could go broke within months."

"I've put my name down to start a catering course at night school. It'll mean starting a term late but I'll catch up. I don't want to be a drain on you. If we separate then let it be a true split and a fresh start for us both."

Lewis was so surprised he kissed her. She was so surprised she let him.

He went out to tell Nia that it was out in the open, and their lives were going to change for the better, leaving Dora staring at the chips she was cooking for their evening meal.

She look around the kitchen, at the clean but shabby collection of cupboards and shelves, and she stared for a long time at the place she had set for herself to eat, apart from the rest of the family. Sadness crossed her face and tears became a threatening lump in her throat but she shook the chips in the fat and forced the disappointment and regrets to subside. She had realised for some time that the situation with Lewis pretending to live at home, while all the time wanting to be with Nia, couldn't continue. She had avoided a solution, afraid of the gossip, afraid of being so indisputably alone, unable to face an empty future in this house that had once been filled with the noisy shouts and laughter of her three children.

Rhiannon would be home for the next few years if she remained true to her promise and waited for Barry's divorce. Viv showed no sign of marrying, he was so wrapped up in the impossibility of a romance with one of the Weston Girls. But things could change. In a few short days they could both have found someone and begun to plan homes of their own and where would that leave her? Rattling around in this house waiting for one of them to take pity on her and call? No one to talk to, no one needing her. She thought again of a dog. At least it would give her a reason to go out!

These thoughts, which had kept her awake night after night had become less frightening. Some subtle change had occurred to ease the negative outlook on her future. Now she had some definite plans of her own, the fear of gossip ruining her peace of mind had subsided until she thought of it as a mere irritation.

Let people talk. There were few houses in Pendragon Island that would survive an investigation into the inhabitants' apparently successful relationships. Many of the people she knew were living very unhappy lives tied to each other no longer by love but by convention and the fear of gossip. She was not going to end up a bitter and resentful woman. Today would be a new beginning, Christmas 1953 the cornerstone of her new life.

She looked at her reflection in the mirror near the sink. Behind her was reflected the tray on which she had been eating her meals to show Lewis she couldn't bear to eat with him. She tutted at her reflection. Eating her meals out here to show her disapproval of Lewis and Nia, it was so childish.

As she set the table she arranged a place for herself at the head of the table. Lewis's place was at the other end, but if he failed to turn up, well, so what? The chips were going to be overcooked or cold anyway. From this moment Lewis was no longer a vital part of her life. Why wait for some catalyst? Now was as good a time for the new beginning as any.

She began humming the catchy Lita Rosa song, 'How much is that doggie in the window, woof woof—'. It had been in her mind for days. Her first words to Rhiannon and Viv as they walked in together, were, "Your dad's leaving and I'm going to buy a dog!"

Ryan was unwanted. The only time Sally spoke to him was to ask him to move out of the way while she reached something or wanted to vacuum the floor! Since the lodgers arrived she was busy making sure they were comfortable and needed nothing, she rarely spoke to him apart from mealtimes, after which he was expected to wash the dishes. What a life. Sitting here being ignored day after day.

Joan was at the Wallpaper and Paint store much of the day, and Megan was mooning about, presumably recovering from the attack on her, which he thought was partly her own fault for wandering around the countryside playing at being friends with those Griffithses. He didn't even have Islwyn to visit for a good moan these days, he was cooking chips twice daily. The last time he'd seen his brother-in-law was when Islwyn had told him about cancelling the caterers for old Gladys's party. That had seemed a joke at the time, he had even emulated it by passing

232

on Viv's idea about selling carpets along with the wallpaper and paints, to the attractive woman in the new decorators' supplies.

They'd had a good laugh but all it really meant was less chance of the Weston's Wallpaper and Paint recovering and Old Man Arfon being able to restore his wife's allowance.

Joan and Megan tried to keep the attack on Megan secret but news got out as it always does in a small town, and because of the sympathy constantly on everyone's lips, she stayed in. Jack and Viv were her only visitors. When Terry came, anxious not to be suspected of involvement, Megan refused to see him.

"I don't want to see anyone until my wounds have healed and the bruises have faded."

"You're sure Terry wasn't the attacker?" Viv and Jack asked at the same time. Viv's fists tightened indicating how willing he would have been to deal with the man.

"Terry wasn't with me, I was on my own and the man in the lane wasn't him," Megan spelled out, carefully avoiding another lie.

"I wonder who it was and if it was the same man who attacked our Rhiannon?" Viv muttered. "I think we should watch that lane and see who uses it, besides the Griffithses and us."

"Forget it, please," Megan pleaded.

"Only if you agree to come to Grandmother's party. There's bound to be more gossip if you don't," Joan whispered. "So far people only think you were beaten. If they suspect you were—"

"Don't go on about it, Joan. I want to forget it."

"And you'll come to the party?" Joan insisted.

Megan began to smile then. When asked to share the joke she pointed to Jack and Viv; bruises from their fights still clearly visible. "What will people think of Grandmother? Blackmailed by us into inviting the Griffithses, then us turning up with an assortment of bruises fit for a match against Randolf Turpin!"

"We can use pancake make-up. Whereas these two," Joan said glaring at her cousin and Viv, "they'll just look like a couple of thugs."

Unable to persuade Megan to accompany him, Terry sent a note with his apologies to Gladys stating he would not be attending the party. His cousins, Edward and Margaret also declined a few days later as they were unable to find anyone to take their place in the restaurant at Montague Court. When Joan and Jack went to see her on the Tuesday, she seemed on the point of tears.

"Why not give some of your old friends a ring, Grandmother?" Joan suggested. "A written invitation takes effort to answer, a phone call seems more friendly and makes it easier to say yes."

"Or no," Gladys said. "Besides, a telephone call is not polite. A written invitation gives people time to consider."

"They've had long enough. Come on, hand me that list and I'll telephone a few to start you off."

234

"Grandmother wondered if you could confirm that you are coming on Friday, Mrs Moffat?" Joan began and, giving little time for hesitation, received an acceptance. From then on, she and Jack took it in turns on the telephone, and by quoting the names of those who had accepted, made it easier to persuade the rest.

"You are an ill-mannered lout and I wouldn't want you or your sister there if you begged," Joan said on one occasion and she grinned unrepentantly at her horrified Grandmother. "That was Felicity Greg's brother Felix. I only rang to tell her I didn't want her there. His attitude helped. They've both been so clearly avoiding us since – the trouble – I thought I'd make sure she continues to do so!"

"Really, Joan," Gladys admonished. But there was worse to come with Jack, when a one-time friend made it clear he did not want to renew acquaintence with the Westons.

"You, Desmond Bowen, are a shit," he said slamming the phone down.

"What did you say?" Gladys demanded.

"D'you want me to repeat it?" Jack asked.

"No I do not!"

In spite of several refusals, two hours later, their Grandmother's list was completed, and happily, Gladys said, "Thank you, dears. Now I won't have to invite those awful Griffithses!"

"You didn't invite them Grandmother. We did, verbally, weeks ago. There's no escaping them, I'm afraid."

"Have a word with them, Jack. If they do come, you must see that they behave!"

She rang for Victoria to tell Arfon she wanted to see him, and as he was only in the study along the hall, Victoria sighed with irritation. She desperately needed the money Mrs Weston paid her but how she had to work for it!

"I'm glad they've seen sense at last, my dear," Arfon smiled when she told him how her list had grown. "Now all you have to do is look forward to enjoying yourself."

"I thought we might add to the atmosphere by having lighted candles along the tables. What d'you think?" she asked Joan.

"*Candles*?" Arfon shouted. "Are you *mad*? What would the papers make of the Westons burning down the Hall? Dammit, Gladys, behave yourself!"

Gladys marked with a star the most attractive young men and with a circle the most eligible girls. This was her best opportunity for finding a husband for Joan. She was certain Terrence and Megan would sort out their differences. He was such a charming man.

Jack was the problem. Soon to be thirty, it was imperative she found him a suitable partner. A shy young girl might be best, someone who could be moulded into the right kind of wife for a man likely to rise in his profession. He surely wouldn't stay a teacher all his life? She worked on her lists smiling happily for the rest of the day.

The following morning, with only two days to go

before the party, Megan made it quite clear that if Terrence were invited she would not attend. Gladys assured her he had already made his apologies, but she wondered if Megan really did want to see him and decided to find out what had happened between the young couple.

Without the customary phone call, Gladys called on Old Mr Jenkins and asked to see Terrence. The old man looked shabbier than before. His suit was food-stained and tobacco discolouration on his moustache had deepened. He wore slippers and one was cut to ease what looked like a bunion. Very unseemly when entertaining a lady, Gladys sniffed.

"I think my granddaughter and he have had a little tiff, and I wondered if I could do anything to help put it right," she explained when the maid had brought them coffee.

"I don't know whether it's right to interfere," Mr Jenkins said lowering himself into the most comfortable chair. "If they can't sort it out themselves there's no future for them anyway, in my opinion."

"But they were getting on so well."

"Look, I'll talk to Terrence and ask him to come and see you if you wish, but that's all I can do." His irritation showed and he had used the word 'interfere', so she quickly made her excuses and left, without drinking the bitter and unpleasant drink everyone seemed to serve these days.

"I won't be sorry not to be related to the man," she told Arfon later. "He's very – ramshackle, my dear."

"These posh families often go in for eccentricity when there's no money left," Arfon agreed.

Mr Jenkins had not been angry with Gladys but with his grandson. When would the boy start acting sensibly, and conform to what most consider reasonable behaviour? He studied the letter that had come by that morning's post and a deep frown was added to what Gladys had thought ill humour aimed at her. It had been addressed to Terrence but also, to anyone who knew his present whereabouts. Guessing it would be trouble, he had opened it and was still undecided whether to confront the boy or await further developements.

What he had wanted to say to Gladys when she called to ask about Terrence was to warn her to keep her granddaughters away from him. But he couldn't be that disloyal.

Terry was still trying to talk to Megan. He waited for her at her home, but it was Thursday before he succeeded, when she made one of her rare forays out of the house. As she crossed the park to meet her sister she was huddled in a loose coat, with a hood that concealed her face but he recognised her at once.

Apologising was not going to be enough, and he decided that lies would definitely help. He might not have bothered, but stories about someone attacking her worried him. So far no one had accused him but if they did he would find it impossible to prove he was nowhere near the lanes at that time. He had been home but his grandfather had been in his room and the maid had taken herself off to see her boyfriend.

He had to see Megan and ensure she would make it absolutely clear he was not the man who attacked her. Then he would make plans to go back to London once Christmas was over. It had been good to get away but he knew there was no life for him here in this small seaside Welsh town.

"Megan, please listen to me."

"What can you possibly say that would make it worth my time?" she asked coldly.

"I want to explain."

"Explain why you rushed me into something I was not ready for? That you attacked me without constraint?"

"Attacked?" The word frightened him. "It wasn't me in the lane that night. You know it wasn't!"

"Your attack was no better. Seduction of an inexperienced woman is just as cowardly."

Her words sounded idiotic but being taken by surprise, they were the best she could do. What if he did think she was crazy? All she wanted was for him to go away so she never had to see him again.

He walked alongside her, looking down at her pert face, her eyes hidden in the shadow of her hood. "I have something to tell you, Megan, will you please listen to me?."

"Why should I?"

"Please?" He saw her nod almost imperceptibly and went on. "I thought I could control my feelings for you, but in the end I couldn't. I wanted you so badly I lost

239

control. I love you, Megan and I love you enough to be sure it won't happen again. Please forgive me."

"I can't."

"Then I'll go away, back to London where I won't be reminded of what I lost." He took both her hands in his and kissed her gently on the cheek and walked away.

He glanced back hoping she would be following him, or at least looking back, but his lies and charm were wasted. Megan felt nothing but relief.

When Gladys heard they had met and talked, hope rose in her that at least one of her grandchildren would be settled but hope was quickly dashed. What was the matter with them that they hadn't found someone and settled down like ordinary people? Still, she consoled herself, there was still the party and with seventy-four people attending, there was certain to be someone there for each of them. She must remind them to mingle. If only those awful Griffithses weren't coming. They were sure to be trouble.

Basil Griffiths was a doting father and spent as much time as he was able with Eleri and their son Ronnie. Working as a nightwatchman he had time during the day to walk out with them, pushing the pram, bent over from his skinny height, smiling and talking to the sleepy occupant of the pram.

"Like an 'S' hook he is," Eleri teased when they made one of their regular visits to the Griffithses' cottage. "Peering in to the pram, chatting away, hardly looking where he's going."

"He knows my voice and knows what I look like. He knows he has a loving family around him, so what's wrong with that?" Basil defended.

"Nothing love," Eleri said affectionately. "Wonderfully lucky he is, having a dad like you."

"When is your day off next week, son?" Hywel asked. And the expression of almost foolish sentimentality was wiped off Basil's thin face.

"Oh no! Not this year, our Dad. Please! I'm a working man now. And a father. I don't have the time."

"Chickens to feather and clean, ducks and pheasants the same, plus a few rabbits to skin. Your Mam and I can't manage on our own and you know how useless our Frank and Ernie are."

Eleri kept her eyes downcast. She dreaded being asked to help with the ritual slaughter although she had no qualms about eating the resulting meals. She felt ashamed, knowing that if she were responsible for killing her own meat she would be a vegetarian.

"Thursday the twenty-third," Basil muttered. "And you'll have to teach Frank for next year. It's his turn after all the years I've done it."

"Right then. We'll make a start first thing."

"What d'you call first thing? I work nights remember."

"The orders are written in this book," Hywel explained. "And I've written cards to put on each

241

bird so we don't get them mixed up, like when Frank delivered them. Remember that fiasco?"

"You opened the Christmas cider barrel a bit early if I remember. Said you had to try it, make sure it was all right. That might have had something to do with it," Basil reminded him.

They went on arguing good-naturedly until Basil glanced at the baby and said, "He looks flushed. He's too warm." Then, "His breathing isn't right. Look, Eleri, he seems distressed."

"Nonsense, he's fine." But he was not. At eleven o'clock that night his tummy was rising and falling with every breath in an unnatural way and the doctor was called.

"I told you," Basil was wailing when he was called from work to be with his small son. "I told you, but you wouldn't listen."

While Eleri watched little Ronnie as he struggled to cope with the infection the following morning, Basil ran on his long legs to tell Dora that his wife wouldn't be able to help with the Westons' party that day.

Gladys was cheerful, singing a song she had heard on the radio many times, 'She Wears Red Feathers and a Hooly Hooly Skirt', and was embarrassed when anyone heard her. "Such a silly song," she complained to Sally and Sian who had come to show their mother new dresses bought for the following evening.

When Victoria came to tell her Dora Lewis had called to see her, she felt a flood of irritation. "What's wrong with the woman that she needs to come to

242

me every whip-stitch? Either she can do the job or she can't!"

Gladys ordered, demanded and shouted but Dora insisted that with baby Ronnie ill, she would not expect Eleri to help.

"I could help, Mother," Sian said. "After all, it's a party for the young people, I won't be missed."

"How ridiculous, Sian! How can the Westons hold a party and allow you to be seen dealing with food?"

"Only help in the kitchen is needed," Dora said. "I can probably deal with the cooking beforehand and set it out at nine o'clock as you planned. Mrs Fowler-Weston could stay in the kitchen out of sight."

"I couldn't allow it. How can you think of demeaning yourself in such a way, Sian?"

Dora's eyes began to glitter dangerously. If Mrs Weston said one more word to suggest she was lowly enough to be seen but not her daughter . . .

"I don't think it matters whether I'm seen or not. Skulking around trying not to be noticed would be far worse and why should I? Preparing food isn't anything shameful. Most women do that every day."

Dora relaxed with a low grunt of approval. Sian was outspoken to the point of rudeness but she wasn't bad.

"I'd be happy for you to help serve the buffet tonight," she said. "With the food preparation this afternoon too if you had a mind."

"That's settled then." Sian kissed her mother to show she understood her reluctance and added, "I'll

243

enjoy helping Mrs Lewis, Mother," She turned to Dora and suggested, "Why don't you come to my place at five o'clock, then we can sort out what has to be done?"

In the sweet shop in Sophie Street Rhiannon was busy. With just a week to go before Christmas Day, mothers were searching for small gifts to put around the tree or to hide in stockings to be hung on bed posts. Jimmy had been around to replenish her display of small tins, and the selection of china gifts she had begun to stock had been a great success.

The shelves and the window needed reorganising and she decided that she would spend the early part of the evening working on them. Being busy, and with no assistant to help since Eleri's baby had arrived, was no excuse for the place looking less than spotless and inviting, she told herself.

It was the eighteenth, the day of the Westons' famous party, but that was no great excitement for her. Mam was more animated than she. What was there to be thrilled about?

Barry would be fussing over Caroline and not herself. Jimmy would be pointing out how unattentive he was to her, and how little she and Barry had in common, and coaxing her to make plans to see him over Christmas. What a prospect. The more she thought of it the less she wanted to go. Several times she had reached for the phone to call and tell Jimmy she had a cold and wouldn't be going, but as he had seen her only a few hours before, he would hardly believe her.

At five o'clock, just before the usual flurry of customers as people left work, Barry came in. For a moment she wondered if her plans were about to change. If he invited her to the party she would not refuse. He was so busy with his photography that a rare evening was not to be wasted.

He struggled out of the van carrying a large parcel wrapped in brown paper. Was it her Christmas present? Excited, and already abandoning her idea of working late she went to greet him.

"I want you to see this, I made it for Joseph but I'm not sure if it needs painting or varnishing," he said, dashing her hopes. He unwrapped a beautifully made wooden train, on which a child could sit and work his way along with his feet.

"I'm sure he'll love it," she said with genuine admiration. "But I think he might like some bright colours." Together they designed the pattern for the toy, in between serving customers.

When he left half an hour later, he made no suggestion for spending the evening with her. "I'll take it up to Mam's and use the garage to work on it," he said retreating to the van without even a kiss.

It was long past the time she normally closed, but customers continued to trickle in and she was in no hurry. All she had to do was bath, comb her hair and put on her dance frock. Gertie Thomas closed her shop on the opposite corner and strolled across to buy some Turkish delight. Maggie Wilpin left her chair in her doorway and stood chatting to Gertie, in the shop doorway.

245

"You coming over for tea Christmas day as usual, Maggie?" Gertie asked. "Don't know what meat I'll have. I'm leaving it till Christmas Eve and seeing what the shops are selling off cheap. I've saved my ration for a couple of chops if I don't get a bird."

"We usually have a chicken from the Griffithses but it's hardly worth it for just me and the boy," Maggie replied. "His dad'll be out of prison in January, so Gwyn thought we'd be better waiting for then and have a real celebration."

"If he's out long enough," Gertie said with a sniff.

Stepping back from the conversation, Rhiannon wondered what Christmas would be for her. Going on recent performance, Barry would be involved with Caroline and her son. Dora would be deep in books on catering she had borrowed from the library, Viv would be out with his friends, and Eleri, celebrating her first Christmas with Basil would hardly need her company.

There would be the usual gathering at the Griffithses' in the evening of course. Barry was certain to be there. But would he have time for more than a word? Like her mother she was beginning to think New Year 1954 would be a time to take stock and consider where she was going.

Chapter Twelve

Terry Jenkins was unhappy. He had returned to London but not where he had lived before. He couldn't pick up with the life he had so recently left. That part of his life was over. One more change of address must surely mean they wouldn't find him. As for Megan, he couldn't face trying to explain to her his reasons for leaving, he wasn't certain of them himself. She had told him goodbye, but he knew that if he had stayed he could have changed her mind, there was something there, some fiery glow between them that could have been coaxed into a flame. But no, better to put it all aside and make a fresh start somewhere no one knew him. But most people of his age already had their lives sorted out and there didn't seem to be a place for him.

He missed Megan. She was good company and was beginning to be more than a friend. Much more. He was ashamed at the way he had forced her into making a commitment too soon. What was the matter with him that he couldn't handle a relationship with a woman?

Putting the past behind him and going back to South

Wales had seemed a good idea but now it was one more place to which he couldn't return. But perhaps that was where he was going wrong, not facing things? Never giving things a second chance?

Running away from his previous mess hadn't solved anything, and running away from Megan hadn't either. Perhaps it was time to stand still and face things.

Without waiting until his enthusiasm for the plan faded, he sat down and wrote Megan a letter.

Megan opened the letter from Terry when she was alone. She didn't want Joan giving her advice she didn't need. She wouldn't see Terry again, of that she was certain. But the letter was a temptation she could resist. She could pretend she hadn't opened it. It was brief, stating only that he would be returning to Pendragon Island and was determined to speak to her. If his invitation still held, he would be at the Weston's party on the eighteenth.

She screwed up the paper and told herself she was angry, but that was untrue. She was aware of her body warming with excitement, and there was a hint of a smile as she squeezed the page in her hand.

She told Joan about it later and as her sister began to warn her of trusting him, she said, "It might be fun, just to talk to him."

"Then make sure you speak rudely, and loud enough for everyone to hear!"

"Oh yes. I'll make him wish he hadn't bothered to come."

But that too was untrue. The separation hadn't lessened her feelings, but intensified them. She was remembering how her body had reacted to his touch and the memories were electrifying.

Dora was not looking forward to working with Sian on the day of the party. Her name might be Heath but she was still one of the Westons. Even reminding herself that Sian's husband Islwyn was now working in a fish and chip shop didn't prevent her feeling uneasy.

The brief chat in Sian's miserably small kitchen had not been long enough for the two women to find a way of understanding each other and Dora promised herself that if Sian once tried to lord it over her, she would tell her firmly that with a criminal for a husband she had no right to tell others how to behave. With that uncompromising attitude she set off for Trellis Road.

She didn't cycle as she had so much to carry. Much of the food had been delivered to Sian's house but Dora had already gathered quite a lot before Ronnie had become ill. Struggling with two bags and several carriers, she was encouraged to think more hopefully on this strange partnership when Sian saw her coming and hurried along the road to help her. That generous thought was not enough to make them temporary friends, but it helped ease the first few minutes.

Almost in silence they gathered together the ingredients and equipment and began their preparations. But with a kitchen so minuscule and with tension between them it was not long before trouble errupted.

"Don't make the sandwiches so full," Sian warned. "They'll split and look awful, mind." Then later: "You've made that sardine mixture too soft, Dora. Sandwiches made with that will collapse before it reaches a mouth."

Dora gritted her teeth but her eyes flashed warningly. Then Sian said almost kindly, "Don't you think that's enough egg on that pastry? It'll be like a cardboard box. And we'll run out of egg before we've finished at the rate you're using it."

Dora held her temper with a struggle, then she said loudly, "I've been cooking for a family for as long as you have Mrs Heath and I'll thank you *not* to tell me how to deal with a fiddling little task like this."

Sian raised her head and glared as if to add to the threat of an argument but, perhaps realising how condescending she had sounded, she smiled instead and said, "I bet you didn't do it in a kitchen as small as this one."

"Mine isn't much bigger," Dora admitted, "but if I have my way it will soon be at least arranged efficiently and contain some decent equipment."

With both women greatly interested in cookery they were soon discussing the changes planned for Dora's professional kitchen and when they had finished their preparations so far as they were able, Sian walked back with Dora to look at her kitchen and hear more of her plans.

Rhiannon came in for her lunch and Viv dashed

in and out and still Sian and Dora talked. With the kitchen replenishment and the departure of Lewis discussed, as well as Sian's dilemma with Islwyn, and with all the food for the party organised, they parted for an hour or two, each surprised by the knowledge they had made a friend.

Dora hadn't been completely truthful about Lewis. She had told Sian that she had told him to leave. Perhaps, when they knew each other better she would tell her how much it hurt to have to say goodbye to someone with whom she had expected to spend the rest of her life.

"Not bad, that Sian Heath-Weston or whatever she calls herself," she said to Viv when he returned from meeting Jack and the others. "Sorry I am for little Ronnie being ill, but if he hadn't been, I might never have talked to her and found out how much we have in common. Strange how things happen, eh?"

"Basil wasn't at The Railwayman's. But Frank said the little chap is much improved."

"I know. I went to see him before I went to sort out the food with Sian."

"Sian?" Viv queried. "You call her Sian?"

"I never waited for her to invite me to use her christian name. She called me Dora so why shouldn't I call her Sian? I did call her Mrs when she made me angry, mind," she grinned. "Lot of snobs they are and that Gladys is the worst. I think I went there intending to put Sian in her place, but she wasn't all pompous like I expected at all."

"Joan and Megan are all right too, Mam."

Dora looked at her son with a frown. "Maybe, but it wouldn't do for you to be getting any fancy ideas about the Weston Girls. Gladys still thinks the Westons are a special breed, far above the likes of us, mind! So watch yourself at this party of theirs."

"Yes Mam," Viv said, with a wink. "I'll munch with manners, simper my sentences and dance with decorum." And with luck, he added silently, I'll walk Joan home.

Barry was excited about Christmas that year. He couldn't remember when he had looked forward to the season with greater pleasure. He had moments of guilt, knowing it should have been thoughts of parties and social events with Rhiannon that gave the occasion its excitement, but baby Joseph was old enough to enjoy the fun. Seeing the Christmas period through his eyes was going to be magical.

He wasn't keen to attend the Westons' party that evening, in fact he knew that if he had been escorting Rhiannon he would have made an excuse. But Caroline needed a change of scene and he couldn't disappoint her.

That thought hung in the air and alarmed him. What was happening to him? His emotions were being taken over by a small child and, he admitted in a kind of awe, by the child's mother.

"I wonder why the Griffithses were invited?" he wondered as he and his mother were putting the finishing touches to the tree in Nia's house in Chestnut Road. "When you think what a snob old

252

Gladys Weston is, it doesn't make sense. Glad I am, mind. Caroline is so looking forward to going."

"I think the young people have persuaded her. Lewis heard from Viv that they threatened to stay away unless they were allowed to ask Viv, Frank, Basil and the rest. I don't think Gladys is getting all her own way with her grandchildren these days."

"The old order changeth?"

"– yielding place to new, something like that, yes."

"Talking about changes, Mam, what are you and Lewis going to do? I mean where will you live?"

"The flat for the moment. I don't think I could face coming here. Lewis and I are both married and not to each other. There might be changes on the way, but I can't see the day when my living with a man who is married to someone else will be accepted without disapproval, can you?"

"Will you sell this house?"

"Probably, but not for a while. Why? Are you and Rhiannon making plans?"

"How can we, Mam? My divorce from Caroline will take years."

"And she'll wait for you?" she asked but before he could answer she added, "And you, will you want her to wait?" She stared at him but he didn't reply.

"I'm taking Caroline to the party," he said later. "I invited Rhiannon but she's going with Jimmy Herbert, you know, the sweets rep who worked for Bottomleys."

"I know him." She stared at her son, a frown

253

wrinkling her brow. "Which came first, Barry? Rhiannon accepting Jimmy's offer or your telling her you were taking Caroline?" Again there was no reply.

Barry was in a state of restlessness. He loved Rhiannon, certainly he did and she would be a perfect wife for him. Running his mother's business that would one day be his, managing children and the shop without difficulty. They had discussed it and the future was clear. Or was it? He felt himself drawn more and more to Caroline and young Joseph.

It's only the baby, he told himself. When I have a child of my own this attraction for Joseph will fade and be forgotten, but it would be years before that could happen.

If only he and Caroline were truly man and wife he could start building his future now. Instead he saw years ahead, barren years of marking time. Shaking the thought away, convinced it was melancholy due to his need of Rhiannon, he asked his mother, "Mam, where's the best place to buy flowers? I thought I'd surprise Rhiannon and there's no surprise in giving her chocolates, is there?"

"I hope that isn't all you're buying her for Christmas? A fiancée – even an unofficial one deserves more than that."

To his horror Barry realised that with only a week to go, he hadn't even thought of Rhiannon's gift. "Got any ideas, Mam?" he asked.

Dora and Sian arrived at the Hall at seven. There

254

wasn't much to do until it was time to set out the food. The sandwiches were made and were wrapped in damp tea towels. Sausages and pasties were protected by greaseproof paper and stored in biscuit tins. Other tins contained various cakes, some bought and some made with the aid of scrounged and illegal butter and sugar.

"Won't it be a relief when this food rationing is finally ended," Sian grumbled as she and Dora stacked the food on one of the trestle tables set out in readiness. "I think the first thing I'll do is spread butter on toast so thick I won't be able to see over the top!"

"My fantasy is to buy a joint of meat that will only just fit into the oven and invite as many people as will sit around the table to come and help me eat it."

"You enjoy cooking don't you? This new career of your won't just be a convenient way of making a living?"

"I get great satisfaction from preparing a meal and putting it in front of someone who appreciates it." Dora smiled grimly. "Not that Lewis ever came into that category. Too busy dreaming about Nia Martin! Then I went out to work during the war and Rhiannon took over the running of the house while I continued with my insurance round, so I didn't do much cooking for a long time. I missed it."

The day had been dull, a typical December day with the daylight failing to arrive to bleach away the night-time mists. The party was due to begin at eight and with the cold air seeping in through doors and windows it was hard to imagine anyone being able to take off out-door coats and expose bare arms in party dresses.

Jack and Viv dashed in to check that the bunting hadn't fallen down and that the lighting was in order, before dashing out again to get ready to return as guests.

Dora and Sian sat in the gloomy hall, huddled around a small electric fire while all around them shadows hid the artificial magnificence, the veneer of jollity, that would soon set the mood for the evening. Both women were tired but satisfied that they had done their best to ensure that their contribution to the party would be a success.

"I feel I need to find a way of earning money," Sian said.

Dora looked at her wondering how to deal with the embarrassing subject. As usual, she decided that pretence was not the way and she replied, "Because of him refusing to go back to the Wallpaper and Paint and accept my Viv as his boss? And now making chips for the hoi polloi."

"Yes, I think that's a fair summing up!" She looked at Dora, small, red-haired and with those intensely blue eyes that so often threatened anger. "The wages are low. I think the time has come for me to do something."

"Good on you!" Dora said.

"Did you know the Rose Tree Cafe is up for rent? I'm wondering, just wondering, if we could take it over and run it between us?"

"You and me work together permenantly, you mean? Well, I'd thought to start my own business catering for parties, something like we've done here," Dora frowned.

"I have a little money. Not much as we've had to use my savings since Islwyn—"

"Since he spent weeks out of work and still refuses to find a proper job," Dora finished for her.

"You don't mince words do you, Dora Lewis? I don't think it's necessary to be quite so rude!" Sian stood up and walked a little way away, arms folded in an angry posture.

"Look, Sian," Dora sighed. "If we are even to think about working together we have to stop pretending. I'll start us off. I didn't throw Lewis out. He left me for the woman he's been in love with for years. She even had his baby. Did you know that?"

"A child by – by Nia Martin? I'm so sorry, Dora."

"Yes, well, it's true. Her son Joseph who died at the same time as our Lewis-boy, he was Lewis's son." Her eyes glistened as she saw the shock register on Sian's face and she defensively added, "And there's your husband, so guilty at the way he cheated on your father and allowed the family's business to crumble, he couldn't face looking for a proper job. He still can't, except for the lowly chip shop. And he probably only threatened that, hoping your father would take pity on him and help."

"Dora!"

"Those are the facts and it's no use dressing them

257

up in pretence. We have to get on with things without them." Her expression softened then and more calmly she asked, "What about this cafe then? D'you really think we could do it?"

"I don't know what Mother would think of me working after all these years. She'd be upset."

"Pity for her! She's swallowed her son-in-law working in a chip shop! The Rose Tree Cafe can't be any worse!"

"Oh it would be. It's where all her friends go for coffee and afternoon tea."

"Good! They'll all come nosying around and give us a good start then, won't they?"

"You think we should consider it?"

"Why not? The money Lewis promised for the new kitchen would be used in a different way, but I think I could persuade him to agree."

"I'm sure you can," Sian said wryly.

The doors opened, lights came on, there were voices of the staff entering, their chattering and laughter advancing before them, sounding hollow in the empty room. Someone put on a Sid Philips record while the band found their places; and if you were able to ignore the coldness, the dull room was immediately transformed into the venue for people to have fun.

"Come on, Sian," Dora chuckled. "No more time for dreaming, the bell's sounded for round one!"

Jimmy Herbert had called at Temptations just as Rhiannon was closing. It was six-thirty and, even

258

on a Friday evening she usually closed earlier than that. With a party which she did not want to attend, she wasn't anxious to get home. He found her looking into the corner of the window and frowning.

"What's up? You look very serious?"

"There are three chocolate bars missing and that bottle of humbugs was almost full. Someone's helped themselves."

"Forget it for tonight, Rhiannon, love. We're going to a party!" He hesitated then asked, "Would you mind if I came home with you and waited until it's time to leave? I don't have time to go home so I came dressed ready to go." She looked at him and felt a warmth that surprised her. He was wearing what was obviously a new suit. Mid-grey and with a blue shirt, and darker blue tie. His eyes were shining, his hair was neatly combed and even his moustache had been forced to submit. His black dancing pumps shone like mirrors and he had a neatly folded handkerchief in his breast pocket. He looked very handsome. The party didn't seem such a bad idea after all.

"Jimmy, you really look the part," she said stretching up to receive his salutary kiss.

"I didn't want to let you down, this being the Westons' 'Do'," he said modestly.

"Mam is out, she's helping with the buffet, but she'll have left something to eat. I'm sure there'll be enough for two." They went into the house and at once Rhiannon realised it was empty.

"I'd forgotten," she said. "Viv will have gone to check on the hall with Jack."

She felt shy as she prepared a light snack, and as he stood beside her while she washed the dishes and he stacked them away. The shyness changed to something different later, when she was upstairs washing and changing into her party dress. Alone in the house with him gave her a frisson of excitement. An exhilarating sensation of daring as she stripped off, bathed and re-dressed in her party clothes.

It was near half-past seven when Viv dashed in and demanded tea and the freedom of the bathroom, from which he emerged frozen, having washed and shaved in the icy cold room, a brief fifteen minutes later.

They set off together, the three of them walking arm in arm.

"I bet the room will be divided into two camps, them and us," Viv prophesied.

"I don't know any of them apart from Rhiannon and Barry, but I'll be careful I don't offend," Jimmy said seriously.

"There's the Westons, see," Viv explained, "and they've always treated the rest of us like inferior beings. But after Old Man Arfon was found guilty of setting fire to his shop and his son-in-law was found to be dipping his hand in the till, they haven't found it as easy to lord it over us. They try, mind," he chuckled, "they try."

"Dad says fortunes are changing," Rhiannon added. "The Westons' days are numbered. They can't afford to keep the whole family from what the old man made during the war and the shop run by Viv, and they'll soon have to work like the rest of us."

"Damn me, Rhiannon," her brother smiled, "I haven't had the nerve yet, but I'd love to go in and ask Islwyn for a bag of chips!"

"He's better than Megan and Joan's dad who won't work at all."

"You're right. Ryan just idles his time away, moaning about what I'm doing and trying to cause trouble," Viv said. "He's hanging his hopes on his mother-in-law. He knows she won't let the Weston Girls go without anything."

"I don't think even Old Gladys can do anything for them now," Rhiannon said. "Dad thinks they're finished."

"I'm not so sure. It's the Weston Women who will get the family back on its feet," Viv predicted, repeating Joan's words. "You have to admit that the Westons are strong, and sensible enough to do something, even if Gladys does insist it's common to work!"

The hall was already full when they arrived and Rhiannon left Viv and Jimmy, to deposit her coat and touch up her make-up. Joan and Megan were dressed in summer dresses with frilled sleeves and long, full skirts. Megan's was blue and green on white. Joan's yellow and orange on cream. Rhiannon looked down at her long brown dress which she had bought three years ago and at once felt dowdy.

But the dances were lively and Jimmy a superb partner and she forgot her dress and the inhibitions the Weston Girls created in her and relaxed into the party mood. Tonight was going to be fun, flirting

261

with Jimmy and being envied by other girls. She hadn't realised just how handsome he was with his fair curly hair and saucy blue eyes. Tall too and with his smart, well-fitted suit he was quite a dish.

Her euphoria didn't last long. A Tom Jones, was announced and two circles were made, men in one women in the other and they moved in opposite directions until the music stopped and each had to dance with the person facing them.

Jimmy was lost to her and, not in the mood to face anyone else, she moved off the floor and sat pretending not to care, watching the dancers swirling around to the music of the seven-piece band with an increasing feeling of dejection. She was relieved when she saw Barry arrive and she stood and waved to him, but he waited by the cloackroom door until Caroline joined him and took her straight on to the floor.

When Jimmy left his partner at the end of the dance and walked towards her a fit of pique made her pretend not to see him, and she went into the kitchen to see her mother. When she came out he was dancing again, this time with Megan. Confidence pouring out of her by the second, she wanted to go home.

Gladys sat with Arfon in a corner near the band.

"Can we go home yet?" Arfon asked her for the third time and she slapped his hand playfully and told him 'no'.

"I want to see who Joan and Megan dance with so I can invite them to call," she told him. "So far they've only danced with Jack, and that Viv Lewis and that awful Frank Griffiths! I knew we shouldn't have invited the Lewises and the Griffithses, dear."

The food was a success and once it was cleared away, Sian and Dora came in to watch the dancing.

"Come and say Hello to Mother," Sian ordered and Dora trotted after her to where Gladys was 'holding court' to some of her grandchildren's friends.

"Mother, Daddy, you know Mrs Lewis, Viv's mother."

"Of course I do dear. Hello, Mrs Lewis. The food was quite satisfactory, wasn't it Arfon?"

"Not good? Only satisfactory, Mummy?" Sian said. "Pity about that, Dora and I are thinking of going into the catering business together."

"Not now, dear. I'll listen to your little jokes tomorrow."

Sian and Dora shared a smile and returned to the kitchen. "She's going to be the biggest hurdle," Dora warned. "Chip shops and cafes are not what she expects of her children."

"Leave her to me. I'll persuade her we sink in splendour or learn to swim."

"I don't think she likes either alternative, she'd rather you stayed clinging to a rock!"

Jack left the hall before supper was served. Taking some food parcelled up by his mother and Dora, and grabbing a few balloons, he went down to Goldings Street and presented an instant party to Victoria for her younger brothers and sisters. The new baby had arrived and was sleeping peacefully in a drawer taken out of the large chest at one side of the fireplace. It had been been cosily filled with pillows and hand-sewn blankets and the pretty coverlet had been embroidered with flowers.

Most of the children were in bed but hearing the visitor arrive they crept down the bare wooden stairs and peered hopefully around the corner.

"All right, just five minutes," Mrs Jones told them and for half an hour they enjoyed the balloons, the food and the attention of Victoria and Jack. It was with genuine regret that Jack took his leave and made his way back to the Hall.

He could hear the sounds before he reached the door but it was not music and for a moment he decided that the supper interval was still in progress, yet the voices were not happy and cheerful, but raised in anger. He ran in through the door and saw a fight in progress. A quick glance around the room showed his grandmother hiding her face and others standing near the stage in groups, aghast at the spectacle. Men had their arms protectively around their partners, women squealing but trying to see what was going on.

"The Griffithses! I knew we shouldn't have invited them," Gladys wailed. "Always fighting. Known for it they are."

But it wasn't Frank and Ernie. They stood near the doorway looking as disappointed at not being involved in the affray as Gladys was at being a witness to it.

"What happened?" Jack asked and Frank pointed to where Terry was being frogmarched out of the room by someone Jack vaguely recognised. He ran to intercept the two men as they were about to leave the room and then, as the stranger turned to back his way through the swing doors, he saw that it was Gethyn Howells, a friend from army days.

"Gethyn? What the hell's going on, man?"

"This Terry Jenkins, that's what's going on! Left my sister a week before their wedding, he did! What's her and the baby going to do now? I want him to tell her why he did it. Right?"

Jack followed them out, stopping in the doorway to gesture to the band to begin playing. As the door swung closed behind him he heard the drums starting a rhythm that was picked up by the saxophone and the leader was calling for everyone to "Take your partners for a quickstep."

Outside, Jack saw Terry being held against the wall by Gethyn. Gethyn's fist was raised as he shouted questions at Terry.

"Hold it!" Jack shouted running towards them. He succeeded in calming the couple down and insisted that they went to the pub to talk it through.

"He's not going anywhere. I want an explanation. Right now." Gethyn said angrily. "Searching for him for months I have. Sent letter after letter and they came back unknown at this address. When I rang his grandfather I was told he was still in London."

"I was in—" Terry tried to explain.

"Hiding behind an old man, there's brave you are. Running from a woman and hiding behind an old man!"

It was a while before Gethyn allowed Terry to speak and when he did, Jack had no doubts on the truth of it.

"I just lost my nerve," he told them. "I just lost my nerve. Renting a flat, plans to save for a house, taking responsibility for two human beings, I couldn't manage it. I'm sorry, Gethyn. Angharad didn't deserve it."

"Deserves to be rid of you, mind! You got that part right! But why run off and leave her to face the questions and the sneering laughter, eh? Call yourself a man?"

"If this is true," Jack said, "you owe it to Angharad to go back and tell her."

"I can't marry her," Terry said.

"She wouldn't have you! Not after this. Someone who lets you down once will do it again!"

"I'd better get back inside and give some sort of explanation to my grandparents," Jack said.

"And to Megan. I came hoping to talk to her, you see." Terry muttered.

"Fat chance of that!" Jack retorted.

There was a murmur of anxiety when Jack returned to the Hall but seeing him walking calmly across to talk to Gladys, the dance continued and the conversations returned more or less to normal, although several pairs of eyes swivelled, hopefully following his progress. The band did its best to re-create the lively atmosphere by choosing cheerful dances, and the evening continued on a happy note. All but Megan seemed to relax and put the frightening moments aside. She was

266

white-faced and embarrassed by the scene, wondering if anyone knew it was her Terry had come to see.

Unaware of her sister's discomfort, Joan laughed and said, "So much for Terry wanting to talk to you." She passed on what she had learned from Jack about the incident. "What was he doing, coming here? D'you think he came here to tell you about his fiancée?"

"Leave it, Joan," Megan said. "Let me get through this evening before we have an inquest, will you?" She forced a smile and went towards one of the young men who was obviously going to ask one of them to dance.

Barry and Caroline left soon after. Barry led Caroline over to where Rhiannon sat with Viv and Jack and Jimmy and the Weston Girls and said goodnight to them all with equal politeness. He hadn't danced with Rhiannon once, having explained that he didn't want to leave Caroline standing alone as she was so shy.

Jimmy said nothing but watched Rhiannon's reactions with interest.

Gladys was taken home by Arfon just before the last waltz was called and she hated having to miss the buzz of conversations she knew would mull over the evening's bizarre happenings, once they had gone.

"If there'd been a convenient cupboard to hide in in that cloakroom, I'd have used it, Arfon, dear!" she said through a mouth tight with anger. "What will people think, Arfon?" she asked sadly as they went into their house. "Sian announcing to all and sundry that she and Dora Lewis are going into partnership

267

to run a cafe, and that Terry, who I thought was so gentlemanly, causing a fight over something as sordid as a jilted girl and the police being called by her brother to sort it out! What a fiasco!"

"Nonsense, those who refused to come will be as mad as hell to have missed it!" Arfon chuckled.

During the interval, Jimmy sought out Dora and asked if he could stay the night.

"The couch will do, Mrs Lewis and I won't be any trouble."

Staring at him for a moment, Dora finally nodded but warned, "You stay on that couch, mind. One of them stairs creaks and I'm not about to tell you which one!" She chuckled as she told Sian, "Jimmy blushed so bright that I thought we could manage without the electric! And poor Rhiannon was shamed, but she'll get over it, give them something to laugh over later on, it will."

Dora left the Hall with Sian, as soon as the dishes had been cleared after supper. They walked through the cold, dark streets chatting about the events of the evening and wondering what was the truth behind the fight involving Terry Jenkins.

"Mother was expecting trouble, but not from that quarter," Sian smiled. "I think she was almost disappointed that the Griffithses behaved impeccably."

"Why didn't you stay?" Dora asked. "Your mother would have been glad to have you there."

"I've had enough. I'm tired! Us working girls need

our sleep," she said. "Now. After the weekend, we'll start making enquries about renting the Rose Tree Cafe. Right?"

"Right. Lewis will help with – sorry," Dora said. "Forget I said that. You and I will be able to deal with it ourselves. Won't we?"

"Every last nut and bolt," Sian assured her as they parted.

Dora walked from Trellis Street down to Sophie Street in a trance. Could it really happen? Could she and one of the Weston Women work together? Run a business together? Lewis had always told her she was good at figures and would be an asset to a small firm, well, he was going to be surprised at how right he was!

Chapter Thirteen

For Megan, Christmas 1953 was fraught with worries about a possible pregnancy. She told herself it was unlikely, that what she and Terry had done could not result in a baby growing inside her. She made promises to herself of things she would do, of faults she would cure if only the worst didn't happen. She prayed and made promises to God that she would be a better, more considerate person if only He would get her out of her present mess. But days passed and there was no sign to give her relief.

One of the decisions she made, which had begun as a promise to God, was, if she were reprieved from the burden of motherhood, she would find work and earn some money instead of expecting her parents to keep her.

She thought about this for some time without reaching an idea of what she could do. A long and expensive education had prepared her for being kept by a rich husband, nothing more. And there were too few of those to go round!

Messing about with paint tins was out, and so was cooking. Neither activity appealed. It was seeing

Gwennie Woodlas that started her on the right track. Clothes, now that was something she could enjoy. Fashion was a subject she could be very good at, but how to exploit that skill? She didn't reach any conclusions, but at least it took her mind away from babies for a while.

Christmas 1953 was a new beginning for several families. In the days between the Westons' party and everything closing down for Christmas, Sian and Dora had made enquiries, declared an interest and begun preparations to become tenants of the Rose Tree Cafe.

"Islwyn keeps trying to get involved," Sian told Dora. "He's so sure I need his advice. But he feels my elbow every time he comes near and I think he's beginning to realise that this is ours: yours and mine. And Ryan, that idle brother-in-law of mine, he keeps calling in telling me what to do and offering, oh, so generously, to give his precious time and expertise to show us how it's done."

"What a nerve! My Lewis offered to help too, convinced we couldn't manage without a man holding our hand. The funny thing is, Nia also offered. She wished us luck via our Rhiannon, and said if we needed someone to talk things through or even an extra pair of hands in the early weeks, she would be pleased to help in any way she could." She looked at Sian, her bright eyes sparkling with the anger which was always close to the surface, then her expression softened and she smiled. "Funny thing is, I think she

271

was genuine. We've known each other for years, Nia and me, been friends even. Although I didn't think what we had in common included my husband!"

"You aren't bitter?"

"Not now. I tried to keep him, using blackmail, guilt, illness and all the rest, but I came to face the fact that he wants to be with her and not me. I could see the years slipping by, being wasted in regrets and futile dreams. Facing it now, while I'm young enough to make something of my life makes better sense. So, blue skies – or roses – all the way, right?"

"Right."

Lewis stayed with Nia in the flat for most of Christmas. Nia had expected him to stay with his family, but Dora had made no secret of the fact that he was not welcome.

"I've got things to do, Lewis, so unless you're desperate to see us I'd prefer you stay away. Viv will be going somewhere with Jack and the Griffithses, Rhiannon will probably be seeing Barry. In and out they'll all be, so Sian and I can get our heads together and work out our plans."

"Oh! All right," Lewis said in surprise. Dora had always made so much of the family gathering on that special day. He wondered whether it was too late to arrange something with Nia but decided not to ask for fear of spoiling her arrangements. She had family too.

He bought a chicken and persuaded one of his friends, young Cathy at The Firs Boarding House, to cook it, and prepared himself for a solitary day eating chicken sandwiches alone in the flat. It was by sheer luck he learned that Nia would also be on her own.

"Did you know Barry and Rhiannon have been invited to the Griffithses'?" Viv asked him on Christmas Eve. "I don't think Rhiannon's going, but Barry is. He can't wait to show young Joseph the toy he's made him."

"I'll call over there myself some time today," Lewis said. "I've bought a little something for him and for Eleri's baby."

"Strange though, Barry leaving his mother on her own on Christmas Day, don't you think?"

"She won't be alone." Lewis tried not to show his pleasure. "Your Mam doesn't want me around either, so we'll be two outcasts together."

He went to the shops and bought what extra food he could find, then drove up to Chestnut Road to tell Nia they were both free.

All the devious planning meant Dora was able to go to the Griffithses too, being fairly certain Nia wouldn't appear.

"It'll be nice to be a part of a family for a change. Why don't you come with me?" Dora asked Rhiannon. "I can't go unless you do. I won't go and leave you here alone on Christmas Day."

Rhiannon wasn't keen to go, convinced she would be alone anyway, even amid the crowd, on her own, with Barry involved with Caroline and her son.

"There's a good show on television," Dora coaxed. "Arthur Askey, Max Bygraves and Shirley Abicair."

"You might see it, but I doubt you'll hear it," Rhiannon laughed. "That's the noisiest house I've ever known!"

"Better than rattling round here," Dora said and Rhiannon finally agreed.

Dora hummed along with the radio as popular songs and carols were played on 'Family Favourites', then, with the food prepared for the following day she sat and listened to 'Life With The Lyons' and 'Take it from Here', laughing along with the audience and looking to Rhiannon to enjoy the fun.

She sensed all was not well with her daughter but didn't feel able to question her. Rhiannon would talk when she was ready. Perhaps she was fed up both with working in Nia's sweet shop and with waiting for Barry's divorce? She admitted to herself that it would be a relief to see her cut those particular threads.

On Christmas morning Joan and Megan opened their presents, then, following the regular ritual, dressed in new clothes and walked with their parents to spend the day with their grandparents and the rest of the family.

Jack went with his parents and wished he could find an excuse to stay away. He was surprised when the door was opened by Victoria.

"What are you doing here?" he asked as she held out an arm for coats.

"Your grandfather asked me to come and help for the morning. I think your grandmother is exhaused after all the fuss about that party," she managed to whisper. "Don't worry, I'm not cooking!" she added with a smile.

"You aren't washing up either!" Jack said through tight lips.

"Grandmother, why have you asked Victoria to come in? She has a mother, and brothers and sisters who are entitled to have a family Christmas the same as us!" Jack asked, when he'd gone through to the sitting room to see his grandparents.

"It was your grandfather's idea, Jack. He thought it would be too much for me."

"You mean we can't manage without messing up her holiday? Nine of us and we can't cope?"

"Let her go home, Mother," Sally said. "I didn't realise she would be expected to help. We'll manage."

Jack went into the kitchen where Victoria was finishing peeling the potatoes for roasting. "It's all right, Victoria, we've had a family conference and Grandmother says you can go home. Thank you for being so generous and coming in, oh, and they asked me to give you this." he handed her two pounds. "That's for messing up your day."

He watched as she walked down the path, closing the gate carefully behind her before skipping off, like a child let loose early from school.

After the dinner was over, Jack left to call for Viv and Basil. The older members sat to listen to the Queen's speech in which she promised to devote her life to the country and its commonwealth. Megan and Joan crept upstairs.

"Joan, I think I might be expecting a baby," Megan blurted out.

"What? You little idiot. Who is it? Not that awful Terry?"

"Of course not!" Megan snapped. She had to convince everyone he had nothing to do with it. "The attack, you know—"

"You mean you really were attacked in that way? I'm sorry Megan, but I didn't really believe you. I'm so sorry." Joan was horrified. "I thought if you had been really – you know – attacked you would have gone to the police."

"Would you have done?" Megan asked, her head on one side. "Could you have faced sitting and telling a disbelieving policeman you hadn't teased, you hadn't encouraged, you hadn't allowed petting to go too far? Would you have risked that?"

"I'm sorry, Megan," Joan said again and again. "What are you going to do? If you are expecting, the baby won't just go away."

"As soon as Christmas is over I – I'll have to go to the doctor. If it's all right, Mum and Dad need never know. If I am, well, I'll have to face it, won't I?"

"I'll come with you."

"No. No, Joan. We do most things together but this is something I need to follow through on my own." They hugged each other for a long time then went downstairs to a pretence of having fun.

*   *   *

Terry continued to stay with his grandfather and on Christmas Day they both went to Montague Court to share Christmas dinner with Edward and Margaret and their mother. It would be a late lunch, after the few bookings for the celebration dinner had been served, crackers pulled and wine offered as a bonus, a temporary pretence that the people who came out to dine were not alone. The diners included Gwennie Woodlas, who planned to spend what was left of the day watching her television or listening to the radio.

Terry's reception was cool as always. He had been away from the family for so much of his life and his behaviour had been far from pleasing to them. He was expected to eat, make stilted conversation for a while then leave, with the hope they would never have to meet again. At three o'clock, when most of the country listened to the young Queen, the Jenkinses sat to eat. An hour later he stood to collect his coat but Mr Jenkins stopped him.

"We have a proposition to put to you, Terrence," he said. "With no parents to look after you and my neglect – apart from the occasional letter – we feel that as a family we owe you something."

"No you don't. I don't want anything." Terrence said at once. The old man wasn't going to suggest staying with him, was he? He wasn't sure what he wanted from life but it was not that!

"We know you've been in the army and spent some time as a jewellery salesman but, if you're prepared

277

to learn something new, Edward here will train you as a waiter and purchaser of wines."

"Wine is becoming more and more a part of a meal and I see that trend increasing," Edward said. "It's a vast subject but one you will find interesting if you're prepared to study."

"Can I think about it?" he said. He had no intention of staying with these dull people who wanted to 'do good' by him and look after the prodigal. Once 1954 arrived he would be off. He wasn't sure which direction he would take but he would end up where not even the diligent Gethyn could find him! There was no way he was going back to face his responsibilities. Not now he'd escaped from that ruffian! But before he did, he would have one more try to see Megan.

Christmas for Rhiannon was a mixture of pleasure and pain. The joys and excitements of the season with its atmosphere of warmth, goodwill and friendship filled her with the usual happiness. Yet there was a worry underlying the rejoicing. She knew she had to sort out the relationship between herself and Barry Martin, which the Christmas period had somehow brought to a head. She no longer had first place in his heart.

Was he really planning to divorce Caroline? Or had she won him over, she and baby Joseph? Had he changed his mind about marrying her? The signs showed he was beginning to want to stay married to Caroline and make the marriage a real one.

Jimmy called on Christmas afternoon and asked her to visit his parents on the following day.

"No, Jimmy. I can't. But thank you for the invitation," she said at once. She didn't want further involvement with Jimmy, and meeting the parents was a giant stride in a friendship bordering on love. It was more important to get the situation with Barry sorted and, Boxing Day, when the excitement was over and people had time to relax, would be a good opportunity to talk it out with him. "I'm going to see Barry," she explained with a feeling of guilt. She had been unkind, leading him on to expect more than she could give.

"Why don't you come with us to the Griffithses' tonight?" Dora asked Jimmy, ignoring the frown of warning on her daughter's face. "They've got a television and Norman Wisdom is on, and Julie Andrews."

Jimmy looked at Rhiannon questioningly but she smiled warmly and added her invitation to Dora's. How could she not appear pleased?

The living room at the Griffithses' small cottage was overflowing and Rhiannon laughingly pointed out to her mother that the television had once more been relegated to the shed. Lengths of thick tree trunks stood, lined up along the walls to form extra seating and the conversation was already loud and lively.

There was soon an opportunity to talk to Barry and Rhiannon asked him to meet her the following day.

"Fine," he said in a voice that didn't match the word

and the enthusiastic nodding of his head. "Some time in the afternoon?"

From this, Rhiannon guessed he had arranged something for the morning, so she said, "No, I'll be busy then. I'll meet you at the shop in the morning, say ten o'clock?" She saw him hesitate as if to argue but a glance at her determined face obviously changed his mind.

"Ten o'clock," he agreed. "We can have a few hours to ourselves then, can't we?"

"Half-past," she said, just for the hell of it.

They sat together for a while but there was the feeling he would rather be somewhere else. Rhiannon watched him sitting beside her, stiff-backed, his shoulders tense, his ill-at-ease mood emanating from him in waves of misery. She knew that what they had to say to each other would only take a few minutes.

The evening in the overheated room made everyone rosy-faced and thirsty even though the beer and cider flowed continuously. Conversations became quieter and the food was abandoned. The women congregated in the back kitchen and drank tea and the men brought out the crib board. It was time for her to leave.

Barry offered to drive her home but she refused, preferring to walk across the fields and lanes with her mother and Jimmy. It had not been one of the best Christmas Days she had known but there was the sensation of achievement. Nothing had been resolved but culmination of the problem was in sight.

*   *   *

280

On Boxing Day Dora went to the small terraced house on Trellis Street to spend a few hours with Sian. Sally and Ryan were there having been invited to tea. Dora and Sian took out paper and with Sally sharing their ideas and Islwyn firmly discouraged from taking even a mild interest, they scribbled in notebooks and began drawing up a financial plan.

After being firmly snubbed when he offered to help, Ryan walked out with a great show of irritation. The day was dry but with a sharp breeze and he tightened the scarf around his neck and walked across the docks to the beach. There were a few people about, mostly those walking their dogs. He passed one or two families out with their children, little girls pushing new dolls prams, boys and girls riding new tricycles with fathers anxiously running alongside.

He felt useless and old. Once he had enjoyed being a father to his two lovely girls. He had been someone of importance in the town, married to one of the Westons, managing the family business in harness with his brother-in-law, a valued member of a couple of the town's better clubs. Until Islwyn had ruined it all.

He walked along the promenade past the empty shops and cafes, scuffing his shoes in the sand spread on the ground by a slight breeze. His wife was busy earning a little money fussing over her damned lodgers. Joan was spending hours every day helping Viv in the shop where he had once reigned. Now his sister-in-law Sian was going into business, he was feeling more and more useless. Not that Sian would earn much. Not in a tinpot cafe and with one of the Lewises for a partner.

What was she thinking about, getting involved with Dora Lewis? Viv Lewis's mother for heaven's sake! If she had deliberately tried to insult her husband and himself, she couldn't have better succeeded!

As he walked past the row of closed cafes, the heavy smell of stale fish was on the air, a memory of past summers and a reminder of those to come. He sneered as he thought of his brother-in-law cooking chips in the Fortune Cafe. And of his wife demeaning herself clearing up after lodgers. What a mess. What fools they were to advertise their reduced circumstances. Better to be unemployed and put on a show, pretend all was well.

Near the first-aid hut he faltered and changed his route. Instead of walking back to the docks and home, he went back and up on to the cliff top. The wind was stronger there and he felt the chill of it reaching inside his coat, and sliding down his neck. Tightening his scarf again he walked on. He didn't walk fast and soon became chilled. When he came back down to the promenade he wished he had not walked so far. Turning away from the docks he walked along the road, hoping to thumb a lift, although the roads were practically empty.

As he passed the old harbour he heard a motorbike and realised it had stopped on the corner where there were a few seats. As he drew nearer he sighed with relief. A man stood near it whom he recognised: his nephew, Jack. He hated motorbikes but at least it would get him home in the warm a bit sooner.

He waved and called and Jack walked towards him.

"How about a lift home, Jack, I'm frozen, boy."

"Sorry Uncle Ryan, but I have a passenger already."

"Who, that Viv Lewis? He can walk. Do him good!"

"No, not Viv, Uncle."

Ryan looked at the seat and saw a young girl and he blustered an apology. But then he saw who it was.

"Jack, what are you doing with her?" he whispered behind his hand. "Your Grandmother's maid out on the back of your bike?" He began to laugh. "I bet she doesn't know. Give me a lift or I'll tell her," he chuckled, jokingly.

"Victoria wanted to visit an aunt and I offered to take her. Sorry I can't give you a lift. See you soon," Jack nodded to him and Victoria gave him a weak smile and they drove off leaving him with the increasingly daunting trek through the town. Too late, he thought of borrowing money from Jack for a taxi.

He did manage to get a lift and when he returned to Trellis Street he told Sally what he had seen. "Jack and that Victoria Jones, bold as brass, riding through the town on that machine of his for anyone to see them." He was stiff after his long walk or he would have gone straight to Gladys. Tomorrow, he promised himself, I'll go and tell her tomorrow.

Jack guessed that the secret of his visits to Victoria would soon be revealed so he went to see his grandmother as soon as he had seen Victoria safely home.

"It was seeing her in that empty house with hardly a mouthful of food at the time her father died," he told Gladys. "I was so impressed with her braveness, and the way she and her mother coped with such dire trouble."

"I know, dear. You persuaded me to take her back, remember, *and* increase her wages!"

"I've seen a lot of them since. I even sneaked over there on the night of your party, Grandmother. I took balloons for the young ones and food for them to have a party of their own."

"Kind of you Jack, dear. I wish you'd told me, I'd have probably been able to find something more."

"You would, I know you would," he smiled at her affectionately. "Kindness itself you are, Grandmother and don't think I don't know it. I've heard of the clothes and toys you've given them."

"Oh, nothing really," she said deprecatingly. "Nothing I couldn't spare."

"Two of her brothers have found jobs now. One left school last summer and the other leaves this coming July. Mrs Jones is working as a cleaner in the offices of the Town Hall and takes the baby with her so they are at least solvent."

"Why are you telling me this, Jack?"

"Because I want you to know that I intend asking Victoria to marry me."

When Ryan called an hour later and told her he had seen Jack and Victoria out together, he was deflated by Gladys's reply.

"Yes, Ryan, I know. What a lovely girl she is, don't you agree?"

When he had gone and Gladys and Arfon discussed the startling news, Gladys sighed and added wistfully, "Pity is I'll be losing a very good servant. She can't work here once Jack has proposed, it wouldn't be right, would it, dear?"

Barry and Rhiannon met as arranged and he drove them to the beach, where they sat on the edge of the cliff path and looked down at the empty beach below. The sea was restless, the tide changing from flow to ebb in a criss-cross of disturbed currents. The choppy movement looked as if something was fighting below the surface which erupted into the wild dash of spray as the larger waves hit the rocks on the distant headland.

Rhiannon asked what his plans were. "Do we still have a future together?

"You know I want us to be together, Rhiannon, but—"

"Don't prevaricate, Barry. You and I both know that the love we had for each other is under strain. If you have changed your mind about us marrying, I expect you to be honest."

"I know it's a lot to ask, for you to wait years for me to be free. I made a mistake and you are suffering because of it. Everything is in a state of limbo. I've been a fool."

"Answer my question," she insisted. "Or answer this one. Are you hoping to make your marriage to Caroline a real one?"

"Rhiannon! I've never even kissed her, not like I kiss you that is."

"But you want to? You want to be a real husband? A real father to little Joseph?"

"That's ridiculous. Caroline loved my brother, not me."

"He's been dead for a year and you've filled his place in most ways, why not completely?"

Rhiannon had the weirdest feeling that he hadn't really considered it, yet to her, his feelings for Caroline and the baby were as apparent as white clouds on a blue sky. "I just want you to know that you can consider yourself free from any promise made to me," she said walking away.

He didn't follow but sat there staring into the sea as if the answer to his loneliness in the present and the hollowness in his future were written there for him to read.

She was waiting at the van when he walked up a few minutes later and they drove home in silence, each considering the dramatic transformation in their expectations for all their tomorrows.

Gladys was feeling let down. So much money had been spent on the party and it had all been for nothing. No reunion between Megan and Terry and after that mysterious fight which had so humiliated her, that was undoubtedly a good thing. Among the guests none had shown an interest in Joan, who had shamed herself by refusing many invitations to dance and had spent most of the evening with Viv, even allowing him to walk her home.

Now Jack, her lovely Jack, had announced his

intention to propose to Victoria Jones, a family servant. Surely he'd change his mind? Surely the girl would refuse? With her sons-in-law such failures, surely her grandchildren could do better than this?

Megan called to see the doctor on the Wednesday after Christmas and on a sudden whim, announced herself as Miss Joan Fowler-Weston. She glared at the man as if he were in some way responsible for her having to be there.

"I think I am going to have a baby," she said, trying to speak in Joan's sharp tongue.

He questioned her and gave a brief examination and shook his head.

"It seems unlikely, Miss-er-Fowler-Weston but if you will leave your – er – sample with me I will make absolutely certain. I will telephone within the week and give you the result."

"No," she said, in Joan's voice. "I will come here. If I'm mistaken, there's no need for anyone else to know."

The nurse had a hand on the door, already partly opening it, to hand in the cards for the next patient. With his hand on the bell to summon her, the doctor hesitated. He didn't know the twins very well, their being extremely healthy and trouble free, but he could have sworn it was Megan and not Joan he had been talking to. That scar, the result of the accident when Joseph Martin and Lewis-boy Lewis had died, surely that was Megan?

The nurse lived near Glebe Lane and on the way

home she met the twins' mother. "Hello, Mrs Fowler-Weston." She stood in front of Sally to bar her way.

"Good morning," Sally frowned. "Was there something? I am in rather a hurry."

"I just think you ought to know," the nurse said with obvious embarrassment. "Your Joan's been to the doctor. I'm not supposed to say, but I think a mother should know."

"Know what?" Sally was impatient.

"Your Joan. Had a test for – er – pregnancy. I'm sorry, but I thought you should know. Being a mother myself and all—" she excused. "Don't tell the doctor I said, mind, or I'd be sacked for sure."

Forgetting the shopping she needed, Sally turned round and ran into the house, her face pale with shock. "Ryan, Joan thinks she might be expecting!" she gasped and realised too late that Jack was standing in the corner.

Jack ran to Sophie Street, remembered Viv would be at work, ran to the shop and up the stairs to his office. He banged on the door and when Viv answered it aimed a punch to his chin. Viv dodged it with ease and demanded to know what was the matter. Jack was weakened by his running but his anger was in good health and in between ragged breaths he called Viv a list of names that broke records for unrepeated length.

"Joan's been to the doctor to ask for a pregnancy test and you're the only one she's been seeing,"

Jack gasped out, still trying to hit the smaller and quicker Viv.

Without trying to convince him otherwise, Viv gathered his overcoat and led Jack down to the shop. Calling for his assistant to watch the shop for a while, he led Jack to the yard, where Joan, huddled in thick jumpers and a coat belonging to her grandfather, was marking the paint tins they were to sell cheaply in the forthcoming January sale.

The truth was soon revealed and Sally and Ryan and the others discussed the best way of helping Megan, who refused to say a word. Sobered by the thought of Megan's predicament, Jack offered profuse apologies both to Joan and Viv. They arranged to meet Megan that evening and assure her of their support.

Then Jack asked for some of the old paint Joan was marking down, to do up Mrs Jones's house.

"Bloody cheek," Viv growled. "You come in here, sling unconfirmed rumours at me, try to knock me into the middle of next week, then scrounge some bargains. Damn it all, Jack, you'll be asking me to paint the walls for you next."

"Well, if you're free this weekend . . ." Jack said before moving out of reach.

Chapter Fourteen

Rhiannon hated the period after Christmas. The need for sweets dwindled as most families still had chocolates and sweets given as presents, so the shop was quiet. This year, besides the lack of business making the days drag, it was made worse by the end of her unofficial engagement to Barry. He still lived above the shop and his constant comings and goings were an embarrassment. She still had a sense of loss and when he came into the shop she tried to hide her face for fear he would see the regret and yearning.

In a purely selfish way she was glad every time she saw him staggering up the stairs, reminding her he was still living apart from Caroline. She didn't doubt they would one day be together, seeing them over Christmas, sharing their love for Joseph, had made that clear, but she hoped it wouldn't happen until she had accepted the end of her hopes of becoming Mrs Barry Martin.

At five-thirty she closed the shop, not waiting for the stragglers as she usually did, but hurrying out, away from the possibility of seeing Barry and Caroline together. As she closed the shop door she glanced at the window and saw that one of the pyramid display of toffee tins was missing. She frowned and replaced it. That was the second time this week she had noticed something missing. Over the past weeks several bars of chocolate had gone, and she was certain that a seven-pound jar half filled with winter mixture had not been sold. There was a thief among her customers, but how was she to find out who, and, what would she do when she had?

It was a mild, tranquil night, the icy wind that had tormented them all day had dropped and the cool air was a mere caress. She stopped, with her key in her hand and walked back down the road to the corner from where she could look between the houses, to the lights just visible in the docks and on the sea.

"Dreamin' again, young Rhiannon?" a voice called and Rhiannon stepped across the road to speak to old Maggie Wilpin.

"Lovely clear night, Maggie," she said.

"When you're as old as me they're all beautiful," Maggie grunted.

"Isn't it time you went inside?" Rhiannon coaxed. "You must be cold sitting still with only an old coat around you."

Maggie grunted again and Rhiannon asked her why she sat there so late into the night.

"The nights are long, and if I stay here for part of them I can cope with the darkness better. Besides, I'm waiting."

"Waiting?"

"Waiting for Gwyn's dad Charlie to come home. He said he'll be home in January."

"Couldn't you wait inside? Gwyn would be glad of your company, wouldn't he?"

"He's out with his friends. Won't be home till eight, then he goes straight to bed. Hardly worth lighting the fire these days."

"You do have a fire, don't you?"

"Yes, I need it to cook on since the cooker clunked out on me. Gwyn's dad'll sort it when he's home."

Charlie Bevan was the husband of Maggie's grand-daughter Morfedd, who had left home when Charlie had been called up. Morfedd had since divorced him and Maggie had taken them in, her granddaughter's husband and his small son. She was tired. How much longer would she have to wait for Charlie?

When Rhiannon reached home she asked her mother if they could buy some coal for Maggie. "I don't think she lights a fire unless she has to. Gwyn spends most of his time out of the house and she doesn't think it's worth lighting it for herself."

"Ask Viv when he comes home. He'll go and see if he can persuade her," Dora said. She had been making soups, experimenting with the idea of offering light lunches as well as the snacks for which the Rose Tree Cafe was well known. Taking the saucepanful of creamy tomato, made with the help of Janet Griffiths's offering of cream, she said, "Here, Rhiannon, love, take her a bowl of this. Old Maggie likes my soups. And my hot pasties."

"How many times this week have you given her food, Mam?"

"No matter."

Joan and Megan's mother told the twins she wanted to see them, together and at once. She knew that it was the day on which the results of Megan's test would be known. She had said nothing to her sister. Time for that if the predicament were confirmed. She doubted whether she would ever be able to tell her mother. She'd have to emigrate first! The subject to be discussed, she told her daughters, was Megan's visit to the doctor.

"It's all right, Mummy," Megan said at once. "I've had the results and there isn't going to be a baby. I – I was mistaken. Worry, the doctor said it might have been."

"Oh, so we can forget it can we? Pretend it didn't happen?" Sally said quietly.

"That's best, isn't it?" Megan said, unaware of the cold anger in her mother's eyes.

"Are you now going to tell me who he is?" Sally's voice grew only slightly louder but Megan stared at her in surprise. Unlike Auntie Sian, her mother rarely raised her voice.

"I don't know."

"What? How many men have you been with?"

As her mother looked about to collapse into tears, Joan said, "It's all right Mummy. Remember when someone attacked her in the lane? Megan's been afraid ever since, that the man might have left her pregnant."

293

"You mean he – actually—?"

Pulling her mother to one side Joan said, "I don't think he did – that – he didn't do – you know what. But Megan was in such a state and she's very ignorant about what creates a baby."

Sally's shoulders relaxed and she stared at her daughter with relief showing on her face. "Poor love," she soothed. "Why didn't you come to me?" Then she turned to her other daughter and said firmly, "And I hope you are ignorant of what's needed too!"

"Oh, I am, Mummy. I just read more, that's all." Joan grinned and was relieved when her mother smiled too.

When they were alone, Joan said angrily, "And that's the last time I get you out of a mess like that, Megan. I haven't forgiven you for using my name yet!"

"Sorry Joan, but I was so frightened I didn't know what I was doing."

"D'you mean on the visit to the doctors? Or when you and Terry Jenkins went further than you intended?"

"What are you talking about?" Megan gasped. "It was that man in the lane!"

"And I'm a chimney sweep with gold teeth!" Joan snapped. "You can at least be honest with me, after I've squared it with Mummy."

"All right. It was Terry, but I was afraid they'd make me marry him and I didn't think I loved him enough for that."

"*Didn't* think?" Joan queried. "What about now? Aren't you sure any more?"

"It's funny, but in a way I was disappointed, about not having a baby. It was as if the decision about what to do with my life had been made for me. Now it's all in the melting pot again and I have to make some plans for the future."

"You're bored, Megan. Get yourself a job. The Weston Women are no longer able to live a life of idleness, and I for one am glad."

On New Year's Eve there was a dance. Viv was going and he asked Rhiannon to go with him. "Jack will be there, and Eleri and Basil are going. The length of him! Can you just imagine what he'll look like dancing with plump little Eleri? That'll be a sight to see, all curled up like a pug dog's tail, he'll be."

She shrugged non-committally but decided later that she would. She didn't want Barry to think that she was stuck indoors pining for him. Although Barry wouldn't be there. He didn't like dancing.

When she walked into the dancehall the first couple she saw was Barry and Caroline, partnered in a waltz. Barry obviously didn't object to dancing when Caroline was his partner! Oh why hadn't she asked Jimmy? He would have come with her and now she was faced with either dignified retreat, or having to sit and hope someone beside Viv would ask her to dance. At New Year there wouldn't be many there who hadn't come with a partner. She looked hopefully for Jack and had another surprise. Jack was dancing with Victoria Jones!

She spent a lot of that evening in the cloakroom or dancing with her brother. Basil asked her for a dance and in his usual bumbling way he shuffled her around the floor and demanded to know why she was alone.

"What's happened to that Jimmy?" he asked. "Nice enough bloke, mind, better than hankering after Barry. Can't make up his mind, that's his trouble. That baby it is, you know. That little Joseph has the fault for Barry spending so much time at our place with our Caroline."

Eleri heard the end of his comments as he escorted Rhiannon back to her seat.

"Oh shut up, Basil, love," she sighed. But they looked at each other and smiled. Rhiannon sighed too, for the dream of someone looking at her as Basil looked at Eleri.

Barry and Caroline left before Auld Lang Syne, and he was silent as they drove back to the Griffithses' cottage beyond the town.

"Is something wrong, Barry?" Caroline asked. "Is it because Rhiannon was there and you weren't able to take her home? I could have come with Basil. He'd have seen me safe. He still would if we turned around and went back."

"You want to know what's wrong?" he asked and he answered for himself. "Everything's wrong."

"Tell me."

After a few false starts he blurted it out. "I want to be married to you. Properly married. I want to share the fun of bringing up Joseph, you and me together. Now, what d'you say to that then?"

"Oh Barry. It's what I want too."

After a benign start, winter was soon gripping the country in a bitterly cold hand. Ice and snow caused problems in many ways: people falling and hurting themselves, transport delaying the arrival of goods, farmers being unable to lift crops. Many and varied businesses were hit as people stayed in rather than face the discomfort of the icy pavements and the keen wind. Even the January sales failed to coax the usual numbers of people out to hunt for bargains.

Viv managed to sell most of his surplus and damaged stock, the best going to Jack to decorate the small house on Goldings Street. Jack did most of the work, helped on occasions by Basil and Eleri, and Viv.

"Selling it to you at rock bottom prices then having to hang the stuff. Talk about cheek," Viv moaned as he put the last piece of wallpaper in place in Mrs Jones's bedroom.

"Stop moaning. You'll be glad of my tuition when you have a place of your own," Jack said. "That is if anyone would have you!"

"Hark who's talking! An old man like you. I've given up waiting for an invitation to *your* wedding, boy!"

The banter continued but Viv's heart was heavy. The prospect of his marrying were slight. He loved Joan but how could he expect her to marry him and accept the little he could offer? The Westons may be broke, but they were still the Westons, and subject to the ambitions and attitudes of people with money.

Viv's words also had their effect on Jack. The following morning when it was time for Victoria to leave Goldings Street and go to start her day's work for his grandmother, Jack was waiting for her at the corner of Goldings Street and Trellis Street. It was too early to call. With all those little Joneses to get up, get dressed and breakfasted, he would have been in the way.

He no longer worried about his parents or anyone else seeing them together. Today he was going to propose. He waited until the front door opened then ran down to greet her.

"I want you to put on your warmest coat, Victoria," he said as she stepped out of her front door. "You and I are going to take the day off." He silenced her anxious "But—" with assurances that his Grandmother knew all about it and had given her blessing.

He walked with her to forty-four Trellis Street and they set off on the motorbike in freezing cold air into the countryside that glistened with frost. Out through villages huddled between starkly beautiful fields and hills, along lanes in which dead vegetation had been given new life by winter's glorious touch.

He had no real destination in mind, he was just putting off the moment when he put the question and she would say either Yes, or No. Once said, a

No would be so final that he wanted to drive on and on and not hear it.

She wouldn't say Yes. Why should she? A pretty little thing like her? And so young she had plenty of time to choose someone more suitable. For a moment he almost decided to forget the whole thing, take her on a good day out, treat her to a meal somewhere and return her home with the dreaded words unsaid. He even turned the bike around and began to head for home.

At a crossroads he stopped and hesitated, then he drove to the pebbly beach and stopped near the entrance to the big park. Giving himself no further time to dither, he helped her off and then held her close and, with tension almost closing his throat said, as if he were barking out an order, "Victoria, will you marry me?"

She stared up at him, her eyes bright in her red, chilled face. "Say that again?" she whispered, a smile wrinkling her wind-burned cheeks in a delightful way. He relaxed and smiled too.

"I love you, you silly little thing, you must have known. Will you marry me?"

"What will your mother and grandmother say?"

"Grandmother already knows and as for mother, let's go and tell her now, shall we? She'll be at the cafe." He kissed her, laughing at how cold their noses were, then took her to Rose Tree Cafe to tell his mother their news.

At the entrance, he stopped in the porch and said in alarm, "Victoria, you haven't said Yes!"

"Yes," she said, but there was doubt in her voice and he waited as she added, "If your mother raises no objections. I won't want to cause trouble between you and your family."

"Victoria, that must be the flattest acceptance ever!" He held the door of the cafe closed and said urgently, "You do love me?"

"I always have," she said seriously, "but I never dreamed you would ever love me."

He kissed her gently, playfully, and opened the door of the cafe and gave his mother a wide smile.

Dora and Sian had opened the Rose Tree Cafe on Monday the eleventh of January. Rhiannon had received a daily report on their progress but she had not yet visited it. On the day Jack proposed to Victoria, Jimmy walked in to Temptations and invited her out to lunch.

"I don't have time, silly," she said, "I only close for an hour."

"An hour's plenty," he said. "I want to take you to the new place over by the lake."

He grinned then and her heart warmed to him. He really was very thoughtful.

"Rose Tree Cafe, you mean," she smiled. "Mam's place."

"Not new but definitely under new management."

The cafe was hardly full, a few tables were occupied by one or two people brought there, as Dora and Sian had guessed, by the desire to see if the rumours were true and one of the Weston women was working there. The lunchtime menu had never been large, it had been more a place for snacks, and it would take time to spread the news of a better choice.

Because they had so little time, Rhiannon and Jimmy ate tomatoes on toast. Not very tasty tomatoes as they were imported and had ripened unevenly, and with the tops stubbornly hard. But they both cleared their plates and finished off with tea and a cake.

"We'll do better once the rationing is finished," Dora said apologetically. "If it does ever!"

"Welsh lamb roasted with honey, good warming cawl, lavabread and bacon, and other wholesome recipies that are traditionally Welsh. These will be our speciality," Sian added. "So, spread the word."

Gwennie Woodlas came through the door in a flurry of crisp skirts and a whiff of perfume. "Meat and two veg and easy on the gravy," she demanded with a smile.

"Will soup and something on toast do, Gwennie? We aren't starting the full lunch menu for another couple of weeks." Dora went off to serve her. If they could please Gwennie Woodlas, then others would follow her lead.

When Jack came in pushing Victoria gently before him, Sian was coming out of the kitchen with a tray of teas.

"Jack? Is something wrong?" she asked at once. "Your grandmother?" Then she saw his smile, and relaxed.

"Grandmother is fine, and we're here to start our

301

celebrations, Mum. Victoria and I are going to be married."

Sian had heard a whispered rumour, but it was still a shock to see her son looking so happy with her mother's servant. She managed to hide her first reaction as she looked away and put down the tray, then she turned, kissed them both and offered her congratulations to her son.

"How lucky you are, Jack, to have found such a lovely bride. Welcome to the family, Victoria."

The hubbub of conversations had died down but was revived and Gwennie hurriedly finished her soup and hurried off to begin spreading the news. At the doorway she stopped and called back.

"Oh, by the way, Sian. Will you be seeing your Sally? If you do, tell her Megan's been to see me and I've offered her a job, helping me in the gown shop."

This startling piece of news seemed unimportant after her son's announcement and it was almost an hour later before she remembered and telephoned her sister then her mother.

Barry was waiting for Rhiannon when she got back and at once she began to explain her late return.

"No matter," he said. "I just want to talk to you. It's about Caroline and me."

"You want to stay married to her."

He went into long and detailed explanation but she heard none of it, she just wanted him gone so she could allow the fact to penetrate. It was a freedom of a sort.

Better to be free than tied to someone who no longer loved her.

Barry and Caroline married for real, and a wedding to come, when Jack married Victoria. What a surprise. Jack and Victoria. She wondered if Viv knew. She hoped not. It was fun being able to tell news like that.

She felt the usual excitement at the thought of a wedding, but amid the joy was the shadow of her own hollow life. It was time she was settled, and with Barry gone from her life she stared into an empty future.

That evening as she was closing, Rhiannon watched with extra care to see who came in and who paused near the doorway from where they could reach into the window. Gwyn came as usual with Barry's evening paper and he stopped to talk.

"Our dad'll be home soon," he said.

"I'm pleased for you, Gwyn," Rhiannon said, replacing the jar of Midget Gems on the shelf after selling two ounces. "Let's hope he gets a job and stays out of trouble this time, eh?"

"He will. He promised in his letter that he won't leave me again."

Charlie Bevan had been caught and imprisoned after robbing Temptations, and at the time, Rhiannon had been gratified to know the thief was being punished. But now, listening to Gwyn, who had been deprived of his father for months, she felt unexpected guilt.

The guilty were never the only ones to suffer. A thief had been caught and locked up, but his innocent family

303

were poor and without friends, because of something they had neither done nor condoned.

Maggie Wilpin had been sitting outside her door waiting for Charlie's return, lonely and trying to care for the boy. Gwyn himself had been like a lost soul, wandering the streets long after his friends had been safely settled in their homes, also waiting for the father he obviously loved and of whom he had been deprived. She gave Gwyn a sweet from the jar of pear drops and silently hoped that Charlie would survive without being tempted back to crime. For Gwyn's sake, and poor old Maggie's.

She closed up fifteen minutes later, after a late rush of customers. In the commotion of serving she hadn't noticed anyone hesitate at the door, but another chocolate bar was missing.

She no longer wanted to catch the thief and be responsible for making another family suffer. Better she asked Barry to fix a board across to make the small window harder to reach.

A few days later she did catch her thief. Coming down the stairs from the flat, where she had been to get some hot water, she was in time to see Gwyn Bevan's arm reach into the window and grab a tin of old fashioned humbugs left over from Christmas.

With a growl of anger, she grabbed him by the arm, swung him around and whacked him hard on the backside. Gwyn was almost thirteen but he was small and looked more like a ten-year-old. His voice lacked nothing because of his size and the yell he gave startled her and, more angry because of it she hit him again.

"Here! What's going on?" A man burst through the door and grabbed Gwyn then stood protectively between him and the glaring Rhiannon.

"That's what's wrong! Look at that!" She pointed to Gwyn's hand which still held the decorative tin. The boy uncurled his fingers and the tin dropped and rolled along the floor.

"I'll see to this," Rhiannon said. "There's no need for you to involve yourself." She did not want this interfering stranger to go for the police.

It was only then that Gwyn turned and looked at the man who still held him. "Dad!" he shouted. "You're back!"

"And not before time, either," Charlie Bevan said grimly.

Later that evening, Charlie Bevan came to apologise. "I'm sorry if I frightened you. What you did, giving Gwyn a slap and a fright wasn't wrong. He deserved it. I'm home now and I'll make sure it doesn't happen again."

"I'm not going to the police, if that's why you're here," Rhiannon said. "I wouldn't. Not after being responsible for you being sent away last time. He's been so lonely and lost. I'm sorry," she said and was surprised to hear him laugh.

"Bless you, Miss Lewis. I'm glad you did. It was the last straw, see, and someone I met in there made me face up to what I am, and ask myself if I want to go on like I am for the rest of my life. I don't. And unless I'm very unlucky, I won't see the inside of a prison ever again."

"I'm still sorry I deprived Gwyn of his father. Maggie's done her best but—" Charlie appeared not to hear her.

"This man I met," he went on, "he made me look hard at some of the old men in there, men who've spent more than half their lives in prison, not seeing their kids grow up, not being an example to them, only someone used as a threat. 'You'll grow up like you father if you don't watch out'." He shook his head. "I don't want that." He stared at her, his blue eyes dark in the artificial light, his hair cropped and shining golden on his head. He was tall, almost as tall as Barry, and he looked strong and determined.

"You've punished Gwyn?"

"No, but I made him talk about it. He was stealing the sweets old Maggie liked, and taking money when he had the chance, to buy food to coax her to eat, or so he says."

"That's all over now you're home."

"If I can get a job."

She looked again at his tall, straight figure, the clear confident expression in his eyes. "Somehow I think you will."

Gladys was settling the last of the party payments and as she totalled the final cost she thought what a waste of money it had been. Neither Megan nor Joan had met anyone they had since bothered to

306

meet. Only Jack of the three had found his future spouse and she had been here all the time, a servant in her house. And one who used to complain about Jack patting her bottom!

It had seemed so simple, give a party, and all her problems would be solved. The romantic setting would encourage the young people to find someone they could learn to love, and soon her grandchildren would begin their courtships with attractive and wealthy young people. After all, it was at a dance that she and Arfon had met. It was where most people found their partners. Not her grandchildren of course! They had to be different! She moaned silently. Jack choosing a servant. Joan and Megan choosing no one at all!

As she licked and sealed the last envelope with its account and money inside, she heard the door and the voices of Joan and Megan. She rang the bell for Victoria, gave a very mild curse remembering she was no longer there, and went herself to the hall to greet them.

"Darlings," she said hugging them. "Come into the kitchen and we'll make some tea. What d'you think of Jack's news?"

"It's a bit embarrassing," Joan said, "it will be difficult for us to remember not to ask her to fetch and carry for us."

"Joan dear, you mustn't!"

"We won't Grandmother," Megan laughed. "We like Victoria and she'll be good for Jack. That's what counts."

"Yes, dear." Gladys sounded unconvinced.

They discussed the little they knew about Victoria and Jack's wedding plans for a while: the determination of Jack to have a quiet affair, bouncing against Gladys's determination to have a splendid, show-em-how-it's-done occasion.

"I was hoping you two would meet someone at the party and start to make plans of your own," Gladys said sadly, "but you didn't seem to see anyone who took your fancy."

"Oh I did," Joan said with a far-away look in her eyes. "I danced with the man I intend to marry."

"You did?" Gladys brightened up considerably.

"No one new, someone I've known a very long time but only just realised I want to marry."

"Tell me, dear. We'll invite him here for Sunday tea."

"He doesn't know yet, but I intend to marry Viv," Joan said, looking at her grandmother with a rebellious spark in her eye. "Viv Lewis."

Gladys smiled through her tears.

Rhiannon was closing for the evening when Maggie Wilpin came across to talk to her.

"That grandson of mine. Was he stealing from you?" she asked.

"No, it was a misunderstanding, Maggie," Rhiannon said at once. "He was looking, that's all. He'd picked up a tin to look at the picture and I went at him, thinking he was taking it. Other stuff had been taken, you see. Your Gwyn was looking. Only looking he was."

"Humbugs wasn't it? He knows I like 'em," Maggie said sadly.

"Gwyn's dad came and we sorted it all. Nothing to worry about."

Maggie nodded doubtfully. "I don't want him to grow up making the same mistakes his father did."

"No. Neither does Charlie," Rhiannon assured her.

"You think the boy'll be all right, now Charlie's home, do you?"

"Sure of it, Maggie."

Gertie walked across from her grocers' shop on the opposite corner and called to Rhiannon, "Give a hand carrying the veg in for me, there's a good, lovely girl." Then she saw Maggie.

"That Charlie Bevan's home at last then, Maggie."

"Thank goodness," Maggie replied. "He'll watch the boy from now on. I can rest at last. There's glad I'll be to hand over to Charlie and take things easy. I'm awful tired, Gertie."

Later that evening, when Rhiannon ran down to post a letter for Dora, there was a mist that hid icy patches on the ground and she walked carefully for fear of slipping. As least Maggie would be inside now Charlie was home to look after her she thought. Then she saw a shape in the doorway of number eight which she guessed was Maggie. What was the matter with Charlie that he'd let her stay out there in the bitter cold? He owed it to her to care for her proper after all the months she had looked after Gwyn.

She went across and saw that there were two people sitting there. Charlie was hugging Maggie and he was crying. Sitting in the seat where she had spent so many lonely hours, Maggie had relaxed in the knowledge that Gwyn would now be safe, and had quietly died.

Dora was looking through her post one morning while she ate breakfast with Rhiannon and Viv.

"Barry's moving out of the flat above the shop, Mam," Rhiannon said as casually as she was able. "He and Caroline are going to make their marriage a real one. I'm not upset, I've seen it coming for a long time."

"Looking down at the town from above it must look like a game of draughts!" Dora snapped as she handed Viv a letter from Lewis. "Your father's going to live in Chestnut Road with that Nia Martin in February. No shame they've got, them two! Your Barry's moving from the flat above Temptations to live in the flat your father was renting, with Caroline and Joseph. And, to cap it all, Jack is asking Nia if she will rent the flat above the shop to him and Victoria!"

"There's more, Mam," Viv said taking a deep breath before saying. "Last night Joan and I decided we will marry towards the end of the year."

"You and that—" Dora quickly adjusted her reaction after a dig from her daughter and instead

310

said, "Sudden like, isn't it, Viv? I thought you and the Weston Girls were more like enemies."

"Blaming them for the death of our Lewis-boy helped me cope with his death for a while," Viv said. "But we've worked together more and more and I've seen the real Joan. We're perfect partners. I didn't think she'd ever think of me as more than the man who runs her grandfather's business, mind, but last night, well, we talked openly and honestly about how we felt and . . . There you go, another move in the giant game of draughts. I'll be looking for a flat where we can start our married life."

"Good on you," Dora said. "I wish you joy. Both of you." She stood up and hugged her son and added, "I really do, my boy. I really do."

"And me, Viv, but I won't half miss you," Rhiannon added as she too hugged him.

Gladys and Arfon sat watching the television news and thinking about their own.

"I can't pretend to be thrilled, Arfon," Gladys said. "Victoria Jones and Viv Lewis as relations. It will be hard to live down."

"Once the Town Cats get to hear of it, you mean? Just make sure you get your version in first, make it known how thrilled we are, my dear. The best form of defence is attack, so they say."

"We've been the main subject of gossip in the town this past year or so, haven't we? When will it end? I had such dreams, Arfon. Good marriages for my lovely Weston Girls and a gentle well-brought-up girl for dear Jack."

"I think Victoria will surprise you, Gladys. She has the makings of a fine wife. And as for the rest, well, Ryan and Islwyn have let us down, but the Weston Women have dragged us out of the mess we were in. With Viv's leadership of course. We mustn't forget how much we owe him."

Gladys nodded and smiled. "They have been remarkable, haven't they? Megan going out all on her own and getting herself an apprenticeship with Gwennie Woodlas of all people. Joan learning the family business and working beside Viv. Sally running her home as a rather high-class guest house and Sian working beside Dora Lewis and making a success of the Rose Tree Cafe."

"And you, my dear," Arfon said touching her hand affectionately. "You were so right to hang on to this house, our home. There were many times when I wanted to sell up, give up, accept defeat, but you wouldn't let me. Your determination kept us all going, helped us through. The Weston Women are a remarkable bunch and you the most remarkable of them all."